THE WOUNDED SNAKE

Fay Sampson

severn House

This first world edition published 2019
in Great Britain and the USA by
SEVERN HOUSE PUBLISHERS LTD of
Eardley House, 4 Uxbridge Street, London W8 7SY.
Trade paperback edition first published
in Great Britain and the USA 2019 by
SEVERN HOUSE PUBLISHERS LTD.

British Library Cataloguing in Publication Data
A CIP catalogue record for this title is available from the British Library.

ISBN-13: 978-0-7278-8930-0 (cased)
ISBN-13: 978-1-84751-998-6 (trade paper)
ISBN-13: 978-1-4483-0211-6 (e-book)

Typeset by Palimpsest Book Production Ltd.,
Falkirk, Stirlingshire, Scotland.

AUTHOR'S NOTE

Those familiar with this area may notice similarities between Morland Abbey and Dartington Hall outside Totnes. But there are substantial differences too. I have drawn on features of other historic buildings in the south-west of England and added elements from my own imagination.

I have greatly enjoyed the hospitality of those houses, the lively and historic town of Totnes, and the real-life Buckfast Abbey. My apologies for inflicting such violence on the first two. I recommend that you go there and enjoy them in happier circumstances.

The staff of Morland Abbey and the officers of the Devon and Cornwall police portrayed here are, of course, entirely fictitious, as are all the other characters.

My thanks to Joyce Perry for her careful reading of the script and her thoughtful suggestions.

ONE

Hilary forged ahead under the gateway arch to the inner reaches of Morland Abbey, leaving Veronica to pick her way more uncertainly over the cobbles in her wake. She gave a sigh of remembered joy. Ahead lay the green lawn of the cloister garth. On its right, the Tudor house, built from the stone of the medieval abbey, faced a newer block across the grass in the autumn sunshine. Beyond them rose the fractured arches of the once great abbey church. Further to her right, the octagonal Chapter House and the soaring roof of the ancient tithe barn delighted her.

'Splendid! Shame about the church, but I have to admit Sir George Woodleigh made a splendid job of rebuilding the East Cloister for his private home. Sixteenth century and still going strong.'

'Hilary, you're parked on a yellow line.'

'Only till we find our rooms and move our cases.'

She turned confidently to the door at the side of the arch. Veronica caught up with her.

'We had instructions to go round to guest reception in the West Cloister. They said we could park there to unload.'

Hilary looked round at her friend. The tall, fair widow's fine-boned face looked younger than her fifty-eight years. *Not*, thought Hilary, *like me*. Older, shorter, dumpier, with short brown hair which still managed to look untidy. Veronica hovered at Hilary's shoulder like a guardian angel, trying to keep the somewhat older woman out of trouble.

'Hmmph!' Hilary tried the closed door in the gatehouse that she had confidently expected to lead to reception. She looked behind her and then at the distance between them and the far end of the cloisters. She wondered for a moment whether she should move the car after all. Then she set off at a determined pace across the lawn, until Veronica pointed out the notice asking them to keep off the grass.

'People walk all over the lawn in the summer.'

'It's October now.'

Reluctantly Hilary obeyed. They followed the path along the side of the West Cloister, where many of the guest bedrooms would be. She looked enthusiastically across to the East Cloister and the roof of the tithe barn on its other side.

'It was a splendid idea of Sir George's to make the barn into his great hall. I still get a thrill out of sitting in it and thinking of all the feasts and councils of war and the dancing that have gone on over the years within those same walls.'

'But probably not a master class in crime writing,' suggested Veronica, hurrying to keep up with her.

'Hmm, well. We'll have to see how that goes. But there must be some advantage in forty years of history teaching. And I've seen enough of devious – not to say deviant – teenagers to provide a few ideas for villains. Between them, I should be able to come up with a halfway decent historical crime novel.'

'I fancy something more modern myself. Perhaps with a romantic lead investigator. And some love interest as a sub-plot.'

'Don't tell me. You're planning a twenty-first-century Lord Peter Wimsey.'

Veronica blushed. 'Well, actually . . .'

'Never mind. Let's just hope this Gavin Standforth knows what he's talking about. Now, where did you say reception was?'

An arrow pointed them round the end of the west cloister to an open door from which a couple, whom Hilary assumed from the back of the man's balding head to be about their own age, were emerging. They unloaded suitcases from their car parked alongside and towed them indoors.

'Our partners in crime,' Hilary observed.

'I looked our leader up on the internet,' Veronica said. 'Gavin Standforth. He's written quite a lot of books. Just one bestseller, a couple of years ago, and a sequel which didn't do as well. I ordered it for my bookshop, and people bought it on the strength of the previous one, but some of them dropped by afterwards and said it wasn't a patch on that. Before that he had a publisher I didn't recognize.'

Hilary snorted. 'Probably self-published. Couldn't get a decent publisher to take him on. Then he struck lucky. May never be able to do it again. Still, you never know. It may say "master class", but in my experience masters of any profession aren't necessarily the ones who teach best.'

She ducked into the reception office. A young woman in a crisp black suit and white shirt sat behind the desk.

'Hilary Masters and Veronica Taylor,' Hilary announced.

The woman ran her finger down the list. 'That's right. You asked for singles, I believe. We've put you in the East Cloister. Some of the top rooms are a bit more cramped there, and they were built before anyone had thought of en-suites. But you'll each have your own separate bathroom.'

'Perfect!' said Hilary. 'The old East Cloister is definitely the one with character.'

'Here's the programme. We're thrilled about the opening session. Dinah Halsgrove is just about the biggest name you can get in crime writing.'

'I must say she was a big part of the attraction. She must be over ninety now. But still turning out quality thrillers.'

'She's ninety-two. And as sharp as a button. Marvellous, isn't it?'

'I hope I'm that productive in thirty-four years' time,' laughed Veronica.

'Don't we all?'

'There's tea in the private rose garden first, behind the Great Barn. You can meet your fellow enthusiasts. Here are your keys. When you've unloaded your luggage, you can move your vehicle across to the main car park.'

Hilary and Veronica emerged into the sunshine. The door the receptionist had indicated lay on the other side of the lawn between bushes of lavender. Hilary kept an injured silence as they had to retrace their steps outside the courtyard to where she had illegally left her car.

They hauled their luggage over the path around the lawn. The delicately needled branches of a tall tree spread over the grass. Its ancient roots knuckled their way up through the cobbles that fringed the path.

'*Metasequoia*, otherwise known as the dawn redwood,' Hilary announced. 'Rare example of a deciduous conifer.'

'Hilary! You're supposed to be retired from teaching, remember?'

Hilary swung round on her friend, dropping her case. 'Being a teacher isn't something I did. It's what I am. I thought you understood that. I like to *know* things.'

'Yes, Hilary. Sorry.'

Hilary saw the fondness in Veronica's smile and was glad of it.

Conversation ceased while they hauled their suitcases up two flights of narrow stairs.

Hilary panted as she reached the top. 'What sort of people come on a course in crime writing, do you think? Innocent, butter-wouldn't-melt-in-their-mouths types, looking for vicarious thrills? Or more sinister characters, keen to discover devious ways to do the deed themselves?'

'Hardly the latter,' Veronica suggested. 'It would look a bit obvious, wouldn't it, if someone committed a murder and it was found that they'd recently been to a master class on murder mysteries?'

TWO

Hilary struggled through the glass-paned fire doors to the second-floor landing. She consulted her key tag. 'Right. It looks as though I'm on this side of the corridor, and you're over there.'

She opened the door to her room. Her delighted cry brought Veronica across the corridor from her own room.

A massive ancient beam arched over the interior, springing from the whitewashed stone wall. Wooden pegs studded it. Others angled upwards to meet under the highest point of the roof. There was no ceiling. The shape of the room mirrored the slope of the slate roof outside.

The bed was enormous. There was a small fireplace with a chequerboard of decorative tiles. A dormer window looked out over the cloister garth.

'I seem to have struck the jackpot,' Hilary cried. 'They must have run out of single rooms.' She stroked a loving finger over the deeply pitted timbers. 'What do you think? Tudor, or recycled beams from the fourteenth-century abbey? I don't know whether Gavin Standforth's books are any good, but he certainly knows where to hold a conference.'

'Lucky you. I don't suppose my room is anything like as grand.'

Hilary waited a few minutes for Veronica to find her own quarters before she returned to the corridor. She crossed to a door a little further along.

'Come in,' called Veronica to her brisk tap.

This room was indeed smaller, and the bed was a single one, but the room's sloping ceiling showed its own signs of antiquity. Hilary went to the deep-silled window looking out on the other side of the East Cloister, away from the lawn. She found herself looking directly across a path at the magnificent tithe barn.

The rough stone walls were pitted at regular intervals by small embrasures to let in the light. But the walls themselves were dwarfed by the soaring height of the slate roof. She sighed with satisfaction. The monks might not have built the tithe barn to serve as a great hall, but it was hard to imagine a more splendid one.

She opened the window and leaned out, squinting along the path between the cloisters and the barn to her left.

'I was right. My memory hasn't let me down. This path leads to the Lady Chapel, which is all that's left intact of the abbey church.'

Veronica came to join her. 'I wonder if anyone uses it now.'

'It used to be the Woodleighs' private chapel. Now it would be people who live on the abbey estate, I suppose. It's a fair old step to the village church. Or maybe they just keep it for private prayer.'

'The abbey church is still rather romantic, don't you think, even though Henry the Eighth pulled it down. I like to imagine all those medieval monks, coming down the dormer stairs to pray in the middle of the night. We must take a look at it some time.'

'Meanwhile, tea beckons. I'll meet you in ten minutes.'

Hilary returned to her own bedroom.

'David would have liked this room,' she thought, as she dropped the sheaf of papers the receptionist had given her on the dressing table. But her husband had opted not to come with her. And for Veronica, sharing a holiday break with her Andrew was no longer an option. Death had taken him suddenly, two years ago.

Once Hilary and Veronica were settled in to their rooms, they negotiated the narrow stairs again. A few more people were arriving with suitcases, evidently bound for the same crime weekend. Hilary favoured them with a cheery smile. Others, earlier arrivals or casual visitors to the abbey, were strolling along the paths with a more leisurely air. Some were starting to tend more purposefully round the far end of the cloisters to the garden behind the Great Barn.

'I was going to say that it's hard to tell the criminal minds from innocent sightseers who've just dropped in to enjoy the historic buildings and the gardens. But I imagine those people over there are starting to head for the private rose garden. Tea!'

They entered the back of the barn and passed through a dim corridor out into the sunshine on the far side. This part of the garden was laid out with grassy terraces edged by stone walls and rose bushes, still aflame with crimson blossoms. Ropes across the gaps in the borders barred it from casual visitors. A table had been set out with a crisp white cloth, and tea urns stood beside generous plates of cake.

Hilary accepted a cup of tea from a waiter and helped herself to a slab of rich-looking fruit cake. She looked around with satisfaction. 'I must say, I rather like this feeling of privilege. In the past, I've only ever glimpsed this garden over the wall, or through gaps in the hedge, like ordinary mortals. It's rather nice to be on the inside for once.'

'I suppose that's what this weekend is all about,' said Veronica, setting down her slice of lemon gateau. 'Getting to look at things from another point of view. We may not actually write from the persona of our villain, but we need to have an understanding of what's going on in his mind, to make sense of what he does in the plot.'

'Or *she* does,' Hilary corrected her.

Swivelling her cup of tea dangerously, she advanced on the couple they had seen arriving at reception just ahead of them. 'Hello. Are you here to explore the dark side of your nature, or to celebrate the moral victory of good over evil?'

The man turned his stocky head towards her. He had a round, genial face, which now bore a look of incomprehension.

'Sorry?' He still attempted a smile.

'I was asking what brought you here for this weekend.'

'Oh, well. This is Jo's thing, really. I've just come along for the ride.'

Now that she looked more closely at the sleekly curled blonde by his side, Hilary saw that the woman of the pair, at least, was younger than she had thought. A lively, somewhat babyishly round face was surmounted by unexpectedly dark-framed spectacles, behind which her brown eyes sparkled. It gave her an incongruous mix of innocence and sharp intelligence. Those curls, Hilary decided, must be natural. Nobody under seventy went in for perms these days. She reserved judgement on the colour. The blonde cap seemed out of place with her dark eyes.

'I rather fancy trying my hand at some Scandinavian crime noir.' The smile flashed. 'You know, the sort of thing that's all over the telly nowadays, with subtitles. Sinister twilight in a marshy forest. A body lying in the mud, gruesomely murdered. A multiple cast of tortured characters and a deeply flawed investigator.'

Hilary raised her eyebrows. There was a childish enthusiasm in the woman's face that seemed out of step with her words.

'Hmm, I wouldn't have guessed. Hilary Masters, by the way, and this is Veronica.'

'How do you do. Jo Walters, and my husband Harry.'

'Good fruit cake,' Hilary commented. 'You can always rely on Morland Abbey to feed you well.'

'Have you been here before?'

'Not to anything like this. To the literary festival in the summer, or sometimes just to wander round the grounds.'

'You must be local, then.'

'Near enough. Twenty miles away. Do I gather this is your first time?'

'Yes. It looked absolutely beautiful in the publicity. And Harry's keen on gardening. I couldn't resist the combination. He can wander round the grounds, while I do the dastardly murder. Perfect combination.'

'I know what you mean. Dark deeds in an idyllic setting. It gives an extra frisson, don't you think?'

A squat, straight-haired woman was advancing upon them. She was inspecting people as she passed. She stopped in front of Hilary.

'Your name badge,' she demanded. 'You must have been given one when you booked in.'

'Upstairs on the dressing table,' Hilary confessed. 'I'm not keen on going round with "Hilary" blazoned on my bosom.'

The woman's own badge said in bold letters: THERESA.

'You'll need it to get into Dinah Halsgrove's talk after this.'

'Sorry!' said Hilary, feeling like a scolded schoolgirl. 'I wouldn't miss that for the world. I'll nip up and get it when I've finished this delicious cake.'

The stout woman softened. 'There's more on the table. Help yourself.'

Someone tapped a teaspoon against the urn. The chatter across the garden fell silent. A tall man, with wavy black hair and a silver-grey jacket, threw a professional smile around the group, deliberately including all of them.

'Hello, everybody. Good to see you all. I'm Gavin Standforth, in case you hadn't recognized me from my dust jackets. It will be my delight to entice you into a life of crime over this weekend. Mind you, you could say I'm cutting off my own nose to spite my face. With competition to get published the way it is, why would I want to encourage more of you to become crime writers, and take the bread out of my mouth?'

His audience shared in the laughter.

'You've been given the programme when you arrived. Just to draw your attention to the two highlights of today. First, of course, Dinah Halsgrove's talk will be in the Great Barn straight after this. Then at seven it's down to the quay for our evening boat trip on the Dart. There'll be a buffet supper on board and I'll talk you through some of the things you'll see downriver. I believe most of you have got cars, but if you haven't, see me or Theresa' – he indicated the stout woman who had inspected their badges – 'and we'll fix you up with a lift. If you have any issues on the domestic side, see the Morland Abbey people. They have someone on duty twenty-four/seven, on reception, or in the bar, or failing that on the end of a mobile phone. Anything to do with the programme, come to us. That's me, Theresa, or Melissa, whom you're just about to meet.'

Hilary sensed a commotion behind her. She turned with everyone else. Two women were coming out of the Great Barn to join them.

One was unnaturally tall, her head stooped forward under a fall of light-brown hair. She wore a dress of almost-transparent floral material in shades of green, which fell to her ankles and floated as she walked. The other was considerably older, but trimly upright, with the sort of straight backbone you rarely saw nowadays. Her white hair was cut severely short around a weathered but intelligent face.

'Dinah Halsgrove!' breathed Veronica. 'In the flesh.'

Gavin broke off what he was saying. He strode towards his distinguished guest, hand outstretched, face set in a beam of welcome. He took her by the shoulders and kissed her on both cheeks. Dinah Halsgrove looked rather startled. She did not return the kiss.

'They did well to get her for such a small affair as this,' Hilary grunted. 'There must only be about thirty of us.'

'She's spoken at the literary festival here before, hasn't she? I know that's much bigger, but she probably likes coming to the abbey. Who wouldn't?'

Hilary continued to stare at the meeting between the trim, decisive-looking woman, with such a worldwide reputation for crime thrillers, and the rather unctuous Gavin Standforth with his solitary bestseller.

'Now there's an idea for a crime novel,' she mused. 'Which do you fancy? "Famous detective writer murdered at mystery weekend"? Or "Queen of crime suspected of murder at thriller convention"?'

'I don't buy it,' Veronica laughed. 'Not the second one, anyway. Someone who's written as many bestselling detective stories as she has should be able to plan the perfect murder and get away with it.'

THREE

G avin approached his distinguished guest bearing a plate of cakes and a beaming smile. Dinah Halsgrove waved the offering aside. As if unwilling to accept rejection, he continued to hover at her elbow.

'I can recommend the fruit cake,' suggested Hilary, who had worked her way within speaking distance. 'Morland's finest.'

The novelist turned a businesslike smile on her. 'Type two diabetes, I'm afraid. More difficult to control as you grow older. I already take so many tablets I rattle like a maraca.' She switched that polite smile to Gavin. 'Tea, if you wouldn't mind. With lemon.'

Her host's eager grin vanished. He strode back towards the tea table.

Hilary watched Jo Walters advance on their speaker. Her small bespectacled face was a mixture of trepidation and anticipation.

'I loved *The Case of the Disappearing Rabbit*,' she ventured. 'The ending really took me by surprise.'

Dinah Halsgrove favoured her with a rather weary but courteous smile. 'I'm glad you liked it. Do you write yourself?'

A strange expression came over Jo's face. It might almost have been anger. 'I try.'

'No luck with publication? It's a tough old world in publishing at the moment, I'm afraid.'

She accepted the cup of tea Gavin brought her and moved a few discreet steps back, away from her fans. Hilary heard her tell her long-skirted minder, 'If you wouldn't mind, I'd like a little rest before my talk.'

Presently the two of them headed back inside the building.

Hilary turned to find another elderly woman standing on her own. Also small, also trim, but with short grey hair instead of white. There was something about her self-containment which made her solitude seem something to be respected, rather than pitied. She had not moved to intrude upon Dinah Halsgrove, though she had stood not far away.

All the same, Hilary advanced upon her. 'Hilary Masters. Here with murderous intent. Like you, I assume.'

If the woman looked surprised, her smile was warmer than Dinah Halsgrove's dutiful politeness had been.

'Lin Bell. Yes, I had a go at writing historicals, with no success, I'm afraid. But I discovered an unexpected streak of violence in my books. It made me wonder whether I wouldn't do better in crime.'

'I think we're all going to reveal things about ourselves we hadn't suspected. I can't wait to get started. My friend Veronica over there . . .' She indicated her tall, fair companion, who seemed to be laughing with a pair of young men. 'She's the sweetest creature imaginable in real life. I'm dying to know her thoughts about killing someone.'

The gathering in the private garden was thinning. Veronica came over the grass to rejoin Hilary.

'It looks as if we're being steered into the Great Barn. It's nearly four thirty.'

Gavin's helper, Theresa, was standing by the door, encouraging the course members into the shadows of the stone-flagged corridor. Stewards were standing by the inner doors that gave access to the Great Barn auditorium. There were a great many more people than Hilary had expected. Veronica showed her name badge and was allowed through.

Hilary stepped forward. She put on her most authoritative senior teacher's voice. 'I've left that silly name badge in my room, but I'm booked on the crime-writing course. I've come with my friend whom you've just let through.' She favoured the bespectacled young man with a confident beam.

He blushed. 'I'm sorry. You have to show a name badge or a ticket. I can't let you through without.'

Veronica's back was disappearing down the crowded aisle towards the front of the hall, under the arching beams. The seats were filling rapidly, not only from the garden, but from the great door nearest the gateway as well. Inside the barn, people were starting to perch on the broad ledges that ran round the walls.

'Idiot!' Hilary said to herself. Of course, thirty would-be crime writers would hardly pay the expenses for someone like Dinah Halsgrove. What was it the door steward had said? *Name badges or tickets*. Gavin must have advertised her talk to the general public. And with her reputation, the Great Barn would probably be full.

'Veronica!' Hilary called. But her friend did not look back. She had probably not heard. 'Drat!' The look Hilary gave the young steward should have shrivelled him on the spot. But he was busy checking the badges of other course members behind her and admitting them to the hall.

Fuming, Hilary headed for the door to the cobbled courtyard and out into the blaze of sunlight. To her dismay, a long queue was snaking along the path, moving slowly up the steps into the barn.

Unwilling to admit that it was herself she should be annoyed with, she stomped her way against the flow of arrivals. She muttered her excuses as she broke through the slowly moving queue to the cloister garth and the door that led up to her room.

The two flights of stairs seemed steep, even without a suitcase.

Mercifully, the name badge announcing 'Hilary, Beginning a Life in Crime' was indeed lying on the dressing table where she had a vague memory of discarding it. With a scowl at the mirror, she pinned it on her blouse.

As she descended the stairs she had a nasty feeling that she might now be expected to join the queue of ticket-holders, and not overtake them to regain the privileged access of the other course members coming straight from the private garden.

She struggled with the fire doors at the foot of the first flight of stairs and almost cannoned into someone else approaching along the narrow landing.

The woman drew back with a hiss of indrawn breath.

'Sorry!' Hilary exclaimed. 'More haste, less speed. After you. I assume you're heading for Dinah Halsgrove's talk. Oh, sorry! You're on the staff, aren't you?'

She recognized the woman now, though the landing was in shadow. The silhouette was familiar. That way of bending her head forward to reduce her height. It was the woman in the long floral dress who had accompanied Dinah Halsgrove out on to the lawn. She was, Hilary assumed, another of Gavin's assistants, like Theresa. She must have been sent to meet the speaker at the station.

'No! No, it's nothing. You go ahead.' The woman spoke rapidly. There was an undercurrent of something sharper in her voice. She withdrew into the shadows of the corridor so swiftly it was as if she had never been there. Hilary could not even hear her steps hurrying along it.

For all her haste to join the queue, Hilary paused for a second. It seemed an odd time for the woman to be going to her room.

Surely no one involved with the crime-writing course would want to miss Dinah Halsgrove's talk?

But perhaps it wasn't her own room she was heading for. Hilary's experience of attending conferences here before told her that the best bedrooms on the first floor of the historic East Cloister were often reserved for speakers. Opposite, in the West Cloister, the rooms had a more modern feel. And the rooms on the second floor tended to be smaller, like Veronica's.

Still, there *was* only one guest speaker this time. Gavin's staff might also be occupying rooms on this lower corridor.

There was no time to stand and wonder about this, or why the woman had seemed so startled to meet Hilary on the landing. Almost – Hilary tested the word in her mind – *angry*. It seemed a puzzling reaction, but there was no time now to think about it. She hurried down the second flight of stairs and into the courtyard.

The end of the queue had moved past the door and was moving up the steps into the hall.

'Drat!' said Hilary again. She pictured the Great Barn full now: the front seats at floor level before the speakers' table, the raked seating in the back half of the hall, the elevated ledges that could hold several dozen people. As she climbed the steps, almost the last to do so, she sighed. She was past the age of wanting to sit on a narrow ledge. Instead, she turned to the left, showed her name badge to another steward and was allowed through the door which gave access up more steps to the rear gallery, added by Sir George when he turned the tithe barn into his great hall.

The gallery too was almost full. Hilary squeezed her way past people's knees to a vacant place on the bench near the wall.

She was in no good humour as she peered down into the body of the Great Barn. It should have been an emotive sight. Heraldic banners blazed from poles along the walls. A forest of medieval timbers vaulted overhead. A table and two chairs were set on the rostrum. But for once, Hilary was not in the mood to revel in the setting.

It took her some time to locate Veronica's fair head in the third row from the front. She seemed to have been keeping an empty seat beside her, but as Hilary watched, she relinquished it to the steward's appeal and let a latecomer take the vacant place. Hilary glowered. If she had thought, she could have claimed it herself.

There was a rustle through the audience, then a burst of clapping as Gavin led his distinguished speaker through a door on to the rostrum. Even from this distance, Hilary could sense how thrilled he was to be hosting the *grande dame* of crime writing at what was, after all, an insignificant provincial writing course. It's the barn, she thought. It isn't Gavin Standforth who has lured her here; it's Morland Abbey. She's been here for more prestigious festivals and it has laid its enchantment on her.

Gavin was introducing her. 'You hardly need me to remind you of her achievements. Forty-one detective novels, guaranteed to go straight to the top of the bestseller lists. The distinguished patron of authors' organizations and a prominent spokeswoman on their behalf. Something of an expert, I believe, on the administration of poison.' As he turned to her with a knowing smile, a ripple of appreciative laughter ran through the audience.

'You will understand, I'm sure, if she doesn't occupy the speaker's usual place at the lectern. She has asked if she may deliver her talk sitting down. I hope everyone can hear her well enough. So without further ado, I give you . . . the queen of crime, Dinah Halsgrove.'

The applause as he sat down was even more enthusiastic.

Hilary reflected, with a small ray of satisfaction, that she might, after all, have a better view from the gallery than some of those seated in the body of the hall, with other people's heads in the way.

Just for a moment, the little woman in the cerise shirt and black trousers seemed about to get to her feet. An instinctive movement. She must have spoken at scores of such gatherings over the years. But she sank down again behind the table with the microphones. She looked a more diminutive figure than she had when drinking tea on the lawn. Her sleekly cut hair was snow white. It was a vivid contrast: red, black, white, though the trousers were largely hidden by the tablecloth. The colours of the Celtic goddess of fertility, Hilary remembered: Maiden, Mother, Crone. Dinah Halsgrove had definitely reached the Crone stage and wore it with an imperious authority. And yet, seated, there was something vulnerable in the ninety-two-year-old facing the expectations of her capacity audience.

But when Dinah began to speak, Hilary settled back with what she was surprised to identify as relief. The elderly novelist had lost none of her ability to spellbind an audience. And Hilary knew from experience that not everyone who wrote well could speak about it entertainingly.

'I must have killed more people in my career than some of you have had birthdays.' Gavin's reference to her expert knowledge of poisons had drawn only laughter. Now, there was something in the way Dinah Halsgrove spoke that sent a frisson down the spine. These deaths, it said, were serious to her.

'When I share notes with fellow crime writers, I find that we begin with different starting points. For some it is the setting. Everything that happens springs from that place. Other writers are grabbed by their central character, be that the murderer or, more likely, his pursuing nemesis. For me, it is the crime itself. How exactly is it done, and why? And you will appreciate that, after forty-one novels, it gets harder to think of yet another method as arresting as the first, or another twist in the workings of the human mind. I'm praying – and that's not too strong a word – that the ideas and inventions will keep coming, as long as I'm physically and mentally capable of handling a keyboard.

'Of course, one doesn't just sit and wait for ideas to arrive out of the blue. They come to those who go in search of them, or at least create the opportunities for them to appear. Gavin, dear boy, you are right. I must have done enough study into the range of poisons, their effect on the human body, and the chances of their going undetected, to qualify for at least two PhDs.'

Hilary followed the talk with enjoyment. The detailed examples about the physical characteristics of some poisons, combined with the deviousness of the minds that had used them, interwove strangely with the setting of this magnificent medieval hall. Of course, if she wrote a crime novel herself, it would almost certainly be historical and set in Elizabethan times. That, after all, had been the highlight of her teaching and her personal studies for nearly forty years. In an instant, she peopled this hall below her with the aristocratic Woodleigh family and their guests, their ambitious attendants, their low-born servants.

It was a jolt to be brought back to twenty-first-century science. But the two were not entirely unconnected. At its height, Morland would have had its wise adepts, its herb garden, with plants that could bring both healing or death, depending on the dose. Certainly its share of jealousies, political and personal, to send long shadows down this hall.

Sooner than she wanted, the talk was over. There were questions, but not too many. Gavin was the solicitous chairman, his famous speaker like a personal treasure he must protect from pawing hands.

'I think Miss Halsgrove has given us a feast to savour. Just watch out for poison in your supper.' He laughed again, and his audience followed him. Yet he lacked the underlying menace behind Dinah Halsgrove's words, which meant that what she talked about was not just clever entertainment, but deadly reality.

'She'll be signing her novels in the book room, to your right as you leave the barn. And may I remind the members of my writing course that we meet down on the quay at six thirty. Now, would you please remain in your seats while I escort Miss Halsgrove out.'

They were gone, disappearing below the gallery where Hilary waited.

She continued to watch the scene beneath her as she spoke to the woman beside her. 'Well, she's lost none of her marbles. Not a single note in front of her, yet she could roll off the toxic properties of just about any substance you cared to mention.'

'I know. Fascinating, wasn't it? What must it be like to spend your whole life plotting murders, and how to get away with them?'

There was something familiar in the voice.

Hilary turned her head further. She had been so bothered by her late arrival that it had not occurred to her to look closely at the woman on the bench beside her. Now she recognized the youthful, bespectacled face with its innocently rounded features.

'Of course, you're Jo!' Then, refreshing her memory of their introduction, 'Jo Walters. What are you doing up in the gods like this, when the rest of our group are down there at the front? Did you forget your badge too?'

'What?' Hilary could see the thoughts chasing behind those

dark brown eyes. 'Oh, yes! Yes. I had to dash back for it. Came out again to find myself near the end of the queue.'

'Me too.'

Hilary studied her. Years of questioning the behaviour of teenagers had taught her when a girl was rapidly seizing any excuse that offered itself, to cover what she had been up to. But Jo Walters must be in her thirties, or older. A fellow participant on Gavin's course. Hilary had no authority to question her on what she might really have been doing to arrive late.

FOUR

Hilary followed the crowd towards the book room on the ground floor of the West Cloister. Looking over people's shoulders as well as her limited height allowed, she saw that the room was stacked with copies of Dinah Halsgrove's books. The author herself was seated at a table, pen in hand. Gavin stood proprietorially over her, a trim figure in his silvery jacket, beaming with reflected fame. A queue of would-be purchasers was rapidly forming.

'Excuse me.'

Hilary turned to find a woman working her way through the crowd. She felt a sudden constriction in her throat. It was the same minder in the flowing skirt who had escorted Dinah Halsgrove into the garden. Melissa, she remembered. The woman, Hilary realized with an unexplained shiver, she had bumped into in the bedroom corridor. The one who had seemed so unaccountably upset to meet her.

The woman reached the signing table and set down a glass half full of golden-brown liquid in front of the novelist.

Whisky, Hilary decided. The author had certainly earned it.

In Hilary's efforts to step out of the way, she had bumped into the table behind her. She heard a slither of falling books. She looked round in dismay to find that a smaller display of Gavin Standforth's novels lay in disarray across the table. Some had tumbled to the floor.

'Here! Let me help you.'

Lin Bell had followed Hilary into the book room. That neat elderly woman, who had stood listening, but not pushing herself forward, as Dinah Halsgrove took tea in the private garden. Hilary smiled her gratitude. Together they reconstructed the stand of books as best they could.

Lin picked up the most prominent title. The number of copies outweighed all the rest. '*The Long Crippler.* A brilliant plot. Have you read it?'

Hilary stared at the cover. A blind, snakelike head quested its snout through mysterious swirls of grey. There was something intentionally sinister about it.

'Afraid not.'

'Then I won't spoil it for you. I only wish I'd thought of it myself.'

'Odd title. I suppose it makes sense if you've read it.'

'Apparently the long crippler is the local name for a slowworm. There's a superstition that it lames horses. You'll understand if you do read it.'

'I've always had a soft spot for slowworms. You sometimes find the slinky little things asleep when you turn over a stone in the garden. I thought they were harmless, though. Not a poisonous snake.'

The two young men who had been talking to Veronica in the garden had squeezed into the book room behind them. One was shorter, darker, in denim jeans and jacket. Lank hair fell across the forehead of his taller companion, startlingly red against his black leather jacket and shirt. Hilary judged them to be in their thirties, at most.

The shorter of the pair reached for another title at Hilary's elbow. '*The Long Crippler*'s genius. But the rest . . . Well, this sequel was pretty much run of the mill.'

'Still,' grinned his red-haired friend, 'I bet it sold well on the back of *The Crippler.*'

'Lucky sod. That's all I need. One good break.'

It was an echo of what Veronica had said.

Lin Bell smiled at them, rather thinly. 'Let's hope Gavin can teach the rest of us how to do it, then.'

The queue for Dinah Halsgrove's books had lengthened

considerably. Hilary could not find the end of it. She sighed. Did she really need the author's signature on her latest offering? A good book was a good book, without the trappings of celebrity culture.

She turned away. Time to go back to her room and choose some warmer clothes for the evening boat cruise.

The questing head of *The Long Crippler* seemed to follow her out of the room.

The wooded banks of the Dart glided past. Hilary let most of Gavin's commentary wash over her, though she did perk up interest as they passed the vineyards of the Buddhist community at Sharpham Manor. There, she thought with relish, might be an intriguing setting for a more modern crime novel.

Away from his distinguished guest, Gavin had lost that unctuous smile. He had almost snapped at his long-haired assistant Melissa as he ushered her on board. It was odd. He should have been basking in the success of their first talk.

Dinah Halsgrove, not surprisingly, had not come with them. Nor had the smaller Theresa.

Whatever Gavin had reproved her for, Melissa had replied only with a wide smile and a toss of her long hair. There was something about her defiance that deepened the frown on Gavin's brow.

Still, he had now recovered something of his professional charm, to judge from his voice over the loudspeaker.

'Now, folks, we're approaching the high spot of the cruise for every fan of detective fiction. You see that boathouse, down by the water's edge, and the white house high above it? That's *Greenway*, the Devon hideaway of the original queen of the genre: Agatha Christie.'

There was a rush to the port side of the boat. Cameras flashed in the gathering dusk.

'I don't want to disappoint you, but she didn't actually write any of her books here. It really was a hideaway – the place she came to refresh herself on holiday. Not easy to get to, even nowadays. The National Trust owns it, but they prefer that you don't drive up to the door. So it's the vintage bus, or the ferry, or a pleasant woodland walk.'

Hilary looked up at the white house overlooking the river, then

let her attention slide back to the brown water slipping away
along the side of the cruise boat with an engaging gurgle. She
was beginning to feel hungry. She had seen the buffet supper
laid out in the cabin below, but the beauty of the evening had
encouraged most people to stay on deck for the outward leg of
the voyage down the estuary to Dartmouth.

'Oh, Hilary, look!' Veronica touched her arm.

Hilary lifted her eyes from her contemplation of the river
running past. Ahead a forest of masts from a marina, safely
tucked away inside the entrance to the estuary. Beyond, the
evening sky was piled with purple clouds, edged with gold. A
rose-pink flush caught the smaller wisps of cloud trailing away
to the west.

'Looks like rain,' she said.

'Oh, *Hilary*!'

Hilary grinned. 'Yes, I'll give you that. It's a very fine sunset.
Do you think they'll let us eat when we turn for home? I'm
famished.'

As if in answer, the boat began to swing across the hurrying
current. Gavin's voice came over the loudspeaker.

'This is as far as we go, folks. We shan't quite venture out
into open water. But you can glimpse Dartmouth Castle at the
harbour entrance.' Then came the words Hilary had been waiting
for. 'Supper is laid on the lower deck. The rain clouds may catch
us up before we get back to Totnes, but you'll be snug and dry
down there, and you can still admire the scenery through the
windows while you eat. Evening's a good time to see waterfowl
on the river.'

They descended the steps and Hilary piled her plate with
finger food.

'I wouldn't have minded a hot meal back in the restaurant,'
she remarked to Veronica. 'I hear Morland's chef is a wizard. I
had a peek at the menu. We're into the game season. Venison,
pheasant.'

'I think I saw a mention of wild boar.'

'Instead of which, we've got sausage rolls and quiche.'

'But look at the scenery.'

'Trees. And more trees.'

'Oh, *Hilary*!'

They had reached the end of the buffet table. Melissa stood
serving drinks from a smaller table. Pale brown hair fell from
her shoulders as she leaned her head towards them.

It was the woman Hilary had bumped into on the landing of
the East Cloister. The one who had backed away with a startled
look in those brown eyes. The one who had brought Dinah
Halsgrove a whisky at the book signing. She gave no sign that
she recognized Hilary. She smiled.

'Hot punch? Or there's a non-alcoholic version.'

'Well, that perks things up. I was missing my hot dinner.'

They accepted the steaming glasses.

'Got one for me, Melissa?' Gavin was right behind them. 'I'm
parched with all that talking.'

'No Dinah Halsgrove, I see,' Hilary said to him.

'No, I'm afraid not. Not surprisingly, the dear lady felt she'd
had enough for one day. The train from Sussex, then addressing
a crowd of several hundred and signing goodness knows how
many books. She's opted for a quiet supper in her room. Theresa's
looking after her.'

There was an edginess in his voice that she could not quite
place. He shot a look at Melissa that Hilary failed to understand.

'That would be in the East Cloister, I assume. I know they
often put speakers there.'

'Yes, enchanting, isn't it? The oldest part of the accommodation.'

'We're up in the rooms under the East Cloister roof.'

'Everything OK?'

'Yes, fine, thank you. Mine is verging on the palatial.'

He turned away from her without replying. The professional
smile of this afternoon seemed to be in short supply. Hilary
looked back at Melissa. She was still busy pouring drinks for
the slowly moving queue. A perfectly ordinary woman. There
was no need to imagine a mystery surrounding her, just because
Hilary had startled her, emerging suddenly from the shadowed
stairs, when everyone else was in the hall or waiting to enter it.

Her smile grew rather fixed as she poured Hilary a glass.
Was she too remembering that encounter? Come to think of
it, was she wondering what this stocky woman in the tweed
skirt and silk blouse had been doing in the East Cloister at
that particular time? Might Hilary have been the one acting

suspiciously? It was an intriguing thought. Hilary swigged the hot punch with relish, as she considered this twist in the scenario.

Yet why had Gavin spoken so sharply to Melissa as they boarded?

They were passing Agatha Christie's *Greenway* again on their way upstream. It was strange how a weekend on crime writing could add a sinister colour to your perceptions.

Veronica interrupted her train of thought. 'What's up with Gavin? He just got out his phone and sloshed half his glass of punch over the table.'

Hilary looked round swiftly. Gavin did indeed look white with shock. She edged determinedly closer, nudging other people aside, until she was in earshot.

'No!' Gavin was protesting. 'That's terrible! I'm stuck on this blasted boat, but I'll be back there just as soon as I can. Pray God the news isn't worse by the time I get there.'

He put his phone away and stood there, looking stunned.

'Bad news?' Hilary asked.

He seemed to come back to her from a long way away.

'What? No . . . No, nothing for you to worry about.'

This was clearly untrue. He made his way through the press of people eating chicken drumsticks and slices of quiche, to where Melissa stood behind the drinks table, now clear of customers.

There was a low-voiced consultation. From his body language, Hilary was sure he was speaking angrily to Melissa as he bent towards her. Melissa looked oddly unperturbed. She did not change colour, as Gavin had. She was still smiling. But she bent her long neck solicitously towards Gavin, apparently trying to comfort him. Gavin himself kept glancing forward through the cabin windows to where the cruise boat was slowly forging its way back upriver against the current. Dusk was deepening.

Veronica was at her elbow again. 'I wonder what all *that* was about. One thing's certain. Something's happened. Gavin can't wait to get back to Totnes.'

The boat had hardly nudged against the quay before Gavin leaped ashore. Ignoring the shouts of the crew and the men warping the craft more securely, he sped towards the car park.

Hilary, too, shouldered her way towards the gangplank, with Veronica more apologetically in her wake. It was a short brisk walk to where they had left the car on the quayside. Hilary zoomed out on to the road ahead of everyone else.

Back at Morland Abbey, she shot out of the car and made for the cobbled path to the entrance arch. Veronica's longer legs overtook her. They both stopped short as they came out on to the wide lawns of the cloister garth.

It was not normal for vehicles to drive into this enclosed square of lawn and paths. But parked in front of the East Cloister was a yellow ambulance with green and yellow chequered bands along its sides. The blue lights across the roof were still flashing, evidence of the urgent haste with which it had driven from wherever the nearest accident and emergency hospital was.

They were just in time to see a stretcher being carried out of the door where, only a few hours before, Hilary had gone hurrying in to fetch her badge. She could not see the face, but with a sinking heart she knew for certain who it must be.

With a sense of inevitability Hilary stood back to let the ambulance drive past her, siren now blaring.

Gavin and Theresa were left standing forlornly in front of the lavender bushes. Hilary strode up to them.

'It's Dinah Halsgrove, isn't it? What happened?'

Gavin turned a tragic face to her. 'We don't know yet. Of course, she was ninety-two. It could be anything, at her age. Heart attack, stroke. She'd asked for supper in her room, but when Theresa went to see if there was anything else she needed, Dinah was . . .' His voice faltered.

Theresa beside him finished his sentence, somewhat grimly: 'She was lying, slumped over the edge of the bed. She was out cold. Her skin looked . . . grey. I thought at first . . . well, you can imagine. The ambulance crew seem to think it's touch and go. We'll have to wait till she gets to hospital to know for certain. But it must be natural causes.'

Why should it not be? It seemed an odd thing to say.

'Oh, I do so hope she pulls round,' Gavin exclaimed. 'It would be terrible if the great Dinah Halsgrove were to die at a conference I'd arranged. I could never forgive myself!'

The silly man was verging on the histrionic.

'It's surely not your fault,' Hilary snapped. 'You were halfway down the River Dart. I'd be more worried if I were the chef. Anybody else taken ill?'

Gavin looked at Theresa blankly. The other woman shrugged. 'I was too shocked to think of asking. But the rest of you had a buffet supper on the boat.'

'The restaurant here is open to the public, isn't it? You need to find out if anyone else who ate there this evening has been taken ill.'

'Well, I told the Morland Abbey staff straight away,' Theresa said. 'Fiona, the manager, took care of everything. I presume, if there has to be an investigation, it's in their court now. But it didn't look like food poisoning to me. She wasn't sick or shitting herself. She was just out cold.'

Gavin put out a hand, as if to stop her.

'Oh, Gavin! Snap out of it. Going round looking like a tragedy queen's not going to help.'

'Where's Melissa?' he queried. 'I have to talk to her.'

Hilary looked at Veronica. 'I don't know about you, but I think a strong black coffee is called for, if not something stronger. That punch was more orange juice than anything else.'

They headed for the lofty Chapter House next to the Great Barn, which housed the restaurant and bar.

'Do you really think she'll be all right?' Veronica asked as they followed the path around the lawn. 'Silly question. How could you know?'

'At ninety-two, it has to be a close call.'

Other course participants were coming along the paths now, having made a less hasty departure from the quay. Yet there was an air of alarm and anxious conversation. They must have seen the ambulance speeding away, even if news of Dinah Halsgrove's sudden illness had not yet spread beyond Veronica and Hilary.

At the bar, Hilary opted for both a coffee and a shot of whisky, while Veronica ordered a gin and tonic. They settled themselves at an empty table. This octagonal building with its stone vaulted roof had once housed the business meetings of the monks, before Sir George had commandeered it for his kitchen. Huge embrasures showed where once two fireplaces had fed the Woodleigh household and their guests. High above, a tracery of Gothic windows let in the fading light. They watched the room slowly filling up.

'Mind if we join you?' It was Harry Walters, husband of the blonde-haired Jo.

'No, of course not.' Veronica smiled.

'Bit of excitement,' said Jo, moving in to take the remaining seat. 'We were coming up the drive when this ambulance came tearing down the road. Siren screaming, lights flashing. Harry had to pull out of the way. We were wondering if there'd been an accident in the kitchen. All those sharp knives.'

'Nothing like that,' Hilary told her. 'Dinah Halsgrove was found collapsed in her room.'

There was a startled silence.

'No! Surely not!' Jo's cry brought other heads turning round to listen.

Hilary rose to the occasion, and to her feet. 'Ladies and gentlemen, you might as well all hear it now. While we were on the cruise, Dinah Halsgrove was taken dangerously ill.'

At the back of the room a young woman with a ponytail gave a nervous laugh.

'Are you sure it was genuine? You don't suppose Gavin has staged this for our benefit? A murder, on a mystery weekend?'

The word fell jarringly into the silence. Hilary snorted.

'Don't be silly. No one's mentioned murder. She's not dead.'

She found herself crossing her fingers.

FIVE

Hilary woke suddenly in darkness. She groped for the light switch. An unfamiliar bedside baffled her fingers. Before her brain could catch up with the reason, a more startling truth broke in upon her. She had identified the sound that had woken her.

Someone was trying the door latch.

Scattered bits of knowledge were coming back to her. She was in a bedroom at Morland Abbey. On the top floor of the East Cloister. Veronica was in a room across the corridor. David was not beside her in the big bed.

On an unexplained instinct, she abandoned her attempt to find the light switch. Her senses were sharpened as she swung her feet quietly to the floor. In a few swift steps, she crossed to where she now remembered the door to be.

As her eyes accustomed to the gloom she reached cautiously for the handle. Her nerves were stretched, waiting for the sound to come again. She had almost grasped the latch when she heard it lift.

With the determination of decades spent as a teacher, she forestalled whoever was on the other side. She flung the door wide open.

The hiss that greeted her sparked a memory she could not immediately place.

The corridor was dimly illuminated. Backing away from her was a tall, thin figure spectrally gowned in white. Pale brown hair fell forward around her face.

Fragments of memory were falling into place. She had stumbled across the same figure, clad then in floating green, in the corridor below this. Again, there had been that sibilant alarm.

Melissa. That was the name. Gavin Standforth's assistant. The woman who had fetched Dinah Halsgrove from the station.

'Excuse me!' she said, taking the advantage of surprise. 'Can I help you?'

Generations of schoolgirls would have recognized the menace in that simple question.

Melissa floundered, as Hilary had meant she should. 'No . . . I . . . got lost.'

'Is that the best you can do?'

Hilary was getting into her stride now, beginning to enjoy herself.

Both women were startled out of the encounter by a commotion further down the corridor.

'*Melissa!*' The masculine cry was both suppressed yet urgent. It might not have woken Hilary if she had still been asleep.

She made out the pale figure advancing towards them. Gavin Standforth, in silvery silk pyjamas. Hilary was suddenly aware of her own skimpy summer nightdress. A little of her schoolmistress's authority ebbed from her. She stiffened her back. She was not the one who should feel embarrassed.

Gavin was as smooth as ever, his smile rather ghostly in the lamplight.

'I'm terribly sorry, Mrs Masters. Hilary, isn't it? Melissa, I'm afraid, is prone to sleepwalking. I hope she didn't alarm you. Come along, Melissa. Let's get you back to bed.'

He took the tall woman's elbow. At first, she made to shake him off, but then her head drooped. She let him begin to lead her away.

'Just a minute,' Hilary said. 'Your rooms are on the floor below us, aren't they? Her sleepwalking's taken her remarkably far off course.'

Even as she said this, she didn't know if it was true. How far did somnambulists venture from their beds?

A second later, she knew what was bugging her. That encounter before Dinah Halgsrove's talk, when she had gone back to fetch her badge. Even at the time, there had been a startling malevolence in the reaction which had greeted Hilary when she bumped into Melissa. As though she was not only surprised that Hilary should meet her in that corridor, but angry. Why?

Her imagination took her back to that first moment when she had woken in her bed and known that someone was trying to get into the room. Hilary was not of a nervous disposition, but there was something about that surreptitious movement, coupled with that earlier flash of rage, that made her scalp crawl. She knew with a certainty she could not explain that Melissa had not been sleepwalking.

It took a couple of seconds, as the couple retreated towards the staircase, to realize that Gavin knew that too. He might have manufactured a more plausible excuse than Melissa's, but it was no more true. Whatever had brought Melissa to Hilary's bedroom, Gavin must have known what it was and feared it. He had come hurrying after her with that urgent cry.

She watched their figures dwindle under the last lamp before the stairs.

She turned back to her door and started.

Another figure was standing in the corridor behind her.

*   *   *

'Veronica!'

'Am I as alarming a sight as all that?'

Veronica had slipped a pink cotton housecoat over her rose-patterned nightdress. She managed to look, Hilary reflected ruefully, as delightful as always, even suddenly roused from sleep.

'No! I mean . . . well, it's been a rather surprising night.'

'You seem to have had company.'

'Melissa. Lost or sleepwalking. Take your pick. She was trying to get into my room.'

'And you don't believe either of those. Come into my room while I make us some hot chocolate. You look a bit shaken.'

Hilary followed her into the smaller room with the single bed. She collapsed into the armchair while Veronica put the kettle on.

'I might have believed her, or Gavin, if it wasn't the second time I've had a run-in with her in the last few hours. I don't think I've told you this.'

She went over again that strange encounter in the East Cloister corridor.

'I can't explain just how . . . menacing it sounded. Like a snake you've just startled.'

Veronica carried her hot chocolate across the bed and sat there.

'And you've got it into your head that this might have something to do with Dinah Halsgrove's falling ill. But we don't know there's anything suspicious about that, given her age.'

Hilary heard again the question echoing across the bar last night.

'Unless Gavin staged it for our benefit.'

'And this could be one more clue for us?' Veronica shook her head. 'I don't buy it. Still . . . Gavin found her in our corridor. It's above theirs. Yet it seems he knew where to come.'

Hilary pondered this. 'We'll have to wait till the morning to clarify that. Find out just what was wrong with our distinguished speaker. I can't believe they'd actually harm her, just to jazz up a murder mystery weekend. And I don't see where I could fit in.'

Veronica put down her cup. 'Will you be all right now, on your own?'

It was not normal for people to be so solicitous about Hilary. She did not usually give the impression of being vulnerable. But Veronica had always been perceptive.

Hilary shook her head, not in denial, but to clear her thoughts. 'If Melissa wasn't sleepwalking, why else would she come to my room?'

An uncharacteristic shudder ran through her.

'I'm not a fanciful woman, but I can't help wondering what she might have done if she'd found me asleep in bed.'

The question lay between them unanswered.

It was an uncomfortable thought.

SIX

The next time she woke, a faint grey light showed through a gap in the curtains. But the window was in the wrong place. Hilary struggled once again to make sense of the unfamiliar bedroom. This was not her bed. It was far too wide and there was no David beside her.

An unexplained feeling of dread overshadowed her.

Slowly, the reality slipped into place. She was in Morland Abbey, for a weekend course on crime writing. It was Saturday morning. But the realization did not bring her the pleasure it should. Something had happened that should not have.

Her body was growing aware of what had woken her. She needed to go the bathroom. It was one of the downsides of growing older.

She was halfway to the bedroom door when her sleepy brain clicked into gear. A few hours ago she had made for this same door in total darkness. Someone had lifted the latch.

The reason for that sense of fear flooded back to her.

Melissa. Spectral in her white nightgown. And then Gavin calling to her urgently from further down the corridor.

And now a darker truth came on the heels of that memory.

That was the dread that was hanging over her. She had gone to bed with the news that Dinah Halsgrove had been rushed into hospital after a sudden collapse. Theresa had been sceptical about food poisoning, but still . . .

Melissa? Hilary had surprised her yesterday in the corridor

leading to Dinah Halsgrove's bedroom. Is this what had brought her to Hilary's room in the middle of the night? Because Hilary alone had witnessed that?

It was an unsettling thought. Hilary was not normally given to irrational fears. But *was* this irrational?

Dinah Halsgrove had nearly died – might even now be dead. Was it too ridiculous to imagine that Hilary too might have been found dead this morning? Smothered by her pillow, perhaps.

She shook herself back to common sense. She was very much alive this morning. It was the danger to the author, not to Hilary, that mattered now. Clearly, considering Halsgrove's age, nobody was taking any chances last night. But a cloud had hung over the course participants in the bar. Would the author survive the night? There had been those two young men who had helped Hilary right the bookstall, the improbable redhead and the darker one. They had joked that it might not be natural causes. Was the queen of fictional poisoners going to meet her end in the same way as her dozens of imagined victims?

If that had been meant as a joke, it was a ghoulish one.

But as Hilary had turned out the light yesterday evening and lain in the darkness, another disturbing thought had laid hold of her. If it was indeed accidental food poisoning, whatever Theresa's doubts, would anyone else fall victim to it? Would Hilary herself wake in the night with some violent warning of death?

She breathed deeply with relief, as her cold toes curled against the carpet. She had survived the night. She needed to empty her bladder, but it was no more than that. No stomach cramps, no vomiting. Just a normal, early-morning waking.

Sixty-three was certainly not old by modern standards, but it was still a blessing to be given another day.

As she returned from the bathroom, she crossed to the window and drew the curtain aside. An autumn mist shrouded the quadrangle. She could barely see the West Cloister on the opposite side. No sign yet of the sunrise ready to strike through the gloom. Yet day could not be far off. She turned on the bedside lamp to check her watch. Five a.m.

Still, she sat on the seat in front of the window, without returning to the warm nest of her bed.

A cold doubt was creeping over her. It had seemed a fun idea to come to this evocative setting and try her hand at a kind of writing which had never occurred to her before. But why not? She had enough knowledge for a convincing Elizabethan background, and historical crime novels seemed to be endlessly popular. She had a sharp analytical brain. She could surely set up a viable plot, with a set of colourful characters. She had infected Veronica with the same enthusiasm.

She had not expected to get involved with a real-life drama of life and death on a weekend about violent endings.

Coincidence. Probably not food poisoning. Heart? Stroke? The novelist herself had said she was diabetic and heavily medicated. Given her advanced age and questionable health, anything was possible. There was certainly no need to believe the young woman in the corner who had laughingly suggested it was a put-up job.

Hilary was getting cold. She got to her feet and was hesitating about whether to close the curtains again, when a tremor of sound came up to her from two floors below. Someone was opening the door which gave on to the cloister garth. She leaned forward, with her forehead against the chill condensation of the windowpane. Infuriatingly, she could not see directly beneath her without opening it and alerting the person below to the fact that she was there. But as she craned her neck sideways, she had the impression of a figure running along the path until it merged with the early-morning mist. The quadrangle fell quiet again.

A jogger. David would sometimes get up and go for an early-morning run. She had never seen the attraction herself.

Hilary sat on for a few minutes. Then, with a sigh, she went back to bed and dozed again.

'Are you all right?' Veronica cast a concerned look over Hilary as they met before breakfast.

'Never better,' Hilary asserted, with a confidence she no longer felt.

'Last night you were thinking Melissa had evil designs against you.'

'You can imagine anything in the middle of the night.'

Breakfast in the restaurant was more subdued than it should have been, given that they were about to embark on their writing course.

'Have you heard anything?' Veronica asked her neighbour. It was the young woman with the ponytail who had advanced the theory last night that Dinah Halsgrove's illness was not real at all, but a carefully planned drama to fuel the murder mystery weekend. 'Do we know if Dinah made it through the night? I've been praying they got her to hospital in time.'

'If it really *was* genuine.' A long-legged man of the girl's generation threw his limbs across the bench and set his glass of grapefruit juice beside hers. Dark hair fell forward over an earnest, bespectacled face.

'I'm with Tania. It's got to be suspicious. It's just too far-fetched a coincidence that it should happen this particular weekend. Where are the witnesses? We've only got Theresa's word for what happened. And she's part of Gavin's team. The rest of us were miles away on that boat. I bet they're setting up a crime for us to write about.'

Hilary's thought flew back to Melissa lifting her door latch. Could that be part of it? The thought came as a relief.

She surveyed the pair of fellow writers. The young man was wearing navy shorts and a sweatshirt saying *Wirral Whippet*. It was, Hilary thought, rather late in the year for shorts. The woman he had called Tania was more warmly dressed in a black tracksuit, with white flashes on the sleeves and legs. There was a rather ostentatious athleticism about the pair.

'You forget,' she said crisply. 'There was an ambulance with a crew of trained paramedics. There were the Morland Abbey staff. Or are you suggesting the ambulance service was in on the hoax too?'

The young man flushed a little and shrugged. 'Do we know it was a real ambulance? There must be mock-up ones you can hire, you know, for films and such. Someone with Gavin's background would know how to set that up.'

Harry Walters' voice rose from the next table, addressing the middle-aged waiter. 'Is the English breakfast safe to eat? I don't want to be the next one ending up in hospital.'

The waiter's voice was icy. 'I can assure you, sir, the cooking area has been thoroughly cleaned. The plates and cutlery are sterilized, as they always are. Chef's going mad at the suggestion that it might have been his food. From what I've heard, the lady wasn't even sick.'

Hilary turned back to the conspiracy theorists.

'So where's Miss Halsgrove now, if you think she's not in hospital?'

'Probably safe at home in Sussex,' Tania suggested. 'If she was too tired to go back last night, they could have smuggled her away early this morning, before any of us was up and about. Rob's right.'

Hilary remembered that sense of someone opening the East Cloister door below her. Of a figure on the path before the mist had swallowed it up. Should she say anything?

But that figure had been alone and running. Hardly that of an elderly woman with luggage being escorted to the car park.

There had to be some other explanation. Just an early-morning jogger.

The mist had lifted, promising a fine autumn morning.

They gathered in Lady Jane's Chamber, at the end of the East Cloister. It was a high-ceilinged square room at the far end of the first-floor corridor. Its size was better suited to the thirty or so course members in this morning's group than that splendid auditorium of yesterday's talk.

Hilary looked around at the assembled participants. There should have been an air of anticipation, a nervous appraisal of their wished-for talents, the hope that Gavin would set them on an enjoyable – and even profitable – path. But a feeling of anxiety was palpable in the room, that had nothing to do with their literary abilities.

'He's here!' Veronica whispered.

All heads turned as Gavin Standforth appeared in the doorway. He paused, as if for dramatic effect. Hilary took in the yellow cravat at the neck of his crisply laundered shirt, today's cream jacket and trousers. She had not read any of his books, but he looked a picture of the successful author. Then she remembered the others saying he'd had just one bestseller, among a mediocre output.

Yet the practised pause might have been to catch the flash

of waiting cameras. He had obviously enjoyed the fame, once it came to him.

Harry Walters broke the tensely expectant silence. 'Well? What news?'

Gavin allowed his face to flower into a confident beam.

'The news is good, I'm sure you'll all be relieved to hear. Dinah has passed a peaceful night under sedation, after they pumped out her stomach. Apparently, she was even confessing to feeling hungry when she woke this morning.'

There was a ripple of enthusiasm, even a solitary cheer.

The red-haired young man leaned forward to whisper to his neighbours.

'Stomach pump? So they *did* think it was something she'd taken.'

'So,' said Gavin, coming forward to the speaker's table at the front. 'We can turn our minds back to the purpose of this weekend. How to release the secret crime novelist locked up in all of you.' He let his smile travel round the breadth of the room.

In spite of herself, Hilary found her own face breaking into a smile of acknowledgement. She had indeed discovered such an ambition in herself.

She pushed away the urgency of Gavin's voice in the night summoning Melissa away from her door.

'Doesn't answer all the questions, does it?' said a man behind Hilary. She turned to survey him. Elderly, military. Those seemed the right words for him, even from the viewpoint of her own sixty-three years. Tall, square-shouldered, straight-backed. A green gilet, hung about with pockets, over a grey sweater with leather shoulder pads. His remaining grey hairs were severely clipped.

His voice had the confidence of having rung out over many parade grounds.

'Colonel Truscott,' he announced. 'What we all want to know is what made the dear lady so ill. Was it the food? I gather the chef is throwing a wobbly at the suggestion. Or a bug? Is it likely that anyone else will catch it? You hear dreadful things about this norovirus thing. Wouldn't want to go down with that.'

'I'm sure there's no need for you to worry.' Someone else had appeared at Gavin's side.

Hilary drew a sharp intake of breath. Melissa. The woman who had opened her bedroom door in the middle of the night. The stooped head of brown hair.

She studied the taller woman for any sign of apology for last night's intrusion. Melissa's eyes made no contact with hers. If she was genuinely sleepwalking, would she remember? Probably not. Gavin was avoiding her eyes too.

Melissa smiled, somewhat tightly. 'Her symptoms don't suggest anything of the sort. I can assure you that no one else has been taken ill. You don't need to fear that the cause was in the kitchen.'

'So what was it?' cut in Tania, the conspiracy theorist. 'This is getting interesting.'

Gavin gave her a murderous look. 'Let's just enjoy the rest of the weekend. I'm going to divide you into three groups. If you'd like to arrange yourselves on the left, in the middle, and to the right of the room. That's right. About nine or ten to a group.'

Hilary and Veronica edged their chairs sideways into the left-hand circle, nearest the door.

'Right. You can sit yourselves down. Now this lot,' he beamed across at Hilary and Veronica's group, 'are the Toads.'

'Charming!' said Tania, the sceptical young woman they had met over breakfast.

'And you,' he turned his smile on the centre group, 'are the Snakes.'

An answering hiss rose from this group, as of people relaxing and getting into the spirit of the game.

All the same, to Hilary, the genial look he gave them seemed rather forced.

'And you,' he said to the right-hand group, 'will be the Slowworms.'

Hilary pictured the smooth-skinned reptiles she sometimes found in damp and shadowed places in her garden. Not true snakes, despite their appearance. Harmless. Even beneficial to the gardener. But alarming to those who had a horror of snakes.

'I wonder why these?' Veronica reflected. 'Because all reptiles are rather creepy? I fancy something more furry, like a fox.'

'I don't know,' Hilary replied. 'I'm rather fond of the toads in my garden pond. Croaking away among the lily leaves and defying me to see where they're camouflaged.'

The red-haired man in the leather jacket leaned across. 'You're forgetting. What about the dust jacket of his book?'

Into Hilary's mind came a picture of that blindly questing head thrusting its way sinisterly across all those book covers on the display stand. What was that enigmatic title? *The Long Crippler.* The connection clicked into place. It was another name for a slowworm.

Gavin was calling them back to attention. 'Now, you're probably wondering about the three names. There's a prize for the first one to tell me where I got the idea from. A signed copy of my latest book . . . No, not you, Ceri,' he said as a woman from their own Toad group shot up a hand. 'You're local. That's an unfair advantage. And don't tell anyone else. Let them do the detective work for themselves, if they're curious and clever enough.'

Hilary found her curiosity pricked. She turned to the woman two seats away. Black, tightly curled hair and a green skirt of a knobbly fabric that seemed to have curls of its own. What could it be that an inhabitant of Totnes would already know?

'Now,' Gavin was saying, 'Dinah was talking to us yesterday about the many things that can inspire a detective novel: place, characters, a particularly bizarre plot idea. Today – and where better than in a place like Morland Abbey – I'm challenging you to begin your crime novel with a strong sense of place.

'Of course, there's plenty to start you off right here. You've got the house, the splendid ornamental gardens and the wider grounds beyond. But feel free to venture further afield, as long as you leave yourself enough time to drink in the atmosphere and get a fair bit of writing done. It wouldn't take you long to walk down to the river. There are footpaths on the other side of the drive that will take you there. I'm not talking about the tidal estuary where we sailed last night, just the path along the waterside through the woods. Or it's only a short drive to the edge of Dartmoor – *Hound of the Baskervilles*, and all that. Then there's Totnes itself – a fascinating and ancient town. Lots of ideas there. It's up to you. Then just sit and soak in the vibes for a while, until you are ready to write. You've all brought notepads, I trust.' The groups nodded. 'Just one word of caution. Try to avoid clichés like the wind whistling over the moor on a stormy night, or a shadowy barn with the scuffling of rats. Crime can be even more chilling when it springs out of just that situation where we feel happy and safe.

'It's just after nine. We'll gather back here at eleven for coffee, and then break into groups to see what you've got. You'll be surprised how even the mildest mannered of you can see dire deeds, if you look deeply enough and let the dark thoughts come.'

His grin illuminated the room. This time it seemed more genuine.

'Hmm,' said Hilary to no one in particular. 'Is that what we're here for? To discover the darker side of our nature?'

'Better to bring it out into the open,' laughed Tania's companion, the bespectacled Rob in shorts. 'It's what people *aren't* saying you need to beware of.'

People were getting to their feet, pushing back chairs. There was a buzz of anticipation, mingled with apprehension, as they headed for the door.

To her surprise, Hilary was intercepted by Gavin as she followed Veronica to the door. His smile stretched wide. Tense, Hilary thought.

'I apologize for last night. Melissa is highly strung. I hope she didn't alarm you.'

'You said she was sleepwalking. Though why she was outside my room on the top floor needs a bit more explaining.'

She kept her eyes on him and saw him flinch.

'Nothing sinister in that, dear lady. It could have been anyone's room.'

Hilary's attention was snagged by the sense of a sudden movement beyond Gavin's shoulder. He turned and saw Melissa beckoning him vehemently. With a muttered apology to Hilary, he joined Melissa and she seized the arm of his cream linen jacket. She was gesturing in what looked like agitation. Hilary followed her gaze. She seemed to be focussed on the Snake group in the centre of the room as they moved to join the mass of people by the door. But, try as she would, Hilary could not make out just whom Melissa was drawing Gavin's attention to.

She had, however, seen Gavin's start of evident alarm. Then the press of bodies around her shut them from her view.

What and whom could he have seen?

* * *

'What do you think?' Hilary asked Veronica as they descended the stairs. 'Here, or further afield?'

Veronica turned on her with a patient smile. 'We don't both have to choose the same setting, do we? I rather fancied that garden walk above the tiltyard – you know, the flat lawn with the line of yew trees.'

'Of course I know what the tiltyard is. You can still see the terraced banks around it where the spectators watched. Don't be patronizing.'

'Sorry. Of course you'd know. The flower beds along the walk above it are lovely this time of year, all misty vistas of mauves and blue, shot with gold. Rustic benches. Just the place for a romantic rendezvous.'

'I thought we were supposed to be writing a crime novel.'

'I knew it wouldn't be your sort of thing. You may be into something unpleasantly dark and forbidding, but I'm sticking with my heartthrob investigator and the smitten heroine. What better place for them to meet than in this garden? And who knows what might be lurking behind those yews? As Gavin says, it doesn't have to be the cliché of a sinister setting. There *is* something more shocking about murder in an idyllic place, don't you think?'

'Perhaps you do have a darker side to you, after all,' Hilary chuckled. 'Right then, I'll leave you to it. I'm off into town, to see if I can find a short-stay car park and soak up a different sort of medieval vibe than I get here. Less of the local gentry and more guttersnipes perhaps.'

'What are you looking for?'

'I won't know until I find it, will I? The perfect place for a murder.'

SEVEN

The steep High Street of Totnes was bustling with Saturday morning traffic. It was too late in the season for stallholders in Elizabethan costume, and probably, Hilary reflected, the wrong day of the week. But her well-informed imagination found no difficulty in peopling the narrow thoroughfare with a motley cast of characters from the sixteenth century. Here, a grubby-faced urchin darted in among the shoppers, cutting a purse from the owner's belt. There, an ample countrywoman shouted her crop of red-cheeked apples as buxom as her own face. A grave alderman strode slowly but purposefully downhill with the expectation that the common folk would step aside for him into the muck-strewn street.

The illusion was helped by the fact that Totnes had resolutely stood out against the advance of ubiquitous chain stores. Not a McDonald's in sight, she noted approvingly.

Below her, where the short walk from the car park had brought her out on to the street, the view of the main thoroughfare was picturesquely broken by a steepled arch. Beyond it, the hill led on down to the River Dart. Hilary stopped to get her bearings. She wished she had brought her copy of the town trail with her. She had printed it out from the Totnes website, hoping there might be a free time in the weekend's programme when she and Veronica could explore it. She had not thought to go back to her room and fetch it.

She stood indecisive, wondering which way to go next. The crowded main street might indeed be a potential crime scene, in this or any other century, but it was not quite what she had in mind. St Mary's church? She could see the sandstone tower with its pinnacles close by, between her and the arch which carried the rampart walk. Further downhill, she recollected, was the museum, with its reconstructed scenes of Elizabethan life. Or, going further back in time, there were the remains of the Norman castle at the top of the hill.

Which to choose?

She found herself turning uphill, to where the High Street narrowed still further and rounded a bend. This was an area less familiar to her. Her eye fell on the name of the side street she was passing: Leechwell Street. *Leech* was an old name for a physician. *Leechwell* suggested a healing spring. Her curiosity piqued, she ventured down this side road. It led her past board-faced houses to a black-and-white timbered inn. Ahead, the road seemed to be taking her on to a modern highway. Definitely not what she wanted. But to her left, a much narrower lane plunged steeply downhill. She glanced at her watch. It had taken her less than half an hour to get this far. She still had time.

The lane was hardly more than a footpath, not wide enough for cars. Drawn by a mounting curiosity she could not name, she started down it.

Once she had left the corner of Leechwell Street, no houses fronted the path. The noise of traffic fell behind her. There was nothing but the tall blank stone walls on either side, over which ivy tumbled. They were oddly without windows or doorways. A very close-set lane. Hardly room for two people to pass. But there *were* no other people. She had an uncanny feeling that she was walking out of time, not knowing where and when she might arrive.

The lane curved, making it impossible to see what was ahead. She felt a sudden, irrational longing for someone else to be with her. Her hand went into her shoulder bag and fingered her mobile phone. It was a reassurance to know that David would be on the other end of the line. That is, if there was a mobile signal here between these tall enclosing walls.

Idiot! She had come for a weekend of crime writing. A rational exercise of clues, deductions, ingenious plots. Not a foray into the darker Gothic fantasy. Nothing lurked around that curve ahead, except what her imagination chose to make of it for the purposes of a detective novel.

She reached the corner and stopped in surprise. Whatever she had expected, it was not this. Not one, but three similar lanes converged on an open spot where the morning sun could fall between their walls. Two of the lanes were narrow, walled, windowless, without doors. The third, leading up at an angle to the one she had descended, showed a high white wall and a slate roof. The nameplate said 'Leechwell Cottage'. And between these two lanes, facing the third downhill one, was a large rect-angular basin, surrounded on three sides by ivy-clad stone walls. There was the tinkle of falling water. A natural spring? A watering trough for animals? She looked at the three narrow lanes which converged on it. It was just about possible to imagine a mule laden with panniers.

Hilary moved round to stand in front of the basin.

She had been wrong. Into that wide, shallow well, not one but three springs spouted from low down in the rear stone wall. Each one let fall a small cascade into its separate basin, flanked by a low stone kerb. Water spilled over from them on to the cobbled base of the much larger rectangular enclosure.

The Leechwells were plural.

Three lanes. Three sacred wells – the word 'sacred' formed itself in her mind before her conscious brain had made that decision. Three was a mystic number. Three springs, uniting in one larger pool, their waters separated by these divisions only a stone's width higher than the surrounding basin. Three in one, like the Trinity. The lower stones were dark with algae.

Yet no two troughs were alike. The middle one, in front of her, was a long narrow enclosure reaching across the basin almost to her feet. The one to the left was only half its length, while the right-hand one had been turned through ninety degrees to lie broadside on to the back wall. It seemed as though each of these springs had its own personality.

As she would have expected at a natural well, there was ample evidence that others held these waters sacred. There was a grating above the middle spring. Coloured ribbons had been tied to its bars. Pots of flowers and egg-shaped stones stood on the ledge below this grating. There was a hoop of twisted twigs. Evidence of New Age reverence, or age-old Christian rites?

The water in the larger space around the troughs looked barely deep enough to cover her shoes. In places, the cobbles were dry. At the edge of the tarmac someone had placed a flat-topped stone to enable her to step down into the pool. She took advantage of it and picked her way across to the further wall over the driest stones.

She reached her hand tentatively down into the middle pool. It was slightly warm from the sun shining down on the shallow water. She leaned further over. The water spouting from the pipe in the wall was colder. She wondered just what healing properties these Leechwells were supposed to have.

'Ah, that's the Long Crippler, that is. There's them as is afraid of him, but he's good for sore eyes.'

Hilary started upright. She had not heard him coming. An old man, back bent, so that he stooped his head and helped himself along with a stick. His voice had the rich burr of the Devon countryside.

'I'm sorry! You startled me.' Hilary found herself uncharacteristically flustered. It was not like her to react to fanciful imaginings, but this place, secluded, yet so near the town centre, the odd desertion of these narrow lanes, the water trickling into these curiously walled-off troughs, had got to her.

'I take it this is a sacred well. I hadn't heard about it.'

'Sacred? Well now, I'm not sure what you means by that. But they do say there's something in the water. Couldn't tell you what. Or should I be saying who? There's three of them, see? That one over there's the Toad, and the one on the right's what they call the Snake, and that one you had your hand in is the Long Crippler.'

The Long Crippler. His recitation of strange names would not have been out of place in the scene of the witches' spell in *Macbeth.*

But the rational part of her brain jumped into place. It didn't take her more than a second to realize she had heard those names, or at least two of them, earlier this morning. Gavin had chosen them for the names of their groups. The third . . .

'The long crippler? That's another name for a slowworm, isn't it?'

'Arr. Right enough. Them as you find wriggling away, all blind in the sunshine, when you turns over a stone. That's what we calls them hereabouts. The long crippler.'

The name sent an unaccountable shiver down Hilary's spine. She had always liked slowworms. But why were they called the long crippler?

Something was buzzing at the back of her mind. Of course! It was the name of Gavin Standforth's bestselling book.

'That's a strange name, the Crippler. Is it supposed to do people harm? These sacred wells were usually associated with healing.'

'Arr, so they do say. The Toad for troubles with your skin, the Snake for snake bite and when the Black Dog sits on your shoulder, and him there,' he nodded at the still pool at Hilary's feet, 'he's supposed to be good for eyesight.'

Hilary thought of the reptiles also known as blindworms. It seemed an unlikely association with restoring sight. But then, the warty toad wasn't the picture of smooth, healthy skin either. It must be the magic of opposites.

'But why the Crippler?'

'Don't ask me. I'd nothing to do with the naming of 'un.'

The old man started to move on, up the steep lane by which Hilary had approached. The sound of his stick echoed between the blank, stone walls. Hilary listened, as it faded around the bend.

Why had she not heard him coming? Or had her brain, busy with her surroundings, not registered the tapping of his stick?

She looked down. The bunches of flowers looked incongruously bright against the dark wet stone. There was a curious ambiguity about this place. The sacred with the sinister.

In her experience, holy wells were usually named after saints. She had never associated them with reptiles.

Still, she reminded herself, she had a novel to write. Or at least, a setting to evoke. And where better than this?

She needed a place to sit. There was no bench, no convenient wall or ledge. She looked down at her feet. The stone by which she had stepped down into the pool made the only convenient perch. Hilary lowered herself on to it and rested her feet on the damp cobbles. It was not the most comfortable seat, but it would have to do.

She took out the notebook from her shoulder bag and began to write.

It was not until she lifted her tired wrist and looked down at the pages she had covered with scrawl that the memory of the first time she had heard that strange name came back to her. *The Long Crippler.* She saw in her mind the book room stacked with copies of Gavin Standforth's output. The slowworm on the cover.

Then she remembered that Lin Bell had been at her elbow, telling her the superstition that slowworms were said to lame horses. There was a curious ambiguity about this place.

Healing or harming?

EIGHT

I t was a surprise to look at her watch and find how much time had passed. She was pleasantly surprised by the amount she had got down in her notebook as she had sat absorbing the atmosphere of the Leechwells.

At one point, a pair of boys running down the lane swinging conkers had stared at her perched on the edge of the well and laughed, but Hilary had waved them on with a cheery greeting. Apart from that, the three lanes had remained almost eerily quiet.

Her burgeoning story was set in Elizabethan times, of course – she had expected that. Her characters were thus imbued with the beliefs, both Christian and not a little pagan, which hung about such holy waters. With what a strange mixture of thoughts young Bartholomew, her chief protagonist, must have approached these wells, concerned for his ailing grandfather. The wells were for healing. Why else would they be called Leechwells? But there was something about their guardian spirits – the Toad, the Snake, and that strange local name, the Long Crippler – which prickled the hairs upon his neck. *On my neck*, Hilary admitted to herself. There would have been fear, as well as hope, as he approached the pool. Fear that what ailed his beloved grandfather might not be entirely natural. That it might need a supernatural remedy. Fear of the powers that could grant it.

There had been a young woman, waiting at the well for him. Veronica would like that. Hilary had not intended the romantic angle, but it had presented itself without her conscious volition. Perhaps there was a softer side to her than she cared to admit. She had evoked the setting in front of her – a strange one, even in the twenty-first century – and got as far as Bartholomew confessing to Miriam the doubts that gnawed at him about his grandfather's illness. She had no doubt that there was going to be something sinister about it.

It was a promising start. She wondered where Veronica's imagination had taken her, in the flower-lined walk above the tiltyard.

A more analytical part of her brain wondered whether it was a good idea to plunge into her story like this, without constructing a fully fledged plot. Surely detective fiction depended on careful planning, so that at each stage the author knew the path down which she was leading her readers and where she intended to spring on them the surprise – perfectly logical with hindsight, of course – at the end. As it was, she seemed to be making it up as she went along.

She looked up from the shallow pool at her feet. The three lanes that converged on the Leechwells were still deserted. It gave her an odd feeling that she might have been transported out of her own time into an unknown world.

No doubt the events of last night had influenced her subconscious.

Still, it really was time she transported herself somewhere else.

It was with a feeling of satisfaction that Hilary drove back into the car park at Morland Abbey. It was five to eleven when she hurried under the archway towards the cloisters. People were appearing from different quarters of the house and grounds, converging on Lady Jane's Chamber and the promised coffee. Should she go straight there or carry on around the corner to see if Veronica was still in the romantic gardens where she had hoped to set her story?

It was not a conscious decision. Her feet led her around the garth to the less formal lawns that sloped away on the opposite side to the Great Barn. She turned right, down some steps, on to the walk below the wall of the private garden. A line of massive close-set yew trees confronted her. Lower still, the level rectangle of grass that was once Morland's tiltyard, created by the Woodleighs after the monks' eviction. Hilary's ready imagination peopled it with armoured and helmeted knights showing off their military skills and horsemanship. Henry VIII, she recalled, had been a notable jouster, until he was thrown from his armoured horse, which fell on top of him. It was the ulcerated wounds to his legs and the forced inactivity which followed that had reduced him from a muscular man in the prime of life to the bloated, overweight figure of later portraits.

Veronica, on the other hand, was given to less earthy imaginings. She would surely have found the romance she wanted between a dashing knight and one of the ladies in extravagant Tudor gowns and pearled headdresses who thronged the seats of the tiltyard, now reduced to steeply terraced banks of grass.

It was on that long walk above the tiltyard, with its autumnal line of flowerbeds, that Hilary had expected to find her friend, if she had not already succumbed to the lure of coffee and home-made biscuits.

Vistas of lavender and gold stretched away to where more stone steps led up to higher terraces. At intervals, benches invited the visitor to sit and take in the charming view. Veronica was seated on none of them.

With a click of impatience, Hilary turned to retrace her steps to the cloister garth and Lady Jane's Chamber.

'Hilary!' The cry stayed her.

Veronica was hastening towards her, her long legs covering the ground faster than her normally more dignified pace. She was coming, not along the level path past the flowerbed but up the steps from the tiltyard behind the yews.

Her face was pink, her breathing unsteady, as she caught up with Hilary.

'I've had the strangest morning!'

'Do you want to tell me now, or over coffee?'

'Hilary, this could be serious.'

'OK, OK. Here, sit down and tell me. You look all of a fluster.'

'*Well*. You know I said I meant to sit on one of the seats along this walk?'

'Yes.'

'Well, I did at first. I sat looking out over the tiltyard and the rest of the gardens. Then it occurred to me that, if there *was* a mystery, it wouldn't be happening out here in the open. There was something dark and mysterious about this line of yews. So I found a place – down there at the foot of the trees – where I could sit and imagine I was hearing something, some*one*, on the other side. Only then . . .'

'You did.'

Veronica turned astonished blue eyes on her friend. 'How did you know?'

'What else would you be leading up to? Go on. I'm all ears.'

'It was Gavin's voice. I didn't know who he was talking to at first. He said, "Well, it happened. It didn't result in a death this time. But she's got to be stopped."

'And then another voice said, "How?" I found it hard to place at first. We haven't heard much from her yet and it was just one word. But it didn't seem like that rather breathless way Melissa has of talking.'

'Theresa?' Hilary suggested.

'I guessed it must be her.'

Hilary pictured the stouter and shorter of Gavin's assistants. 'So what next?'

'"We need to play this carefully," Gavin said. "It mustn't look suspicious."

'"So what then?"

'"Leave it to me. I'll shut her up."

'"And what about the old biddy on the top floor?"

'Then their voices began to trail away. I peeped around the yew tree and I was right. It was Theresa with him. I could see them walking along here above the tiltyard, going away from me. From behind, I couldn't see anything wrong.'

Hilary said, 'Perhaps there wasn't.' She put out a hand to stay Veronica's protest. 'All right, all right. I grant you it sounds sinister. As though they were talking about Dinah Halsgrove. Finding another way to . . . silence her. But you have to remember we're here on a crime weekend. We've geared our imaginations up to seeing dastardly deeds around every corner. I can't imme-diately think of an innocent explanation for what you heard, but my mind is telling me that that doesn't mean there isn't one. Maybe Tania and Rob are right, to some extent. It could easily all be part of some scheme they've dreamed up to add extra spice to this weekend. Something that might even get this course in the papers. Draw attention to Gavin's books and any future events like this they may have planned.'

'Do you think so?' Veronica sounded dubious. 'It sounded as if they were talking about a real death – or at least a death they expected.'

'And what did Theresa mean about "the old biddy on the top floor"?'

Veronica's mouth fell open. 'Hilary! You mean you really don't . . .?'

Hilary's honest mind pulled her up short.

'You mean me?'

'Who else?'

'The cheek, coming from her! She's no oil painting, is she? Still, I have to agree with you. It does sound sinister. So what are you going to do? Are you thinking this is something you ought to report to the police?'

Veronica flushed a brighter pink. 'If you must know, that's what I *was* thinking. Dinah Halsgrove nearly *died.* Could they really be responsible for that? Just for a publicity stunt? And why would they have to repeat it?'

Hilary was silent for a moment. 'It does seem a bit extreme, I grant you. Let me do some thinking . . . Look, let's grab a coffee while there's still time. I don't expect there'll be another corpse – sorry, a *real* corpse – before the next session begins. We'll decide about telling the police later.'

They were rounding the corner of the East Cloister when Hilary shot out a hand to catch Veronica's arm. 'I forgot to tell you. I've found out the answer to the riddle.'

Veronica looked at her, puzzled, her mind still clouded by what she had overheard.

'You know,' Hilary said impatiently, 'why Gavin chose those odd names for the groups. The Toad, the Snake, the Long . . . the Slowworm,' she corrected herself.

'Where did you find out?'

'Never you mind,' Hilary said smugly. 'You're obviously not the slightest bit interested in what I've been doing this morning. But I'm going to claim my prize the moment I see Gavin. It was an out-of-the-way part of town, and I didn't bump into any of the rest of our group, so I'm pretty sure no one else will have discovered it.'

Lady Jane's Chamber was full and abuzz with conversation. Evidently their first venture into a writing exercise had loosened tongues as well as pens. People were busy exchanging information about where they had chosen to set their scene and what sort of mystery might grow from it.

'Wait till you hear mine!' Rob in his shorts was saying.

There was a knot of people around Gavin. Hilary strode towards them, keen to reveal her discovery and lay claim to the signed copy of his book.

Before she could reach him, Gavin tapped his spoon against his coffee cup. The many conversations fell silent. Heads turned.

'Well, that didn't take long.' Gavin flashed a wide smile at them. 'I thought it might take you a day or two, since I'd ruled out unfair local knowledge – sorry, Ceri!' His beam spread further to the woman from their group with the dark curly hair and the knobbly green skirt. 'But Colonel Truscott here has proved a shining example of military intelligence.'

'All it needed was to get my hands on a copy of the town guide.' The colonel's smile was more controlled, self-deprecating, yet satisfied. 'It's all there in the Town Trail. Three holy wells flowing into the same pool. The Toad, the Snake and the – funny name, this – the Long Crippler. But of course, you'd know all about that, Gavin. You've written the novel. And a very ingenious one it is too.'

There was a ripple of applause. Hilary stopped dead.

'Too late,' she muttered to Veronica. 'I should have come straight upstairs.'

'You knew that? Did you get the town guide too?'

'Did I heck! I've got a copy upstairs, but I never thought to look at it. I found the place for myself. I've been sitting with my feet in that pool half the morning, writing my first pages of deathless prose. But I didn't see Colonel Truscott.'

'Oh, Hilary! What a shame! I'm sure that deserves the prize more than simply reading about it on a leaflet.'

They watched Gavin lift the colonel's hand in the air, to redoubled clapping. He reached behind him and handed over a handsome hardcover copy of his own book. Hilary could see the large print: 'By the author of *The Long Crippler.*'

'Oh, well,' Hilary grunted. 'I can always get it out of the library.'

'That's not the point, is it?' Veronica gave her a small push.

'You wanted to be first. You wanted to crack the mystery when no one else could.'

'Hmmph!' Hilary snorted.

She did feel thwarted.

NINE

The three groups retook their seats in circles in different parts of the room. Hilary looked at her fellow sleuths in the Toad group. Veronica; Tania and Rob, the athletic-looking couple with the conspiracy theory about Dinah Halsgrove's collapse; the affable colonel, still beaming with satisfaction; Ceri, who was obviously a local resident. In addition, there were those two men in their thirties she had met in the book room. The darker one introduced himself as Ben, and the one with the improbably red streak in his hair, more fuchsia than auburn, was Jake. Had they come together, or made contact on arrival as kindred spirits? She decided they were a couple. Finally, there was the small silver-haired woman with bright-grey eyes, Lin Bell. Possibly a Miss Marple type, Hilary decided. Someone who said little but observed much. Though older than Hilary and Veronica, she had a youthful sparkle about her that showed an eagerness to embrace this new challenge.

Hilary looked beyond them at the Snake group. Jo Walters had attached herself to it. Hilary felt a small pang of disappointment. Harry Walters might have come along just for the ride. She noticed he hadn't rejoined them for coffee. But Jo had shown a lively determination, not only to have a shot at writing detective fiction, but to make a success of it. Scandinavian-type noir, Hilary seemed to remember. Hard to reconcile with her youthful round face and curly blonde hair. Hilary would have liked to hear the results of her morning's writing. Just now, Jo was frowning, her lips pressed together.

Gavin and his two assistants were consulting. Theresa was heading for the Toads. How very appropriate, Hilary thought.

She looks like a toad herself. Squat, earthy, even if her skin was free of those warty nodules which easily distinguish a toad from the smooth-skinned frog.

Hilary looked back to see which group Gavin would take. She was alarmed to see for the second time that air of tension between him and Melissa. Melissa was motioning towards the middle group, the Snakes. Gavin looked flustered, as if not sure what to do. The expression on his face was almost frightened.

They seemed to reach a decision. Melissa came walking purposefully towards the Snakes, her long flowered skirt swinging. Hilary watched her attentively. She favoured the group with a vague smile and seated herself. Nothing seemed out of place now. It must have been Hilary's imagination.

Gavin was introducing himself to those in the right-hand corner. The Slowworms. How very appropriate. For the purposes of this weekend, Gavin had cast himself as the Long Crippler, the title of his most successful book.

Was the Long Crippler truly a healer, as the old man had told her, or a source of danger? Hilary had an uneasy feeling that the figures from the Leechwells had once meant more than today's generation knew.

Veronica beside her was whispering in some agitation as Theresa approached.

'What am I going to do? I've got nothing I can read out. I was just settling down to write about my setting and begin my story when I heard them. Gavin and Theresa. It was such an odd conversation that I wrote down what they said instead. Ever since then, I've been puzzling about what it could have meant. I've jotted down some notes. Just theories. Look.'

She showed her notebook, taking care that no one else could see. The first page was set out as dialogue. But below was a list of briefer notes. The first one read: *Plot to poison Dinah Halsgrove?*

The second: *Elaborate charade for us students?*

The suggestions went on, growing ever more tentative or fanciful.

'I can't read this out.' Veronica's whisper was becoming more of a wail. 'Not in front of Theresa. Even if I wrap it up as fiction, she'll know that I heard what they said.'

*　*　*

Hilary studied Theresa as she joined their circle. A sensible figure in a brown skirt, beige jumper and cardigan, with a string of brown wooden beads. Her stockings and shoes were brown too, as was her rather severely cut hair. Not elegantly shaped to her square head, but trimmed to a level just below her ears. What Hilary's mother would have called a 'pudding basin' cut.

And this was the woman who had called her an 'old biddy'.

It occurred to Hilary, with a jolt of honesty, that the two of them were not unlike in build, though Hilary had taken rather more trouble with her greying brown hair. Yet Theresa, she thought, must be about twenty years her junior.

Their group leader gave them a brief smile, which quickly fell into to a more businesslike demeanour which she seemed to try self-consciously to soften. The writers responded somewhat nervously. Hilary felt herself listening for any sign that the seemingly incriminating words Veronica had heard might be rooted in dark reality, or whether there was a more innocent explanation. She found herself wanting to believe it was related to Gavin's colourful plans for the weekend. To believe otherwise was too heavy a thought.

Could Dinah Halsgrove's illness really have formed part of those plans? It seemed too extreme. Hilary wondered if she was already going off the idea of the murder mystery.

Yet her sharp brain would not let her rest. There had been an ambulance, the paramedics. Or was it an unfortunate accident on which Gavin thought he could try to capitalize? Still, the words Veronica had overheard seemed to indicate foreknowledge.

And a determination to try again.

She was startled back into the morning's purpose when Theresa cast around the group that rather unconvincing smile.

'We have an hour in front of us. Plenty of time to hear what you've been up to, and where it might lead you next. Colonel Truscott?' Her smile brightened for the elderly man at her side. 'You've gone to the top of the class, so perhaps we can start with you.'

'Dan, please. Let's not stand on ceremony. Right, then. Here goes.'

He launched into a reading of his script, in a confident voice rather devoid of variety or emotion. Hilary had to strain to find the atmosphere he was supposed to convey among the bald recital of facts. The colonel – she found it hard to switch her mind to Dan – had chosen to set his crime scene in the town of Totnes, as she had herself, but he had taken himself up to the castle at the top of the hill. He had picked, not the Normans who built the original motte and bailey, but the seventeenth-century Civil War. It came as no surprise to Hilary that he had cast his hero as the gallant Royalist commander of the fortress. The history teacher in Hilary scolded inwardly at the anachronism. Clearly Colonel Truscott was unaware that Totnes had been a Parliamentarian stronghold.

There was something so predictable about this beginning to his story that Hilary began to wonder how much they would all be revealing about themselves in their choices.

The group received his offering with kind-hearted praise. Hilary wondered, rather snappishly, what was the point of the exercise if no one was prepared to offer constructive criticism. She held back, expecting Theresa to make some positive sugges-tions, but the leader of the group was still looking round the circle enquiringly. Hilary drew a breath.

'You've got the makings of a good idea there, Dan.' She forced herself to use his first name. 'The Castle. Royalist commander in lace collar and curly wig.' She would take him aside and correct his history later, rather than embarrass him in front of the group. 'Plenty of opportunity for swords and cannons as things hot up. But don't you think . . . well, couldn't you try a bit harder to bring the castle to life? What's it built of? How does your Lord Portland feel as he touches the stones? How long has it stood there? What previous warfare has it seen? Give it some character. Make the setting a player in your story.'

There was an uncomfortable rustle around the group. Colonel Truscott flushed a mottled red. Had she been too direct? Should she have sugared the pill with more praise?

'Well done, Hilary.' She was startled that Theresa remembered her first name. 'That's the stuff. Come on, the rest of you. You're not going to grow as writers if all you do is pat each other on the head. I've been in groups like this where strong men have retired to the toilets in tears.' Her grin was wider now, making her face oddly more toadlike. 'Ceri. You're next.'

The local woman ran a hand through her dark curls, making them stand up on end. 'Oh, dear. I was looking forward to showing off what I'd got. I'm not sure I dare open my mouth now.'

'Nonsense. Nobody was saying Dan's offering was rubbish. Only that he could do more to bring his setting alive.'

'Yes, sorry. Anyway, I've set mine closer to here.'

Ceri had not gone far from where they were sitting. She had chosen to set her crime scene in the chapel, which was all that remained of the magnificent abbey church. It rose, solitary above the monks' graveyard beyond the East Cloister. It was just possible to glimpse it from Veronica's window. Ceri dwelt lovingly on the lost remainder of the building: its soaring vaults, the stone carvings and stained-glass windows, the choir stalls where the monks would have gathered for worship. Now, all that was left was the Lady Chapel with its monuments to the Woodleigh family. Not exactly sinister, but imbued with shadows of the past and solemn reminders of death.

'That's it, I'm afraid. I ran out of time before I really got a plot going. To be honest, I don't even know yet what the crime *is*.'

'Never mind. The scene is certainly realized. *Something* should happen there. There's time yet to invent some interesting characters to perform dark deeds in your setting.'

And so it went on around the circle. The younger ones had come up with some colourful, even sinister, ideas. Rob's imagination had gone to town with a macabre use of the water wheel at Dartington Tweed Mill.

'Gruesome!' Jake exclaimed, with evident delight.

It was getting near to Hilary's turn. After taking apart Dan Truscott's offering, she could hardly expect the others to show mercy on her.

As she began to read, though, the memory of the Leechwells came back to her. She was there again, with her feet resting on the cobbles just above the surface of the shallow water. The springs falling into their separate basins – Toad, Snake, Long Crippler. The sound of the old man's stick tap-tapping away along the windowless lane. It was all there, as her fictional Bartholomew told Miriam his fears for the life of his grandfather.

There was a rather flattering silence after she had finished reading.

Dan Truscott cleared his throat. 'Seems to me I've taken Gavin's prize under false pretences. It never occurred to me to actually go to the well. You deserve to be the winner, dear lady.'

'Never mind that,' Hilary said. 'Be honest. Does it work?'

There was a rush of enthusiastic endorsement. Only Ceri hung back.

'I don't know. It was quite powerful, the way you wrote it. But you made our wells sound sinister, and they're really not. We love them. A few years ago, we stopped them laying down a car park there and created a play garden just below the well instead. We had a procession with pipes and drums and garlands of flowers, and the mayor had a golden key to the gate, and there were three benign giants looking over the wall to welcome us in. Toad, Snake, and Long Crippler. Our children play there now. I couldn't square all that with the setting for a murder – if that's what you intend to happen.'

'Well, yes. I did rather. Grandfather comes to a sticky end in a few inches of water.'

'I wish you wouldn't do that. Profane a holy well.'

There was an uncomfortable silence. Through it, Hilary was aware of Veronica's mounting nervousness at her side. It was her turn next. And all she had was the brief conversation she had overheard between Theresa and Gavin, and her attempts to think through what it might have meant. Hilary glanced at her watch. Still twenty minutes to go before they broke for lunch. She had better keep things going.

To play for time, she asked Theresa, 'What about you? Do you think what I'm doing is fair?'

'Murder in a holy place? You'd be joining a long line of distinguished writers. Ruth Rendell talks about the extra frisson which comes from the profanation of what should be sacred. It's not for nothing that the murder of Thomas à Becket in Canterbury Cathedral is a draw for pilgrims, even today.'

Hilary was growing embarrassed. In other circumstances, she would have been only too glad to pass the ball on to someone else. But not to Veronica. Not this morning.

Theresa forced her hand. Her brown gaze focussed relentlessly on Veronica. 'Right, then. Mrs Taylor. Valerie, isn't it?'

'Veronica.'

'Sorry. Veronica, your turn next. What have you got to round off the morning?'

Veronica's fingers fidgeted with the notebook on her lap. She had closed it. Could Theresa, Hilary wondered, have read the incriminating words earlier, upside down from across the circle?

'I'm sorry,' Veronica faltered. 'I didn't get very far. It took me a while to decide the right place. In the end I settled for the . . .'

No, don't say it, Hilary silently begged her. *Not the yews by the tiltyard.*

'Under one of the trees beside some stone steps. They're rather elegant, don't you think, all those stairs with balustrades. You can imagine ladies sweeping down them in rustling silks.'

'Good,' Theresa encouraged her. 'The setting leads you into the characters who inhabit it. Well, read us what you've got, even if it's only a beginning.'

'I . . . I didn't actually . . .'

The door behind them opened abruptly. All three groups turned to look. Two men, one in a suit, the other in a corduroy jacket, paused for a moment, then strode towards Gavin on the far side of the room. The third figure stopped in the doorway. Her head turned to survey them all, observant, vigilant. A uniformed policewoman.

TEN

G avin's face looked ashen when he turned from his consultation with the two men to address the room. *Ashen.* Hilary savoured the word on her tongue. Like the ashes of a fire next morning, a lifeless white streaked with grey. The assured smile of the successful author was gone. But it had become increasingly fragile, even before this. Had what these men just told him come as a total surprise, Hilary wondered, or the news he had been fearing?

It was a moment before the true impact of the shock wave caught up with her. She had leaped to the conclusion that this was somehow connected with the conversation Veronica had overheard in the tiltyard. But what if it was something even worse? What if Dinah Halsgrove, overturning the good news Gavin had given them, had died in hospital?

Gavin was speaking to them, his voice as strained as his expression. 'I'm sorry, folks. This is DI Foulks from the local CID and DS Blunt. Contrary to what some people have suggested to me, I can assure you this is *not* a stunt I have staged for the purposes of this crime weekend. We're not playing a game of Cluedo. These gentlemen wish to question all of us about our knowledge of events here in the last twenty-four hours.'

There was a shudder of dismay around the room.

Ben, the shorter of the pair of men in Hilary's group, shot a triumphant look at the sceptical Tania and Rob. 'Told you! It really is a murder investigation.' His exclamation rang embarrassingly loud.

Hilary heard her own voice rise above the clamour of disquiet and apprehension. It was something they all had to know.

'Is Dinah Halsgrove dead?'

That stilled their tongues.

The detective inspector in the grey suit stepped in front of Gavin. He had a lean, rather canine face, with rimless glasses.

'I've reassured Mr Standforth that Miss Halsgrove is alive, though still not entirely well. That's all I'm prepared to say at the moment. I need to take a statement from each of you, individually. Perhaps . . .' His gaze travelled over the room to the Toads. 'Perhaps we could begin with the group over there.' He glanced at Gavin. 'I understand you were about to break for lunch. So if the other two groups wish to proceed as normal, we'll move on to them after they've eaten.' Again, an apologetic look at Gavin. 'I don't know what you had planned for this afternoon, Mr Standforth, but, given the numbers, I doubt if we'll have completed our enquiries much before four. Would it interfere with your plans much if we call people out from whatever they're doing to question them?'

'No . . . no, not at all.' Gavin's words were tumbling over themselves, too fast. 'You do whatever you have to.' Turning to his students, he said, 'I was going to work on turning some of the people you've already introduced into your settings into

three-dimensional characters. But it won't do you any harm to
see how a real-life investigation works. Right, people. Back at
two o'clock.' He was trying desperately to sound like a man still
in charge.

'Looks like a late lunch for us,' Hilary muttered to Veronica
as the other two groups filed out of the room. 'Pity. I've worked
up an appetite.'

She turned to look at Veronica, suddenly aware that her friend
had gone very still. Her face was pale, though more like the
pallor of a rose whose petals are faintly tinged with pink. Hilary
laid her own larger hand over hers.

'Don't worry. Of course you have to tell them everything
you heard.' She kept her voice low. 'I don't know what this is
all about, though I'm beginning to guess. They'll have run tests
to find what felled Dinah so drastically last night. They must
have found something. It obviously wasn't any of the usual
emergencies for someone her age.' Her voice sank to a murmur.
'Whether that conversation you heard had anything to do with
it, or it's something else entirely, is for them to decide, not
you.'

She saw Veronica's blue eyes shoot up in alarm. Across the
circle of chairs, Hilary saw Theresa's darker gaze fixed on them.
Had she heard?

The detectives took Gavin first, then Theresa. Hilary watched
her go. Theresa had said almost nothing to her group while she
waited. Hilary longed to hear what was going on inside that
broad brown head. Would she tell the detectives about her
exchange with Gavin on the walk above the tiltyard? Not if it
meant what it seemed to. Or was it possible that there was some
explanation so innocent that she would not think it worth
mentioning? And if she did not, what effect would it have on the
detectives when Veronica told them, reading the verbatim script
from her notebook? Hilary glanced again at her companion.
Veronica still looked strained. Hilary hoped they would not keep
her waiting too long.

They did not see Theresa again. Probably she had gone straight
from her interview to lunch. One by one, others of the Toad
group were called by the policewoman at the door and disappeared

into the corridor. Ceri, Tania, Rob. Ben gave a thumbs-up signal
to Jake as he followed them.

'Don't give us away!' Jake called after him.

'This is not a laughing matter,' Colonel Truscott thundered at
him. 'Show some respect.'

Jake tugged that lock of fuchsia-coloured hair in mock defer-
ence. 'Yes, Colonel. No, Colonel.'

A grin threatened to break the forced gravity of his face.

Hilary was growing hungrier.

As she waited, she felt again the intensity of eyes on her. It
could not be Theresa this time. The little woman had long gone.
When Hilary looked up, it was the quiet Lin Bell who was staring
at her and Veronica.

Hilary's was the sixth name on the list. She shot a look of
apology at Veronica, left in the diminished circle, which now
consisted only of her, Colonel Truscott, the silver-haired Lin, and
the flamboyantly coiffured Jake.

Hilary's thoughts were still with Veronica when she saw DS
Blunt, a burlier figure than his inspector, waiting at the door of
a room further along the East Cloister corridor, not far from the
glass fire door where she had bumped into Melissa. It must be
almost under Hilary's own room. Some way beyond the sergeant,
she remembered, must be Dinah Halsgrove's bedroom.

Hilary had, she thought, little to report herself. She had been
a couple of miles away in Totnes, sitting by the Leechwells,
when that strange conversation above the tiltyard was taking
place.

The room was considerably smaller than the spacious Lady
Jane's Chamber. A table had been set under the window that
gave on to the inner courtyard. There were two chairs behind
it. The lean figure of the detective inspector occupied one. The
other was presumably for his sergeant. Hilary would have to sit
on the third chair, facing the light.

A classic arrangement, she thought. They can see every
movement of my face, while theirs are partly shadowed.

A chair scraped across the floor as the stockier DS Blunt
took his seat.

She gave her name and address to DI Foulks and watched
his sergeant enter the details on a fresh page of his notepad.

Would it not, she wondered, be more efficient to tape-record her statement?

She was jolted back to reality by the inspector's next question.

'Will you take us through the events of yesterday afternoon and evening? You arrived when?'

Hilary's mind had been occupied by Veronica's unsettling experience that morning. She was forced back to a different time and place. She went over their arrival, their joining the group for tea in the garden. Dinah Halsgrove's arrival.

'Did Miss Halsgrove appear normal? Was she eating and drinking like the rest of you?'

Surely he had already asked Gavin and Theresa that? Hilary tried to picture the scene. 'She arrived a little later than us. Melissa – I'm sorry, I don't know her second name – anyway, the tall woman with the long brown hair . . .'

'Melissa Standforth,' the sergeant supplied. 'Gavin Standforth's wife.'

Hilary started. This was news to her. Now that she came to think of it, there was no reason why Melissa and Gavin should not be a husband and wife team, working together on this course. But it had never occurred to her. She could not recall any look or gesture of affection between them that might have implied this. Rather the contrary.

Hurriedly collecting her wits, she said, 'Is she? I didn't know. Anyway, she brought Dinah Halsgrove out into the private rose garden. I got the impression she'd just collected her from the station.'

'And did you speak to Miss Halsgrove?'

'Not really. Well, I believe I recommended the fruit cake, but she said she was diabetic. And, well, she did look rather tired. She's over ninety, you know.'

'Yes, we are aware of that fact. You said she refused the fruit cake. Did she partake of anything else?'

Hilary thought. 'Gavin brought her a cup of tea. I got the impression she was there more out of politeness than anything else. She seemed glad to get back to her room as soon as she decently could. I rather fancy Gavin wanted to show her off to us as his trophy speaker.'

'And then?'

'The rest of us stayed on in the garden. It was a lovely afternoon.'

'So the next time you saw her was when she spoke in the Great Barn?'

'Y–yes.' A memory was coming back to Hilary. 'Yes . . . but . . .'

The inspector leaned forward in a waiting silence, his eyebrows raised.

'It's probably nothing. But they wouldn't let me into the Great Barn without my name badge. I had to dash back to the East Cloister to get it. We've got rooms on the top floor, my friend and I.'

'And?'

'Well, I was rushing back down the stairs when I bumped into Melissa. I guessed Dinah Halsgrove must have a room on the first floor – that's where they often put guest speakers. Probably Melissa was sleeping there too. It's just – well, she gave a sort of hiss when I ran into her. Like a snake that's been disturbed. I don't think it was just the collision. That didn't really amount to much. But she seemed angry to find me there, as though she hadn't banked on there being anyone else around just then. I was in a hurry to get back to the Great Barn, so I didn't think much about it at the time. But it's kept coming back to me. And just now . . .' The thoughts were tumbling through Hilary's mind. 'Well, if I'm right, Dinah Halsgrove's room was just down the corridor.'

'So?'

'Yes, I know,' Hilary finished lamely. 'If she was looking after Dinah, she might have gone back to fetch something for her. It's just . . . well, you seem to be looking for something out of the ordinary. Dinah Halsgrove appeared perfectly normal when she gave her talk in the Great Barn. Rather brilliant, in fact, and I'm not even going to say "for her age". Brilliant, full stop. She didn't come on the evening cruise with us, understandably, but Melissa was on the boat, serving drinks. I'm probably making a mountain out of a molehill. And it wasn't her in the tiltyard this morning.'

'I'm sorry?'

Hilary was aware that her words were racing ahead of her ordered thoughts. 'I'd better leave my friend Veronica to tell you about that. All I know is hearsay. I wasn't there. But that was Theresa and Gavin, not Melissa. So that's all I can give you, I'm afraid. A brief encounter on the landing. Somebody acting like the guilty party. Everybody else was in the Great Barn. Why wasn't she?'

A stray thought crossed her mind. She had not been the only latecomer to the Great Barn.

'As you say yourself, Miss Halsgrove could have sent Mrs Standforth on an errand.'

'I suppose so. You'll have to ask her. She really *is* still alive? Dinah Halsgrove, I mean.'

'Still in hospital. She's not out of the wood yet,' DS Blunt supplied.

'But they've found something that makes them think it was not a stroke or a heart attack, or even a normal case of food poisoning?'

'Thank you, Mrs Masters. You've been very helpful. By the sound of it, I think we need to talk to your friend next.'

Hilary felt herself dismissed. She stood up.

'You may go and get your lunch now. My apologies for needing to delay you.'

At least the chef's kitchen had been given a clean bill of health, Hilary reflected, as she crossed the lawn to the Chapter House restaurant.

She stopped as a sudden thought struck her. She had forgotten to tell the inspector about Melissa's appearance at her bedroom door last night.

How much did that matter?

ELEVEN

She entered the lofty medieval Chapter House, which served as both bar and dining room. The assembled writers lifted their heads from their plates. Conversations stilled. Faces bore an air of nervous anticipation. Hilary felt she should be holding a scroll, about to read out some proclamation. But when they saw it was only another of their own number returned from questioning, they turned back. The chatter resumed.

Hilary made her way under the high vaulted roof to a half-empty table. Many of the earlier diners had already gone. Her spirits lifted a little to find a place beside the sharp-witted Jo Walters, the one who had expressed a desire to emulate the Scandinavian crime noir novelists. Her older husband Harry was unlikely to contribute sparkling conversation, but Hilary would have to put up with that. She wondered what he had done with himself this morning, while the others wrote. He hadn't come back to the session after coffee.

He waved his fork towards the far end of the room. 'Buffet lunch today. Go and help yourself. I must say, they feed you well here. I'm jolly glad they've given the kitchen the all clear.'

Hilary got up and picked her way along the line of pies, cold meats and salads. She realized she was ravenously hungry.

The same lugubrious, middle-aged waiter who had served them at breakfast now stood behind the food tables, offering to help her.

'You people are a lot of trouble,' he told her, delivering a slice of duck and orange pie to her plate.

'I'm sorry. Yes, I suppose we must be holding you up, coming into lunch in dribs and drabs like this.'

'You never saw such a morning in the kitchen. Everything to be inspected and scrubbed down. As if we didn't already have a five-star certificate for food hygiene.'

'Yes, it must have been very trying. Tell Chef from me he's done a splendid job. I can't wait to get my teeth into this lot.'

She took the excuse to steer her loaded plate away to the dining table before he could launch into further complaints.

'So? Any theories?' Jo Walters turned an eager face to her. 'What did the CID want to hear?'

Like Ben in the Toad group, Jo's mood was not as sober as the near-death of an iconic writer might suggest. Hilary wondered whether she had made the wrong choice of lunch companion.

She answered Jo shortly. 'Just what you'd expect. What I could remember about yesterday afternoon and whether I'd seen anything suspicious around Dinah Halsgrove.'

'So there *is* something mysterious wrong with her. Well, there'd have to be, to bring in the CID. And had you?'

The directness of the question shook Hilary. For a moment,

she wondered whether she should come clean and divulge that slight, but oddly disturbing, encounter with Melissa in the bedroom corridor. On balance, she decided she had better keep it to herself. And she certainly was not going to make the conversation Veronica had overheard public knowledge.

Even now, a chill sweat was beginning to break out on her skin. *Could* Theresa have caught that murmured exchange of panic between Veronica and Hilary, as the time for her to read her morning's work drew closer? Hilary did not think so, but she could not be sure. If that conversation between Gavin and Theresa meant what it appeared to, how much danger would that put Veronica in? Was it really possible that the workshop organizers themselves had made an attempt on the life of their famous guest? Not a hoax, but something that could have been genuinely lethal?

The food on her plate suddenly seemed less appetizing.

'Well? Had you seen anything suspicious?' Jo's voice demanded.

'Oh, sorry! No, I was in the Great Barn, sitting in the gallery beside you, if you remember, and then off on the boat like everyone else.'

Jo frowned, a forkful of watercress held suspended halfway to her mouth. 'We were all there, weren't we, as far as I know. It was only Theresa who was left behind to take care of Dinah.'

'It was Melissa who fetched her from the station and was chaperoning her in the tea garden.'

She could not get rid of the memory of that unsettling encounter in the East Cloister.

'The thing is, if she *was* poisoned, we know now that the poison didn't come from the restaurant – and I think we're all assuming it *was* poison, aren't we, otherwise what's the point of all this questioning?'

'Go on.'

'Then somebody must have introduced it into Dinah Halsgrove's supper, either on the tray that was brought to her, or in something else in the room.'

'Like the hospitality trays they leave out for us, you mean? Difficult, though. They used to give you little jugs of fresh milk. But even Morland Abbey has gone over to tubs of UHT nowadays.

And the coffee and tea are in sealed packets. You'd have a job to mix anything into them.'

'A jug of water, perhaps? Whoever did it would have to have access to Dinah's room. Then they could have nipped in afterwards and washed the jug out.'

'She'll have had a key to her room. The question is, did she lock it?'

'If she was expecting someone to bring her supper, probably not.'

Hilary frowned. 'But surely whoever did this – and I'm inclined to agree with you about the source of the poison – they'd need a time when the room was empty, wouldn't they?'

'Not necessarily. Of course, it *could* have been while Dinah was talking in the Great Barn. But, on the other hand, if someone brought you a jug of iced water, for instance, you wouldn't think it suspicious, would you? Theresa has to be the prime suspect.'

'Is there a poison you can dissolve completely in water?'

'You'd have to ask our queen of crime novelists. We're all dying to know just what she *did* take to make her so ill. But the police are hardly likely to tell us.'

'But who would want to do such a thing, and why?' Jo's innocent eyes grew round.

'Not only that, but why *here*?' Hilary mused.

'It's not looking good for Gavin and his crew, is it? They're the only ones who stood to gain from the death of a famous novelist at a crime event they'd organized. Front-page headlines.'

'You think Gavin's behind it?'

'Don't be so naïve, Hilary.' The use of her first name startled her for a moment, until she remembered the name badge she was wearing. Or had Jo Walters recalled it from that introduction in the garden? 'How much do you actually hear about Gavin Standforth these days? Oh, I know he had that one bestseller. If it hadn't been for that, no one would even know his name.' There was a strangely bitter edge to Jo's voice. 'He's traded on that to sell his backlist, but he's hardly mega famous, not like Dinah Halsgrove. Now, if Dinah had died, half the world would have got to hear about that. From Gavin's point of view, there's no such thing as negative publicity. You know how you're browsing through a bookshop, looking for something to buy, and a name leaps out at you. The very fact that you've heard it somewhere makes you feel more positive about buying their book, rather than an author you've never heard of. You may not remember *what* you heard.'

'Hmm. You think he'd really go that far?'

'Don't you?' Again that curious coldness in her voice.

Hilary was spared the necessity of answering by the arrival of Veronica. The taller woman's cheeks were flushed a bright pink. She looked scared.

Veronica took the seat next to Hilary. She rested her elbows on the table and buried her face in her hands.

'I don't know what I've done,' she whispered.

Hilary was aware of the rest of their table eyeing her friend with avid curiosity. Gavin, Theresa and Melissa were watching from their own table.

'What's up, love?' asked Harry Walters. 'Did they give you a hard time?'

The implications of this were not lost on the others. Heads now turned in his direction. Was he accusing Veronica of complicity in last night's near-tragedy?

'Harry!' his wife Jo reprimanded him sharply.

Hilary took charge of the situation. She seized Veronica under the arm and yanked her to her feet, none too gently.

'You need food. All this fuss on an empty stomach.'

She steered Veronica towards the buffet.

'I'm not hungry, really,' Veronica protested in a low voice. 'It's just that . . . well, I've practically accused Gavin and Theresa of attempted murder, haven't I?'

Hilary shot a look sideways to gauge whether either of the leaders, or indeed anyone else, could have heard her. Satisfied that the space between them and the dining tables was wide enough, she lowered her own voice.

'You told the truth. That's all any of us can do. What it means – if it does mean anything at all – is up to the inspector and his sidekick. For what it's worth, I've pointed the finger of suspicion at Melissa too, and on a lot shakier evidence. Here, I can recommend the duck pie. Come to think of it, I might just take a second helping.'

The spoon in Veronica's hand rattled against the salad bowl. The waiter helped them both to slices of pie in an injured silence. The first-comers had mostly left the dining room. The last three members of the Toad group – Dan Truscott, Lin Bell and Jake – had not yet appeared.

Did any of the others have significant information to give? Hilary wondered. Was it only the two of them?

'Try not to draw attention to yourself,' she warned Veronica. 'You did what you had to do. Put it behind you. The last thing we want is for Gavin or Theresa to start suspecting you know something.'

'I rather gave that away at the dining table, didn't I? I hope neither of them heard me.'

Her hand still trembled. Hilary righted her plate for her.

'I don't suppose those who did will think much of it. We're all pretty much on edge. We came here for a fun weekend, and now it's got serious. There's nothing like being questioned by the police for making you feel guilty, even if you haven't done a thing.'

'Are you sure? OK. I'll try to get a grip on myself. I wish Andrew . . .'

It was less than two years since Veronica had been widowed. Hilary let the name die away into the chatter of the surrounding tables.

'I know. I'm lucky to have David. Which reminds me, I haven't brought him up to date with what just happened last night. When I last spoke to him, I was still at the stage of telling him what a wonderful talk Dinah Halsgrove gave, and how she'd been taken ill afterwards. Nothing about the police. I can't believe everything that's happened since.'

'I could talk to my children. But it's not the same, is it?'

As they made their way back to their table, a younger waiter emerged from the kitchen. His long grey apron was wrapped sleekly over his black shirt and trousers. He held a tray of food shoulder high as he disappeared through the outer door.

Of course. It would not have been Theresa who had carried Dinah Halsgrove's supper along the cloisters and up the stairs. It would have been one of Morland Abbey's staff. This one? But what interest could someone like him have had in poisoning her?

She shook her head.

'One word of caution,' she warned Veronica as they approached
their seats. 'Be careful what you say in front of Jo Walters. Her
husband may be a bit of a twit, but she's sharp as a razor. She
slapped him down when he seemed to be implying that you might
be under suspicion. But it won't have gone unnoticed. She's
storing it all away under those vacuous-looking blonde curls.'

It was Veronica who took the initiative as she picked at the
food on her plate. She turned to her table companions with a
falsely bright smile.

'Well, then. The rest of you have still got your interviews to
come. Is anybody here harbouring vital information?'

Hilary could see them all questioning themselves. Did one or
two of them flush? Or was that just the good food and wine
or beer? Whatever they did or did not know, they were clearly
not going to share it with anyone except the CID.

Gavin stumbled through the afternoon session. It was probably
a teaching exercise he had done many times before. He could
manage the mechanics of it, but his heart wasn't in it. He gave
a visible start every time the policewoman summoned someone
else from the groups for interview.

'I'm beginning to think he can't be guilty,' Hilary muttered to
Veronica. 'If he was, he'd surely make a better fist of pretending
to look innocent.'

'Something's upset him, though,' Veronica whispered back. 'It
can't just be the shock of Dinah Halsgrove falling ill and then
the police being called in. He's had time to adjust to that.'

'Hmm.'

'Melissa looks inscrutable. I can't tell if she's upset or not.'

'Gavin said she was highly strung. I'm beginning to wonder
whether he meant mentally ill.'

Hilary looked up and saw Theresa watching them.

She bent her attention to her notepad again. In spite of everything, the pages were filling up satisfactorily with ideas that were
not at all bad.

Gavin had encouraged them to put flesh on the bones of any
character they might have envisaged in their chosen setting.

'Think of someone you actually know. It helps to add those
little extra quirks and physical details which it's hard to imagine

from cold. How do they speak? How do they move? What is it that makes this person distinctly *them*?'

'I'm not sure,' said Lin Bell, her back straight, her eyes bright behind their glasses, 'about the ethics of putting someone I know, perhaps a good friend, in the role of the villain. A murderer, in this case.'

'Don't worry.' Gavin's smile was thin. 'You'll find once you put them into an imaginary situation that they start acquiring a life of their own. You may start off with someone's physical characteristics and personal foibles, but as your story gets under way, they'll increasingly depart from the person you know in real life to become a genuinely new individual. It's rather like a kaleido-scope. You start with all these little coloured pieces of genuine memory, and then you give the tube a twist, and lo and behold, they fall into a completely new pattern no one's ever seen before.'

He's said this dozens of times, to other classes, Hilary thought. The words are just falling off his tongue. His mind is somewhere else.

Gavin's eyes flicked once more to the door as Harry Walters was called. Hilary tried to imagine the cheery husband of the more intelligent Jo being shrewd enough to remember any details which might be significant in the hunt for an attempted murderer.

Still less that he might have attempted anything sinister himself.

At last she laid her pen down from her aching hand. She had not realized that creative writing could be physically such hard work. She felt oddly drained. Still, she was rather pleased with the way her young Bartholomew was developing, more romantic than she had been expecting, but astute, as he investigated the strange death of his grandfather at the Leechwells.

'Thank you, everyone,' said Gavin, with evident relief that the session was over. 'Tea is on its way. Then you're free until suppertime. This evening, we'll meet again to see what you've come up with in the way of vibrant characters, whether that's the investigator, victim or murderer.'

The word fell uncomfortably in the listening room.

Hilary put her notepad away in her shoulder bag.

'Right,' she said to Veronica. 'Get some of that fruit cake inside you. Then there's something I want to show you.'

TWELVE

'Do you mind if we walk into Totnes?' Hilary asked. 'I need to clear my head.'

'That's fine by me.'

They stepped out down the road through the Morland estate. On one side, fields sloped away to the hidden windings of the River Dart.

'I was so looking forward to coming here,' Hilary said ruefully. 'The special atmosphere of the Abbey, that Great Barn, the wonderful grounds. Now, I can't wait to get away from it for an hour or two. I haven't a clue what's going on, but it's not healthy.'

'*In the midst of life we are in death*,' Veronica suggested.

Hilary swung round to give her a hard look. 'Nobody *did* die.'

'No, but . . .'

'You're still worrying about what you heard from the tiltyard, aren't you? Look, you've told the police. It's in their hands now.'

'All the same, I can't help feeling the shadow of something. How do I know if Gavin and Theresa aren't plotting something else? Or could it be Melissa, and they're covering up for her?'

'Dinah Halsgrove should be safe enough in hospital, once she's got over that scare. They've probably got a police officer on the door. I'm sure Inspector Foulks will have that pair in again after what you said, and give them a harder grilling this time. Gavin was acting scared this afternoon. With good reason, I'd say.'

'It's queer, but I didn't feel any reaction from Theresa. She just sat there in our group, watching us write. So absolutely still, but I couldn't help feeling it was *me* she was watching.'

'Have you ever tried to find a toad in a pond?' Hilary asked. 'You know it's there, because you've heard it croaking, but you search and search, and you can see nothing. Then, all of a sudden, what you thought was a dried-up leaf on the surface turns out to be this warty face with two bright black eyes, staring at you. It can give you quite a shock.'

Veronica shuddered. 'I know. It's probably because I *do* have something to hide. I expect I'm imagining that she's particularly interested in me.'

'Of course you are.' Hilary kept a prudent silence about her own fears that either Gavin or Theresa might have belatedly seen Veronica leaving the tiltyard. Might have put two and two together and seen the very real danger that she could have heard them.

What then? *In the midst of life we are in death.* Veronica's words came back to haunt her. It would appear to be the elderly novelist whom Theresa and Gavin had designs against, yet was it melodramatic to fear that Veronica was on their list now? How seriously would the police take the danger to her? Did they even think she *was* in danger?

She looked behind her. The road from the abbey was empty. There were no pavements. It would not be difficult for a car to come hurtling down the hill and fail to stop before it ploughed into two pedestrians.

She pulled Veronica further on to the verge.

They came through the gateposts which marked the limits of the estate and found themselves among modern houses. Ahead, they met the busier main road that took them on into Totnes.

'What I don't understand,' Hilary mused, 'is where Melissa fits into all this . . . if she does. Did you know she's Gavin's wife?'

'Yes, I'd heard that.'

'So is she in on whatever Gavin and Theresa are plotting? Do you think what you heard included her? Or have we got the wrong end of the stick? Is *she* the one being plotted against, and Halsgrove's attack just a red herring? Could the other two be having an affair behind her back, and want Melissa out of the way?'

'That's a bit overdramatic, isn't it?' Veronica protested. 'There are easier ways of ending a marriage nowadays than bumping off your spouse. And it was Dinah Halsgrove who collapsed, not Melissa.'

'Hmm. I suppose you're right.'

'Though there was what Gavin said at the end: "I'll shut her up".'

They crossed the railway bridge and entered the town. Hilary's

eye was caught by a newspaper stand that shouted: CELEBRITY
COLLAPSES AT MORLAND ABBEY.

She grabbed a paper and paid for it.

The front page showed nothing but fighting in Syria and gloomy
news about the economy. She turned it over, and then turned
another page. Finally, tucked away in a small paragraph on
page six, was the news that famous crime novelist Dinah
Halsgrove had been taken suddenly ill during a course at Morland
Abbey and rushed to hospital. *A hospital spokeswoman refused
to comment on Miss Halsgrove's condition. The author is ninety-
two. Conference organizer Gavin Standforth said, 'Given her
age, we are gravely concerned about her.'*

'Hmm. That must have been last night. Too soon for them to
have the news that she was still alive this morning.'

'But Gavin does get a *small* mention.'

'Hardly enough to boost his book sales. It's not as if she'd
died. If it was meant as a novel means of publicity, it failed.'

Hilary led the way across the High Street, past the place where
she had parked that morning.

'This came as a surprise to me,' she confided to Veronica. 'I
thought I knew Totnes. The Brutus Stone, with the legend about
the town being founded by a Trojan. The Norman castle. The
Elizabethan market. Eco-friendly Transition Town with its own
currency. All the New Age stuff, plus a colony of local Buddhists.
There's some nonsense about the church having a leper squint
where the poor outcasts could watch the eucharist through a hole
in the wall. Rubbish, of course. But there was also talk of a leper
path leading down from the old Maudlin hospital. Yet somehow
I'd missed *this* gem.'

She led Veronica down some steps, to the beginning of a
narrow lane.

'This is a shorter route than the one I first found. After I'd
finished writing, I followed my nose downhill, instead of going
back up along the way I came. And, lo and behold, it brought
me out to this very car park where I'd left my trusty Vauxhall.'

The narrow path bent away between ivy-clad walls. The noise
of the town fell away behind them. Their own footsteps echoed
louder than they should have done from the old stones. No one
passed them.

'It's a funny thing about this path. No windows in the walls. Nobody overlooking it. And there's hardly a soul about. In all the time I was here, I only saw three people.'

She could hear them now. The laughter of the two boys as they clashed their conkers. Their jeers as they saw her sitting with her feet in the well. And the old man's stick, tapping its way on up the hill. A stick she had not heard coming.

'Just round this bend and up a bit more,' Hilary encouraged her companion. 'It's worth the walk.'

'You said there were no openings in the wall,' Veronica said suddenly. 'But there's this.'

The blank stone wall had been breached by two brick pillars and a slatted iron gate. Between its vertical bars they could see a garden, with trees and flower beds. There were rustic picnic benches and children's play equipment.

'This must be what Ceri was telling us about. Their campaign to make a children's garden here, instead of a car park. It was a rather lovely story of the inauguration, with the locked gate and three friendly giants peering over the wall. Presumably Mr Toad, Mr Snake and Mr Slowworm.'

'Hmmph! That's all very well. But I can't help the feeling that the original figures were not quite as jolly as that.'

The last stretch was the steepest. Hilary hauled herself up it and stopped dead. There in front of her, at the meeting place of the lanes, was the rectangular pool that contained the three springs, set back within stone walls hung with ivy.

What she had not expected was to find a woman face down in the shallow water of the middle trough, seeming to fill the basin with her long body, her burgundy embroidered skirt, her peasant blouse. Her long lank brown hair trailed in the wet beneath the central spring. The one, Hilary remembered, dedicated to the Long Crippler.

There was barely enough water to cover the cobbled floor. In the three troughs, it stood only a couple of inches deep. Could someone really drown in it?

Hilary stood transfixed, unable to move or speak. It was so like the scene she had been imagining as she scribbled the opening pages of her novel. Bartholomew's grandfather, dead like this in the holy Leechwells.

It was Veronica who broke the shocked silence. 'Oh, Hilary! It's Melissa!'

She ran forward to pull the prostrate woman from the water.

Something seemed to pierce the protective film which had Hilary enclosed in a bubble of disbelief. She lunged to help Veronica lift her sodden burden away from the well. As they laid her on the tarmac and turned her over, they saw what had not been evident before: a bloody wound in her left temple.

'Oh, Hilary! She's not breathing.'

Tossing back Melissa's streaming hair, Hilary bent her face to the cold white one beneath her and began to administer a vigorous CPR.

Veronica was ringing 999. 'Yes. The Leechwells, I think it's called. It's in this narrow lane . . . I can't tell you for certain. My friend is applying CPR . . . Thank you.'

Hilary was aware of silence behind her.

'Hilary?' Veronica must have asked something before.

'Yes? What?' Hilary panted between chest compressions.

'I said, do you think we should ring Gavin? We must tell him, mustn't we?'

'If you've got his number. They used to have good old Directory Enquiries. I haven't a clue what you're supposed to ring nowadays.'

'I think I've got the Morland Abbey number somewhere.'

Veronica searched in her bag and found a green-and-white brochure. 'Here it is. They'll get him.'

'Assuming he isn't all too well aware that his wife is dead.'

'Hilary!'

She was beginning to despair of breathing life into the long, collapsed body. Had Melissa drowned in the shallow water of the Long Crippler, or was it that nasty-looking head wound? Liquid leaked from Melissa's sodden clothes, to seep away across the tarmac under Hilary's knees.

There were rapid footsteps. A woman screamed.

Hilary paused to push the hair from her sweating face and looked up. A middle-aged woman with a jute shopping bag had stopped in horror, her hand to her mouth.

'Is she . . . dead?'

'Not if I can help it.' Hilary's voice came out hoarse. She was tiring. 'Let's wait till the medics get here.'

'You've rung nine-nine-nine?' The woman appealed to Veronica.

'Of course. They're on their way.'

'Well, if I can't . . .' The woman's feet were edging round Hilary and Melissa in the narrow space.

'No. You go. There's nothing useful you can do,' Hilary grunted, returning to her task.

There was another noise coming towards them down the narrow lane. Hilary remembered that sound from this morning. The tap-tap-tapping of a stick on stone. She did not lift her eyes from the steady rhythm on Melissa's chest.

The remembered voice spoke almost above her.

''Er's a goner, idn't 'e? You be wasting your time.'

'I'm doing my best,' she panted through tight lips.

'There's life in them there springs, and then there's death. 'Tisn't always but a hairline between the two of 'em.'

'Thank you,' gasped Hilary. 'That's all I wanted to hear.'

The insistent wail of sirens was beginning to make itself heard from the street beyond. Hilary realized how tired her arms were. She bent one last time to breathe life into Melissa's lungs. The saturated clothing beneath her hands was cold.

There were rapid steps now. Two paramedics in green overalls burst on the scene.

'Right, m'dear. You're doing a great job. We'll take over now.'

To her surprise, Hilary found she needed to be helped to her feet. Her folded limbs straightened painfully. She stood swaying slightly.

'You all right, love?' the female paramedic asked. 'No, of course you're not. You've had a nasty shock. Here. Is there somewhere we can sit you down?'

There was not. Hilary remembered perching on the stone that led down into the well to write her crime scene. She did not want to step down into it now.

The woman addressed Veronica. 'I'd say take her to a tea shop. Nice hot cuppa. But the police will want to have a look at this one. Funny sort of accident, if you ask me. You and your friend will have to wait until they get here . . . What about you, sir?'

She turned to the old man with the walking stick. 'Were you here when they found her?'

The man was taller than Hilary remembered, his grey head stooped forward, not unlike the way Melissa had walked. His voice was gravelly.

'It's the Long Crippler, you see. That'd be where they found 'er. You've only got to look at 'er.'

A shiver ran through Hilary. She realized her own clothes were wet now. They had indeed found Melissa lying face down across the pool, with her head beneath the pipe from which the water spouted into the Long Crippler basin. How could he have known that?'

'Jasmin,' called the paramedic kneeling beside Melissa's still body. 'Give us a hand here.'

A police car was inching its way down the narrow lane from the road above. A uniformed sergeant stood in front of Hilary and Veronica. A constable hurried over behind him, his younger face alive to all that was going on around the well.

'Any luck?' the sergeant asked the paramedics.

'Doesn't look like it.'

'Now, then.' The sergeant opened his notebook and turned back to Hilary and Veronica. 'I take it you'll be the ladies who found her? Names, please.'

THIRTEEN

'You again.'

Hilary should not have been surprised to find herself facing Inspector Foulks and DS Blunt again, this time in Totnes police station. Melissa Standforth had, after all, been a significant figure in Dinah Halsgrove's collapse. It couldn't just be coincidence.

A worm of guilt twisted in her gut. She had convinced herself that Melissa was the most likely person to have administered a near-fatal dose to the novelist. But now it was Melissa who was dead.

'I had the misfortune to take Veronica back to show her where I'd been working this morning.'

She was annoyed that the lean, lugubrious Foulks should make her feel responsible. There was no way she could have known what she would find.

'Did Mrs Standforth know you'd been at the Leechwells this morning? Might she have been expecting to meet you there?'

'No!' Hilary was shocked into vehemence. 'I wasn't in her group when we shared our writing before lunch. I was in Theresa's.'

The grey eyebrows rose. 'Did anyone else know you were going back there?'

Hilary was momentarily uncertain. 'No . . . No, I don't see how they could have. It was just something I suggested to Veronica after tea, when Gavin said we were free for a couple of hours.'

The steely eyes regarded her. 'So, it was just coincidence that Mrs Standforth was found by a member of her writing class?'

Hilary flushed. 'Well, yes . . . Are you suggesting that I was *meant* to find her? Or . . .' She swallowed the inference of his questions.

'I'm assuming nothing.'

Again that thoughtful silence.

Then the inspector sighed. 'Right, Mrs Masters. Let's take it step by step. What time did you go to the Leechwells? Which route did you take?'

'About four forty. Uphill from the car park behind the High Street.'

DS Blunt cut in. 'Did you see anyone else in the lane?'

Hilary thought. 'No. In fact I commented to Veronica on how few people were using it when I was there this morning.'

'So what was the first thing you saw?'

She would rather not have relived that.

Hilary came out of the police station feeling shaken. Her clothes were still depressingly damp. She perched, rather uncomfortably, on the jagged stone wall at the roadside, within sight of the police station door. The late afternoon was cloudier than she would have liked, but she had been reluctant to stay inside, though a kindly policewoman had offered her a seat while Veronica was

questioned. She had an oddly guilty feeling. She did not want
Veronica to come out from her interview with DI Foulks and
find her on the phone to David.

It had been two years now since the embolism that had taken
Andrew's life so suddenly. Veronica had put her altered life
together with a quiet dignity and grace. She had her children:
Morag in her final year of a journalism degree; Penny just starting
maths at Cambridge, and Robert doing something Hilary had
never quite understood with banking in Malaysia. But Hilary
knew that however supportive her own Bridget and Oliver would
be, it could never be the same as talking to David about a thing
like this.

She pressed his number. At least she had learned to keep her
phone charged and use some of its simpler functions. She had
rarely felt more glad of what she still regarded as a new-fangled
gadget than she did now.

A wave of enormous relief washed over her as she heard his
voice. She had not realized quite what a toll it had taken on her
to find that body in the well to which she had led Veronica so
optimistically. Then she had had to rally her shocked body to
apply CPR until the paramedics came to take over. Finally there
had been the dawning reality that Melissa would not recover,
even in expert hands. It was not a simple case of drowning.
There was that bloody head wound. She had already been dead
when Hilary found her, in the Long Crippler basin of the triple
Leechwells.

'David!' The shock must have poured into the emphasis on
his name.

'What's wrong?' His own voice was suddenly sharp with
concern. He knew her too well.

'Only that . . . It's a long story, but the gist is that Veronica
and I went into Totnes this afternoon. I wanted to show her the
healing wells where I'd found the inspiration for my crime novel
this morning. Only when we got there . . . she . . . this is bizarre.
You'll think I'm making it up . . .'

'Just tell me. Let me decide.' A doctor's voice. Calm, controlled,
reassuring.

'There was . . . Melissa. She's the wife of Gavin Standforth,
who's leading this course. We'd been divided into groups, Toads,

Snakes and Slowworms. Like the three springs of the Leechwells in Totnes. And there she was. Face down in one of the basins. Dead. I tried to revive her, but, well, the paramedics couldn't either. I'm terribly afraid – I know this is sounding ridiculous – she's been murdered.'

'You're not the hysterical type. Of course I believe you. Where are you now?'

'Outside Totnes police station. They wanted to ask us all sorts of questions, of course. I'm waiting for them to finish with Veronica.'

'I'll come. I can be there in less than an hour. Or would they let you come home straight away? No, belay that. I expect you're still too shocked to drive safely. I'll come.'

'No!' she said in alarm, though it was what she wanted more than anything. 'It's . . . well, it's Veronica. I don't want to rub it in that I've got you and she . . . hasn't got Andrew. I'll cope.'

'I know you will. I just don't want you to have to do it on your own. But I take your point. God bless you, love. Stay safe.'

Hilary's voice grew gruff. 'Thanks. I feel better already for talking to you. And you're right. Inspector Foulks has already asked us to stay around until the end of the course tomorrow. There's still that matter of Dinah Halsgrove and now this . . .'

'What matter?'

There was a silence while Hilary racked her brain to remember what she might or might not have told David when she talked to him last night.

'You said she'd been taken ill,' David's voice went on. 'But why were the police involved? What's that got to do with a dead woman in the holy well?'

'Oh dear. I forgot I hadn't brought you up to date. The police came to the abbey this morning to question us about that. It appears it wasn't food poisoning, or a stroke, or whatever we suspected. Someone appears to have given her something. Someone here at Morland.'

'This is sounding worse. Look, Hilary, if you've already given the police your statement, I really don't see what there is to keep you there.'

'Inspector Foulks was quite adamant about it. I can see his point. I have to say it looks like murder, and the first could be attempted murder. Look, I have to go. Veronica's just coming out of the police station.'

She started to close down her phone over his farewell words.

'It sounds a ghastly business. But you're being a good friend to Veronica. She'll be shocked as well. Tell her I'll be praying for you both.'

She snapped the call off as Veronica came towards her, her usually delicately pink face pale and drawn.

'What a dreadful day. At least the police have offered to drive us back to the abbey.'

'Thank God for that. I'd made up my mind to get a taxi anyway. I certainly don't feel up to the walk back.'

FOURTEEN

Hilary leaned back in the rear seat of the police car. She was terribly tired. As they sped up the drive, away from the tree-hung River Dart and through the grounds of the Morland Abbey estate, she reflected wryly that what should have been an amusing day in a delightful venue had been overturned by horror.

'At least,' she murmured to Veronica beside her, 'this knocks on the head my idea that Melissa might have been responsible for Dinah Halsgrove's illness last night.'

'I thought Gavin and Theresa were the prime suspects for that. After what I heard.'

'Yes, I know. But let's be honest. It was only a fragment of a longer exchange. It may not have meant what it seemed to. But I still can't put out of my head the venom in Melissa's reaction when I bumped into her. She didn't want me in that corridor. Still, she's dead now. And it can hardly have been an accident. The water in the well's only a couple of inches deep, and it's hardly something you'd fall into by mistake. From the look of that head wound, I'd say she'd either been hit or pushed with some force. And it's extremely unlikely there will be two murderers, or would-be murderers, on the same weekend.'

Something was buzzing at the back of Hilary's mind. A murdered body found in a pool. Why did that seem oddly familiar?

The car drew up in front of the abbey's arched entrance. A policewoman sprang from the front seat to open the rear door. Veronica and Hilary climbed out and stood, rather dazed, on the cobbled path to the inner courtyard.

'Here you are, ladies. And thank you for your assistance. This must have been a shock for you.'

'That's an understatement,' muttered Hilary.

'And remember, say nothing to the others about how Mrs Standforth died.'

As the car turned and sped away, a woman came running out of the gatehouse. Hilary could put a name to her now. Fiona, who had signed them in and given them their keys when they arrived. Only yesterday?

Fiona's usual air of efficient self-possession seemed to have shattered. Her long face had crumpled up into an expression of near panic.

'Not the police again! Has something else happened? It's not bad news about Miss Halsgrove, is it?'

Veronica looked at her oddly. 'You got my message, didn't you? You brought Gavin to the phone. Didn't he tell you why?'

Fiona's face took on a guarded look. 'I didn't like to ask him, since he didn't say. Not after last night.'

'You mean Dinah Halsgrove falling ill?' Hilary put in.

She saw the receptionist's desire to answer warring with . . . fear?

'His assistant, Theresa, phoned through to reception when she found her. I was on duty. If she hadn't gone back to check if she wanted anything else and found her . . . She was in a coma. They said she'd have been dead by morning.'

'A coma?' Hilary asked sharply. 'We assumed at first it was food poisoning, or something very like it. But the symptoms weren't right. Then the inspector talked about a stomach pump. And they seemed to rule out heart or stroke.'

Fiona shook her head vigorously. 'It certainly wasn't food poisoning. The chef had prepared a special meal for her. She has diabetes, you know. When they heard that, the paramedics thought it looked like a diabetic coma. Apparently, you can get that if you take too much medication, insulin and stuff, and you don't have the carbohydrates to balance it. Chef was mortified, but he's been assured it wasn't his fault.'

Hilary's brain was working overtime. 'If she had a low-cal meal, and her normal pills or injection, or whatever she usually takes for diabetes, then I still don't understand . . .'

'They gave her tests at the hospital and called the police in,' Veronica said quietly, 'Maybe they found it *wasn't* her normal dose.'

The implications sank in during the silence which followed.

'That would be clever, wouldn't it? Poison her with her own medication? It seems terrible to say this now, but I thought that's what Melissa was doing in the corridor when I surprised her. Stealing something from Halsgrove's room while the rest of us were in the Great Barn.'

'Still, it tells us one thing,' Veronica mused. 'If Theresa roused the house to call an ambulance, then she can't have had anything to do with Dinah's collapse. She'd have left her to die, wouldn't she? Whatever I . . .'

A warning look from Hilary shut her up.

'And here we are, standing around discussing what happened last night,' Hilary continued, 'which didn't result in a death, thank God, and yet we still haven't told you the worst news, and why we came back in a police car.' She watched the anxiety increase in Fiona's face. 'I'm sorry to have to tell you this, but Melissa Standforth has been murdered.'

She saw the second it took for her words to penetrate. Fiona's hand flew to her mouth. She leaned back against the wall of the archway to steady herself. She had gone quite white.

'How?' The question was a thread of sound.

'She was face down in the Leechwells. But with a head wound as well.' Too late, she remembered the inspector's warning. 'Sorry! I wasn't supposed to say that. Keep it to yourself, will you?'

'We found her,' Veronica added.

'And Mr Standforth knows?'

'That's why I called him to the phone.'

'He never said anything! He looked upset, but he has ever since we found Dinah Halsgrove ill. He went tearing off to the car park, but he never said why.'

Hilary looked at her watch. 'There's the irony. The next thing on the programme is what I've been looking forward to all weekend. A proper sit-down evening dinner in your splendid restaurant. But I seem to have lost my appetite.'

As they went up the long staircase to their rooms, Veronica admonished Hilary. 'The police said we shouldn't tell anyone how and where Melissa died.'

'They're hoping someone might give themselves away by knowing more than they should do? Hmmph! Well, it's too late now.'

Hilary and Veronica changed out of the clothes that were the worse for wear. Hilary's were still uncomfortably damp.

She draped them over the furniture and sat at the window in clean shirt and trousers. She turned up a troubled face as Veronica entered the room.

'I feel terrible. Ever since last night when Melissa opened that door you've just come through, I've had her down as my prime suspect. I wasn't sure exactly what she'd done, but I was sure she was behind Dinah Halsgrove's collapse. And now . . .'

'I know. She can't be the culprit now she's the victim, can she?'

Hilary shook her head dumbly. After a while she stood up. 'I'd put myself down as fairly unshockable. But I can't get that picture out of my head. That dead white face lying in the pool that was supposed to be healing.'

Veronica laid a hand on her arm. 'You can't blame yourself. Whatever the real reason, Melissa was certainly behaving strangely. Anyone would be suspicious. And, as you said before, how did Gavin know she'd be up on this corridor? He's also got some questions to answer.'

'You don't think he . . .?'

'I've no more idea than you have.' Veronica tried an unsuccessful smile. Then her blue eyes took on a faraway look. 'And yet . . . what about that strange conversation I overheard by the tiltyard? Hilary! He and Theresa were talking about a death, even though it hadn't actually happened.' She turned a stricken face to Hilary. 'We thought they must have meant Dinah. But what if it was Melissa all the time? "I'll shut her up."'

'You mean, Gavin was plotting to kill his *wife*?'

They took their places in the dining room, still in a state of shock.

Overhead, the ancient vault of the Chapter House soared almost to the height of the tithe barn next to it. Evening sunlight slanted through tall windows high in the walls. But Hilary found it hard to delight in her surroundings as she should have.

The moods of the others had relaxed somewhat, now that their interviews were over. But the two women found themselves locked in near silence. There was nothing else they could talk about, but it was not the sort of news you could pass on casually over the dinner table, even if they had not been warned to say nothing.

Halfway through the meal, Detective Inspector Foulks walked into the dining room, with DS Blunt at his heels. The inspector's tall, dignified form stood for a moment, sweeping his gaze round the tables. Conversations began to still as the would-be writers recognized him. People looked at each other uneasily. Was it not yet over? Hilary glanced swiftly round. Neither Gavin nor Theresa was present. She had not expected them to be.

'I'm sorry to disturb your dinner, folks. But I have something painful to tell you. This afternoon, one of your leaders, Mrs Melissa Standforth, was found dead, and not, I fear, from natural causes.'

There was an outcry of shock. Hilary and Veronica stayed silent. The looks they gave each other were tinged with guilt. It would seem strange to the others now that they had sat there in silence, nursing this knowledge.

The light caught the inspector's rimless glasses as he turned his head to include them all.

'Now, I know this is more shocking even than Miss Halsgrove's illness. In the circumstances, it may be that some of you will be thinking of moving out of here first thing tomorrow morning. I understand, but I must ask you not to do that. It would help my investigation greatly if none of you leaves until we've finished these new enquiries. You may think you saw the last of me when you made your statements this afternoon. But, as you can imagine, I'm afraid there are some even more serious questions I need to ask you now. This may not be what you expected when you signed up for a crime-writing weekend, but it has now become a very genuine murder investigation. Thank you.'

He and his sergeant walked out of the room, leaving behind a scene of shock and confusion, with none of the course leaders there to take control.

Beside Hilary, Ceri's voice came unexpectedly.

'You two came back to the abbey in a police car, didn't you? Does that mean you already knew about this?'

Veronica looked up uncomfortably. 'Yes,' she said in a small voice. 'I'm afraid we were the ones who found her.'

There was a startled silence.

'Where?' asked Lin Bell.

Veronica glanced unhappily at Hilary. 'I'm not sure whether we are supposed to tell you . . . but it was the Leechwells.'

Ceri drew an audible breath. It came to Hilary suddenly that the local woman had protested about Hilary's choosing the healing wells as the setting for her fictional murder, and about Gavin's seemingly joking appropriation of these names.

Hilary looked along their table. At the further end, the two younger men from the Toad group were now talking animatedly.

Jake leaned towards her. His expression was both earnest and excited.

'You have the advantage over us. The rest of us have never seen a murder victim. What did she look like? What colour was her face? Were her eyes open?'

Hilary's jaw dropped. There was a stillness round the table, shocked, uncomfortable. And yet Hilary's instinct told her there was also an avid curiosity in them all.

She rounded on the unfortunate Jake. 'I can't believe you said that.'

'I only asked . . .'

'I heard what you asked. I had a boy in my class once who was diagnosed as borderline psychopathic. Unable to feel for the pain of others.'

The eyes around the table moved away from hers, back to their plates.

Lin's bony hand reached out to cover Jake's. 'I know what you mean, dear. This *is* a crime weekend. There's a ghoulish part of our mind that does want to know. I know I do. In the interests of research, of course. But you could have been more tactful. Poor Hilary is still suffering from shock.'

Hilary choked on a mouthful of venison and took a hasty swig of water.

'Shock, indeed! If he were a pupil of mine, I'd give him shock!'

The image of Melissa's grey face, her sightless eyes, would never leave her mind.

On her other side, the curly-haired Ceri shuddered. 'I'm not sleeping at the abbey like the rest of you. I'm not sure which is worse – going home alone in the dark, or staying here with a murderer.'

There was an indrawn breath around the table, as though the reality of that had not sunk in until now. They looked around at each other speculatively, then at the tables beyond.

'Us? You know one thing?' Jake asked. 'We're all assuming this has something to do with this course. But what if it hasn't?'

'Of course,' said Hilary, turning back to Ceri. 'You're a local, aren't you? You knew about the Leechwells. You were unhappy about Gavin dragging their guardian spirits into his crime course. And with me because I chose them as my murder setting. You got quite angry.'

The words were out before she realized how they would sound. She felt herself blushing.

'I'm so sorry! I didn't mean . . . Of course, there'll be a completely different reason why Melissa was found dead in the well.'

Ceri's voice took on a sharper edge. 'I thought I'd made it clear that the wells are about healing. Are you suggesting I'd get my own back on the Standforths by profaning them with murder?'

'No. Of course not. That didn't come out the way I meant it to.'

'Where *is* young Gavin, anyway?' boomed Colonel Truscott.

'His wife's just died,' Veronica said quietly. 'In terrible circumstances. I don't suppose he feels like eating.'

'All the same,' the silver-haired Lin looked around her shrewdly, 'you'd think Theresa would have turned up. It's not quite the thing to leave us all leaderless, after a shock like this.'

'I'm not sure how much we need a leader. We're hardly going

to be trooping round to Lady Jane's Chamber for Gavin's evening session,' Ben said, with an apologetic look at Jake. 'It doesn't seem quite the right moment to be reading out our character sketches of a murderer or their victim.'

FIFTEEN

Veronica and Hilary left the dining room early. Darkness was falling over those parts of the quadrangle where the lamps did not reach. A deeper gloom invested the lawns and shrubberies beyond the restaurant.

There was a knot of people on the lawn, disregarding the notice asking visitors to keep to the paths. As Hilary and Veronica emerged, the group surged towards them.

A light, shockingly bright, was beamed on to Hilary's face. A microphone was thrust in front of her.

'You're from the crime-writing course, aren't you? We hear one of your leaders has been murdered. Can you tell us about that?'

Hilary recovered her wits. 'No,' she snapped. 'I can't. The police have asked us to say nothing about it.'

'Is it true she was found in the Leechwells?'

'I said no comment.'

'Oh, yes, these ladies were certainly there. They were the ones who found her.'

It was Jake who had come up behind her. He was grinning more broadly than the situation should have allowed. 'Hilary Masters and Veronica Taylor, for the record. And I'm Jake Penderson.'

'Jake! I could kill you for that!'

Even as she spoke, she knew with dismay that her words were being filmed. She knocked the microphone aside and thrust her hand over the camera lens.

'I'll thank you to leave us alone. We have nothing to tell the press. Ask the police.'

'And that,' said the interviewer, as her cameraman righted his equipment, 'is the scene at Morland Abbey tonight, as the shocked participants of the crime-writing course come to terms with a real-life murder.'

Hilary seized Veronica's arm and marched away.

'So much for keeping the details quiet. The whole country will know before long.'

They left Jake and Ben behind them. The two young men seemed not to be camera-shy.

In the shelter of the shadows beyond the Great Barn porch, Hilary paused to recover her wits.

'According to our timetable, we're supposed to meet in Lady Jane's Chamber at eight. But Ben's right. I suppose that's all out of the window now.'

'Lin had a point. It seems strange, doesn't it, just to abandon us like this? Gavin must be distraught, of course, but you'd have thought Theresa would have stepped up to the mark and shown some leadership.'

'Unless the police are still grilling her. After all, considering what you told them, she and Gavin must be prime suspects now.'

Veronica stopped dead on the path beside the Great Barn. 'Oh, dear. Do you think so? I didn't want to get them into real trouble. I just thought I had to tell the police what I heard.'

'Of course you did, you goof. You couldn't *not* tell them. And that was only when they were investigating Dinah Halsgrove's suspicious illness. Now it's a full-blown murder.'

Veronica shuddered, a slight tremor of her clothing in the dusk. 'That's what I can't get into my head. That Melissa is dead. That we actually saw her body. And someone, another human being, did that to her.'

'The inspector seems to think there's a high probability that that someone is staying in Morland Abbey.'

They began to move along the path again. Hilary found herself darting glances to either side, into shadowed doorways, to places where creepers on the walls cast dark shadows. To the giant cypress tree that spread its branches over the lawn.

'I don't want to worry you,' she said with a false attempt at cheerfulness, 'but from the point of view of the murderer, we two must look like trouble. I find it difficult to believe that the inspector could have questioned Gavin and Theresa as hard as he needed to without giving away the fact that someone overheard them. I just pray that pair don't put two and two together and remember seeing you in the tiltyard that morning. And, to cap it all, we have to be the ones who find Melissa.'

'It's too late, isn't it?' Veronica asked, her voice rather higher than usual. 'I can't un-say what I told the police. And we can't un-find Melissa's body. Somebody would have, anyway. It's happened. Hurting us wouldn't make things better for them, except to vent their anger, and that would get them into a whole lot more trouble.'

'I should think committing murder is trouble enough for anyone. If they think they've been exposed, they may not care what they do next.'

She was scanning the shadows more keenly now.

'We're assuming it *was* Gavin and Theresa,' Veronica said after a while. 'But it doesn't make sense. Why would they?'

Hilary shrugged. 'We've only known them a day or so. How can we guess what sort of relationship goes on between the three of them? Let alone what they thought they could achieve by sending Dinah Halsgrove into a near-death coma.'

A figure stepped out of the shadows in the corner where the Great Barn met the East Cloister. The voice revealed the dark bulk to be Colonel Truscott.

'Good evening, ladies. I gather you're wondering the same as the rest of us. What's happened to our leader's programme? What are we supposed to do now? And let me say I share your opinion. What would the two survivors have to gain from the death of Mrs Standforth? Assuming it *was* one of them, or both.'

A flash of alarm stabbed through Hilary. How long had Dan Truscott been listening to their conversation? Could he have heard what she had said about Veronica overhearing an incriminating exchange between Gavin and Theresa? They had told no one but the police about that.

Would it matter if he *had* heard her? Surely everyone else on the course must be as intent on discovering the perpetrator of the crime that made murder a sudden reality among them, as they had been on their fictional crimes?

'I share your views on the intrusion of television at a time like this. If it's any help, there's a light on in Lady Jane's

Chamber,' the colonel volunteered. 'I say we march upstairs and install ourselves as though we expect someone to take charge of things. We paid good money to come here. Someone ought to stand and deliver.'

'It's got to be Theresa,' Veronica said, as the two women stepped through the door he held open for them. 'Gavin's hardly going to be in a fit state.'

'A rather cold fish, that one,' Dan Truscott agreed. 'Or reptile, should I say, under the circumstances? Sitting there as though she really was a toad, and watching us with those beady eyes. Not exactly the competent but sympathetic midwife type I'd hoped for, to help my infant fiction to birth.'

'This evening would have been interesting,' Hilary remarked, as she led the way upstairs. 'I wonder what we thought about what sort of characters commit murder, or get themselves murdered, or dedicate their lives to solving murders?'

'It would have been something of a revelation,' came the colonel's voice from below. 'I'm guessing that most of us wrote about the investigator of the crime, seeing ourselves as the bringer of justice. But I'd like to know if there are any minds among us who felt drawn to write the murderer's part. I can hardly imagine that any one of us thought of ourselves as the victim.'

Hilary stopped on the landing. 'Are you suggesting that you're not a hundred per cent sure it was one of our leaders who killed Melissa? That it might actually be someone else in the group?'

'Oh, I leave that to the police,' laughed Dan Truscott. 'Sorry. It's not a joking matter, is it, as I pointed out to those two young men. I'll just say there's too much about this weekend we still don't know.'

Light was streaming under the door of Lady Jane's Chamber, which was not completely closed. Hilary drew a deep breath, wondering as she did so what she was afraid of. She pushed it open.

A circle of chairs had been arranged around the room. Facing them, on a lone chair behind the table, sat Theresa.

Hilary stopped, rooted to the floor. She had not come face to face with a suspected murderer before. She found herself staring at the dumpy woman behind the table, for once at a loss for words.

A murderer? Was this the reality? Not the colourful fabrication of a TV drama?

Theresa's brown dress fell shapelessly about her, hiding her legs beneath the table. Her clumsily cut brown hair reached almost to her shoulders. She seemed to have no neck. Her rather square face was expressionless. She stared out at the newcomers with no indication of welcome or surprise.

It was Dan Truscott who broke the charged stillness of the moment. He strode forward, hand outstretched.

'Dear lady! We're all so sorry about what happened. Mrs Standforth must have been a friend of yours. How gallant of you to step into the breach while poor Gavin is overwhelmed with grief.'

Theresa's face did not soften. She made no move to respond. The colonel's hand fell to his side.

Hilary felt a surge of respect for him. For someone who shared their belief that Theresa was one of the two people most probably implicated in Melissa's murder, he was putting on a convincing show of ready sympathy. With a start, she realized that this was what all of them must do. It would not do for Theresa to know what they were really thinking, still less that Veronica had apparent evidence of her involvement.

And yet . . . as Hilary's unwilling feet broke into movement again and she walked towards the circle of chairs, it struck her that there was something odd about Theresa sitting here like this. There was no police officer in sight. Theresa must surely have been taken in for more rigorous questioning after Veronica's statement. And yet the inspector had let her go. But then, the police needed to have hard proof, didn't they? A half-heard conversation, however suspicious it sounded, was not enough to make an arrest.

And so here was Theresa. Free, even if under suspicion.

Or was there another suspect? One Hilary and Veronica knew nothing about?

Hilary heard steps approaching on the stairs. Others were coming. Would-be crime hunters, now faced with this real-life murder. Hilary's instincts overrode her more careful scruples.

Theresa must surely have something to do with Melissa's death . . . and with the near-fatal overdose Dinah Halsgrove seemed to have taken. It had been she who had stayed behind with the novelist while the rest of them were out on the river. Hilary felt the horror of it crawl over her skin. She sat down rather more rapidly than she had intended, to wait for what would come next.

As the room filled up, Hilary looked more carefully to see how many had come. It was not difficult. Theresa had set out thirty chairs. Only four were empty.

What had drawn them all back here, when the writing course could obviously not proceed as planned? Curiosity? The eagerness to know what would happen next?

Still Theresa had not moved or spoken.

When it seemed as though there was no one else to come, it was Lin who rose to her feet. That upright back, the determined lift of her silvered head. Her voice was thin but clear.

'As one of the oldest here, I'd like to say on behalf of us all how very sorry I am for what has happened. It must be devastating for Gavin, and for you too. I'm sure we're all praying for you both.'

Hilary felt a stab of conscience. She had prayed for many things in the last twenty-four hours, but not for Theresa and Gavin. But didn't she have a duty to pray for the guilty too, if she wished to have her own sins forgiven? And what if they weren't guilty, the voice of honesty prompted her. Or only one of them?

The shock of finding Melissa in the Long Crippler pool came back to her with an almost physical force. She felt sick. She could feel again the sodden wool and cotton of Melissa's clothing, the chest compressing and lifting under her hands, the cold lips through which she had tried in vain to breathe life. The streaks of blood on that wet face.

In other circumstances, given her professional career as a senior teacher, it might have been she who was on her feet acting as spokesperson. Now, she wanted nothing more than to sit silently, to be overlooked.

'I'm sure it would be a relief to you if we all just packed up and went home,' Lin was concluding. 'But the police won't let us do that, or at least they have strongly discouraged us from leaving. Like it or not, we're here until tomorrow afternoon, when your course was due to end. But there's no question of you feeling responsibility for us. We are blessed with excellent food, beautiful surroundings. We can look after ourselves.'

Theresa spoke for the first time. A brief, dull: 'Thank you.'

'I don't know about that.' It was the bright Jo Walters who had got to her feet, some distance further around the circle. 'I'm not sure if I should say this, but I was in Melissa's Snake group. There has to be a special frisson about her being found in the Leechwells from which Gavin got our group names.'

So word of the details of Hilary and Veronica's macabre discovery had spread beyond their own dinner table. It was, she supposed, inevitable. And of course, there was that television crew outside.

'We're only human,' Jo continued. 'We can't help being curious about what the heck is going on here. It's not for nothing we came on a crime-writing course. We all have that sort of mind. I think we're struggling to piece together what happened and construct a credible scenario. Who did it to her, and why? And I for one would certainly want to exchange notes with the others. We can leave you out of this, Theresa, but I vote that those of us who care to follow this up should meet here after breakfast tomorrow to compare what ideas we've got.'

There was a cautious ripple of surprise around the room. Some, Hilary saw, were shaking their heads. Others were brightening up, as though attracted by the idea. Tania and Rob, who had speculated that Dinah Halsgrove's illness might be a hoax, were now consulting each other with animation.

Hilary stared at them. A memory was growing in her mind. There had been something macabrely familiar about the way she had discovered Melissa. Savagely wounded, lying in a pool of water.

The image snapped into place. That first morning's session, when they had shared their murder settings. Hadn't Rob envisaged just such a scene? A mangled corpse, lying in the pool below the wheel of Dartington Tweed Mill. His vivid description had unsettled Hilary even then.

As if he read her thoughts, a sandy-haired young man in denims,

sitting with the Slowworm group on the far side of the room,
spoke up. 'Is it true she was found in the Snake pool? That would
be gruesomely appropriate, wouldn't it? Given that she's the
leader of your Snake group.'

New alarm bells rang in Hilary's mind. It hadn't been the
Snake basin where Melissa lay face down, but the one the old
man had called the Long Crippler. Suddenly she was sure that
she hadn't mentioned that particular detail to anyone other than
the police. She looked enquiringly at Veronica, who shook her
head.

Jo Walters looked momentarily startled. 'I don't know. Hilary
and Veronica found her, but there must have been other people
in town who walked through Leechwell Lane this afternoon.
Some of them must have seen her. Someone told the press.'

'She was in the one they call the Long Crippler. Ceri told us,
dear,' said her husband helpfully, from the chair beside her. 'The
local lass, who knows about these holy wells. She must have
been talking to some of her pals from the town.'

Ceri had sat next to Hilary at dinner. She had said not a word
about already knowing of Melissa's death, still less the details.
Could she have been the informant? If so, how had she known?

Everyone's eyes went round the circle. Hilary looked in vain
for the black curls of the woman who had protested about Gavin's
appropriation of the names Toad, Snake and Slowworm for his
murder-solving groups.

'Looks like she's done a runner,' said Jake from the far left
of the circle. 'She's not sleeping here, is she? She'll have gone
home.'

'Lucky cow,' muttered someone on Hilary's right.

Ben warmed to Jo's idea. 'I don't want to sound callous, but
we have to do something to fill the time. Not just hang around
to see if the DI wants to talk to us again. I'm with Jo. If anyone
else wants to meet for a bit of brainstorming tomorrow, I'm in.'

'You never know,' added Jake. 'It might just be one of us who
comes up with the right solution.'

Hilary was galvanized into a speech she had not intended
to make. 'Don't be ridiculous. The police have a forensic patholo-
gist to determine the time and cause of death. They're taking
statements from witnesses who might have seen something

relevant. They can delve into Melissa's history and contacts.' She shot an anxious glance at Theresa, who sat impassive. 'After all, isn't it preposterously self-centred of us to assume her death has something to do with this weekend, when there's the whole of the rest of her life we know nothing about?'

'Well said,' trumpeted Colonel Truscott. 'It doesn't seem the decent thing to be treating the poor lady's death like a detective novel. We need to separate fact from fiction.'

'All the same,' Jo said in a lower voice. 'It *was* a coincidence. Who else knew about the names of our groups?'

Her eyes questioned Hilary.

But Hilary's attention was still on Theresa. She looked now not so much like a toad as a fat brown spider, lurking in the corner of her web, observing, waiting.

At last the woman spoke. 'Do what you like. This room is available. You might as well make use of it. As one of you has said, you've paid good money to come here.'

The words echoed in Hilary's mind. She had heard those words before this evening. With an ominous certainty, she knew who had said them. Dan Truscott had greeted them with this invitation to Lady Jane's Chamber as he opened the door at the foot of the stairs. The door at the top had been slightly ajar. She remembered the brighter light streaming through the opening on the landing.

Had Theresa heard everything else they said?

SIXTEEN

The meeting was breaking up.

'I could do with a stiff drink,' Hilary said with feeling.

'So we'll see you in the bar, then?'

She started. Harry Walters was closer than she had realized. Behind him stood his bright-eyed wife.

Sheep and goats, Hilary decided. *Half of us are numb with shock at this terrible thing that has happened. Not a little afraid, too, to think that there is probably a murderer among us. These are people who are experiencing a natural human instinct of grief. We none of us know Gavin well, but we can feel for him. I still find it hard to believe that he killed his own wife.*

Then there is this other faction, smaller perhaps, but evident. Youngsters like Ben and Jake, not yet, as far as she knew, committed to families. For them this represents the chance of a lifetime. Suddenly, here they are in the midst of a real-life murder case. On a practical level, the chance to study at firsthand how the police go about their work. But more than that, they relish the intellectual challenge of trying to beat the professionals. To identify the villain. To them, it's like trying to solve an Agatha Christie whodunnit, which does not require you to feel too deeply for the human beings involved. Reality sanitized as detective fiction.

But even crime fiction has moved on, Hilary reflected, as she met Jo Walters' keen gaze over her husband's shoulder. We are now into the realms of deeper and darker characterization. Not so much *who*dunnit as *why*dunnit. And it's almost a given that the investigator himself, or herself, is a deeply troubled person, bringing their own dark background into the investigation of the crime. Jo, she remembered, had expressed a desire to write something similar to Scandinavian noir.

And where did Tania and Rob fit into this? Certainly, Rob had revelled in the blackness of his imagination.

And what about me? Am I that conflicted investigator? Hilary smiled wryly at the thought of casting herself as the detective. She knew she should leave this to the CID, but she could already see Veronica's knowing smile. Veronica understood her friend too well. Whatever she said to the younger ones, Hilary Masters was unlikely to keep her keen intellect out of her own hunt for the culprit.

She shook herself back to the present, with the course members starting to head for the door. Let them hold their brainstorming tomorrow morning if they wanted to. Despite her natural curiosity, she wouldn't be part of it. She knew how much some of them were longing to question her and Veronica more closely about their shocking find at the Leechwells. For them, this was an unrepeatable opportunity to hear the details of the macabre discovery, what a murdered corpse looked like.

She really needed that whisky.

'I'll just pop up to my room first. We'll see you in the bar.' She smiled to Harry.

Harry, at least, seemed a genuinely straightforward guy. He wasn't actually here for the crime writing, just accompanying Jo. What had he done with himself yesterday morning, while the rest of them were selecting their crime scenes and writing them up, imbued with suitable atmosphere? Somehow, she couldn't imagine him with a pen in his hand and a notepad, letting his imagination loose in or around Morland Abbey. To be honest, she doubted he *had* much imagination. But she did not despise him for that. A simple, uncomplicated, good-hearted man.

She rather wished now that David had chosen to come along in such a supportive role, even though she had assured him that she and Veronica would be fine on their own.

Veronica was waiting for her.

They made their way along the East Cloister corridor.

As they reached the staircase to the upper floor, Hilary said, 'It was here I bumped into Melissa. But that's all water under the bridge now. I'd got it into my head after that that something was afoot. That she was on her way to do something nefarious, perhaps in Dinah Halsgrove's room. I felt sure she had not expected to see me, or anyone else. But I must have got totally the wrong end of the stick. Far from being the person who very nearly caused Halsgrove's death, she was the next victim herself. And in a far more final way.'

'It's dreadful to think of, isn't it?' Veronica agreed. 'That someone should hate her so much they wanted to do that to her.'

'There was something so theatrical about it. There must have been many ways, and many places, in which whoever wanted to could have bumped her off. But why so spectacularly in the Leechwells? Whoever it was took a huge risk. It's a public street – well, a back lane. Still, anyone could have come along and seen them. Or even noticed them going to and from the well around that time.'

'I don't know. We didn't meet a soul between the car park and the well. You said yourself how eerily quiet it was.'

'True. And I only saw three people this morning while I sat there.'

'The old man with the walking stick?' suggested Veronica as

they reached their own landing on the top floor. 'Don't you think it's a bit of a coincidence that he turned up twice?'

Hilary gave a short laugh, without much humour. 'He hardly looked capable of killing an able-bodied woman like Melissa. All the same, he was a bit of a sinister character, didn't you think? In spite of the folksy Devonshire accent. That stick of his · tap-tapping his way along what some people say is the leper path from the old hospital.'

'Like Blind Pugh in *Treasure Island*. I started to read that aloud to Robert when he was small, and he was so frightened by Stevenson's description of Pugh that he wouldn't let me go any further.'

'There's a rather unpleasant literary past of connecting physical disability to a corrupt mind. But our man with the stick isn't blind. He could have seen something vital.'

'I'm sure the police will have questioned him.'

They parted outside Veronica's door.

'I'll be with you in five minutes,' Hilary called as she turned aside towards her own room.

She pushed the door open and put out her hand to the light switch. The movement froze mid-air. She knew instinctively there was someone in the room.

She had drawn the curtains before dinner. But a column of soft light reached through a gap in them from the quadrangle. She sensed a shadow sitting on the wide bed between her and the window.

She gave a gasp that was more like a scream, and then was furious with herself for such an obvious display of fear.

'It's all right,' came a familiar voice from the bed. 'It's only me.'

'*David!*'

Her senses whirled. It was several moments before her scattered wits made sense of the situation. She snapped the lights on and glared at him, denying to herself how overwhelmingly glad she was to see him, once the shock of finding someone waiting in her room had begun to fade.

David stood up, his receding hair still fairish, even in his sixties, his glasses glinting before his amused eyes.

'I'm sorry. I didn't mean to frighten you. I should have put the light on to warn you. But I was looking out at the cloisters,

just trying to put myself in the picture. I see you've attracted
the press.'

'I told you not to come.'

But she was already near enough for him to put his arms out
and embrace her.

'I know you did. You didn't want to upset Veronica by rubbing
it in that you had me at times like this and she doesn't have
Andrew. But to be honest, I'm as much concerned about her
as I am about you. Like it or not, the two of you have got
yourselves involved with this rather more deeply than I'm
comfortable with. Veronica in particular, by the sound of it. If
Melissa's dead, and Gavin and Theresa find out she heard them
plotting something . . .'

'That's the protective alpha male talking.' She stepped back
from the warm circle of his arms and made herself smile. 'You
really think your herd of hinds is in danger?'

'I'd rather be here than sitting at home worrying about you. I
knocked up the admin staff in the West Cloister. Nice woman
by the name of Fiona. She told me there was a double bed in
your room. No problem.'

'Veronica and I did wonder whether to share a twin, but we
decided to treat ourselves to rooms of our own. I struck gold.
They must have run out of singles. You must admit it's rather
splendid.'

'Never mind the medieval woodwork. What's happened here
since I last talked to you?'

'Only that I've discovered some rather peculiar things about
the people on this course. Ghouls, some of them. They really do
still want to treat it as though it were just crime fiction, and
they're determined to crack the mystery.'

'A flight from reality,' David suggested. 'Because the truth is
too terrible to bear?'

She saw the understanding in his weathered face.

'I'm not sure that's how I'd put it. There are two young men
in our Toad group. Ben and Jake. I really do think it's just a
game to them. They've set up a brainstorming group for tomorrow.
And there's another young couple. This morning, Rob came up
with a murder scenario uncannily like the real one. Is it too far-
fetched to suppose he could have turned that into reality?' She

shook her head. 'Then there's Theresa. Just sitting there, as though she really was a toad, and listening to all of us arguing about it. She hardly said a word, except to let us know that she'd heard more of what we were saying to each other than we intended.'

'And that includes you and Veronica?' David's voice became more urgent. There was a sudden concern in his eyes.

'We were talking to a rather tweedy retired colonel as we came up the stairs. I wish I could remember everything we said.'

'I'm getting more glad that I came by the minute.'

'Hilary?' Veronica's voice came from the corridor, sharp with questioning. 'Is everything all right?'

Hilary flung the door open. 'It's more than all right. Look who's here.'

SEVENTEEN

Away from the East Cloister and the brooding presence of Theresa, the Chapter House bar had a more relaxed feel. Bottles twinkled on the shelves set within the sixteenth-century fireplace. Diners still lingered at one end of the room, but most of the tables and chairs were now given over to drinkers. The space was crowded, not only with members of Gavin's course, but with other guests. Not all of the crime writers who had been in Lady Jane's Chamber were here, but those who had stayed on were trying to put on some show of normality. True, there was something nervous in the laughter, the conversation was more subdued, heads turned quickly to each new arrival. Yet there was an atmosphere of relief Hilary was happy to sink into.

She introduced David to the others at the bar with a mixture of pride and embarrassment. No other woman had her partner rushing over here to offer her support. She did not usually trade on feminine weakness.

David himself smoothed the matter over. 'We live less than an hour's drive from here. When I heard the news, I thought I'd drop over and check what's going on.'

'Can't keep away from the scandal?' Jake laughed slyly.

'Your wife's been giving us a good going over for playing detectives, instead of just lowering the flag to half-mast and letting the Bill get on with it. The word *ghouls* wasn't exactly mentioned, but . . .'

Hilary flushed. 'I'm sorry if I sounded like a school marm. But you have to remember I still hadn't got over the shock of finding Melissa's body. The rest of you only know it as reported fact.' Gratefully she accepted the whisky David offered her.

'But you're not coming clean, are you?' Ben insisted. 'There's loads more you could tell us about the body, but you've clammed up.'

'We just don't want to think about it,' Veronica said. 'We came down to the bar to relax. And the police asked us not to reveal the details.'

Jake leaned forward. 'They do that, don't they? They hope the culprit's going to give himself away by revealing a greater knowledge of the crime scene than he's supposed to have.'

'Something like that.'

'But if you were the ones who found the body, you'd have an excuse, wouldn't you?'

'I'll pretend you didn't say that.'

Ben swilled the last of his beer round his glass thoughtfully. 'I don't know why you stay, then. Good old DI Foulks must have milked you dry about what you saw – or didn't see. I don't see that you've got anything left to keep you here. And here's Hilary's old man having kittens because of what you two stumbled on.'

It's what might still happen to us that's troubling him, Hilary thought, but she kept quiet. She looked around the tables and bar stools where small groups were trying to find solace in alcohol and conversation. Could she be wrong about Theresa and Gavin? Was it thinkable that Melissa's murderer might instead be one of them?

But no conceivable motive presented itself.

'You heard the DI,' she rallied. 'He wants us all to stay until tomorrow afternoon when the course was due to end. Dinah Halsgrove's induced coma was serious enough, but Melissa's death has put things on a wholly new level.'

'Message there,' laughed Ben. 'Crime fiction is bad for your health.'

Hilary shot him a sharp look. Still, she took comfort from the thought that he was right about the usefulness of their remaining at Morland Abbey. After they had found the body, she and Veronica had been questioned rigorously by DI Foulks and DS Blunt. They had nothing left to tell. All they had to do was to sit it out for less than twenty-four hours. Nothing worse could happen, could it? David's presence at her side, in that rather disreputable tweed jacket, was reassurance. She was more glad than she would tell him that he had ignored her orders and come flying down the A38 to join her – and Veronica.

She looked across the table at her friend. It was hard to tell from Veronica's still, high-boned face what she was thinking. Did she too welcome the solidity of David making them a three-some? Or was it increasing the pain that it should have been Andrew at her side?

There was another sudden turning of heads. A newcomer was shadowing the doorway. Hilary had to swivel round to see clearly who it was.

A tall, young policeman she did not recognize stood looking rather awkward, his uniform cap under his arm.

'Mrs Masters?' He let his gaze travel slowly over the well-populated bar.

Now the heads were turning back to Hilary. It took a second for his meaning to sink in. It was her name he was calling. She had been so sure that her ordeal was over. She would not have to go over that horrifying scene again. The stark, unbeliev-able reality of turning Melissa over to find that head-wound smearing blood across her wet face. Her own desperate attempts to pump life into that cold sodden corpse. Chillingly, there came back to her the tapping of the old man's stick echoing off the blank stone walls.

'That's me.'

'DI Foulks would like a word with you.'

She slid off her stool, finding the floor not quite as steady as she would have liked. Every eye was on her. David's hand clasped warmly over hers, then let her go.

'Shall I come with you?' he whispered.

She shook her head.

Almost as though she were sleepwalking, she crossed the floor to the policeman standing just inside the restaurant door. It must be the effect of the whisky, slowing things down, giving the whole scene an air of unreality.

It couldn't be anything important, could it? Just a detail DI Foulks had forgotten to ask her.

Distant, but clear, she heard Jake's voice behind her. 'Well, that's one I wasn't expecting. Do you think they're going to arrest her?'

She could not hear David's reply.

DI Foulks and DS Blunt were encamped once again in the small meeting room in the East Cloister where they had interviewed Hilary about Dinah Halsgrove's collapse. That felt like a lifetime ago. It seemed impossible that it was only this lunchtime. Then, she remembered with a stab of remorse, how she had been all too keen to volunteer her story about bumping into Melissa in this very corridor, the sharp expulsion of breath that had seemed so sinister at the time. Now it was Melissa who was dead. The hiss, which had seemed so snakelike, had been silenced in the Long Crippler pool. CID, and Hilary herself, must look somewhere else for the murderous mind which could intend death to both women. And it seemed more than ever likely that someone *had* meant to kill Dinah Halsgrove.

'Good evening, Mrs Masters.'

Her mind was snatched from the interior guilt of her past suspicion to the two men in front of her. Even this morning, DI Foulks' lean face had had a somewhat weary air. Now he looked positively haggard. That forward-stooped head had deep vertical lines either side of his down-curved mouth. DS Blunt also looked tired.

'You two look as though you need a good night's sleep,' she told them in the voice she would have used for an over-zealous pupil at exam time.

'We have a murder investigation on our hands.'

'I'm not likely to forget that.'

'I'm sorry. It must have been a distressing experience. You needn't worry. We're not going to take you over that again. Your evidence this afternoon was admirably clear and helpful. That's not something I could say about everyone who finds a corpse. No, there's something else. Did you – either before or after you found Mrs Standforth – see this person?'

Detective Sergeant Blunt pushed across the table an artist's impression of what seemed to be a young man, or perhaps a boy, in a hooded tracksuit, navy-blue with a white stripe down the side. The hood was pulled forward, shadowing his face. She was clearly not intended to identify his features from the sketch. Only the tracksuit. Even the trainers below it were depicted in a blurred way which showed that the detectives did not have precise information.

Hilary studied the picture. The slim body, the rather hunched shoulders, the face retreating under its hood. A typical image of countless teenage boys. She had taught many pupils like that. She came back to the tracksuit. The distinctive white line down the navy sleeves and legs.

She raised her eyes to DI Foulks again. What she saw behind his rimless glasses was a brightening of hope. Clearly he regarded her as a reliable witness. She felt flattered. But she knew she must disappoint him.

'I'm sorry. Normally, I couldn't swear I'd remember a lad in a tracksuit with the hood up. It's a pretty common sight. But, under the circumstances, I think it's likely that I would. The lanes around the Leechwells were rather eerily empty. The only people I remember seeing were the woman with the shopping bag I told you about – the one who found us trying to revive Melissa – and the old man with the walking stick.'

'Yes, we interviewed him.'

'You think this boy might be the culprit? But why? If we're thinking in stereotypes, he might have mugged her for her handbag, but it seems a bit extreme to drown her in the well for it. Did you find her handbag?'

She had a dim memory of Veronica retrieving a dripping bag of brown cloth. The sort that could have contained a wallet.

'Let's just say he is someone we are keen to speak to.'

'So someone must have seen him? When? Going to or coming from the well?'

The detectives sat silent. Of course they would not share that knowledge with her. Had they found the woman with the shopping bag, who had been only too keen to hurry on away from the body? They hadn't mentioned her. Did that mean it was the old man with the rich Devon accent, who had told her the names of the three wells: the Toad, the Snake and the Long Crippler? Twice today she had encountered him at the well, once this morning as she was innocently scribbling away at the beginnings of her crime novel, and then in the shocked aftermath of their grisly find. Yes, she thought. If he stalks those almost deserted narrow lanes, he probably notices every coming and going along them.

It was a creepy feeling that she too was now stored away inside that inscrutable head.

DS Blunt slid the paper round to look at it again.

'Of course, we're not a hundred per cent sure it *was* a boy. Our informant thought so. The way the shoulders are hunched, the hood pulled forward. You know how teenage lads are. But without a good look at the face, we can't be certain it wasn't a girl.'

'Or even a slim woman,' DI Foulks finished.

Hilary snatched the artist's impression back again and studied it more closely. But it did not make any difference. She had not seen anyone in that tracksuit.

'Sorry,' she said. 'I wish I could help.'

An even wearier look came over DI Foulks' face. She realized how much hope he must have been pinning on her powers of observation.

'Veronica might remember something.'

'We intend to ask her. Would you be so kind as to request her to join us?'

Hilary walked back out of the cloisters towards the bar. There were spatters of rain in the wind. Gusts brought leaves whirling down from the sequoia tree on the lawn.

What if Melissa's death lay outside the circle they had been focussing on? Not Gavin or Theresa? Not even any of the motley crew of would-be writers who had gathered at Morland Abbey? She certainly couldn't imagine the stockily built Theresa disguised as that slim figure in the tracksuit. Was it a relief to rule her out, or a disappointment? Gavin was probably taller than the witness who had supplied that description suggested.

Could the hunched shoulders have hidden that? Or was this, more likely, someone else entirely? She was frustrated by the knowledge that, if it was, she had no hope of guessing who it might be, or why he should want to kill Melissa Standforth. She simply did not know enough about Melissa's background. Certainly, the figure with the blurred features in the artist's sketch seemed to be the only known person who had the opportunity in the time before Hilary and Veronica found her.

Of course, it had always been obvious, if you thought about it, that Melissa had had a life of which the course members at Morland knew nothing. Only the police could gather the information they needed to solve this. Would Gavin help them?

She was almost at the door of the bar before it struck her that she was trying to play detective in just the same way she had berated those like Ben and Jake and Jo for treating this as though it was no more than a crime novel they were determined to solve before they reached the final chapter.

EIGHTEEN

I t was a shock to walk back into the bar and see the expressions on the faces that turned swiftly to meet her. She read surprise, curiosity, an altered perception of Hilary Masters.

So they haven't arrested her, after all?

Could they really have believed that jokey suggestion of Jake's? It *had* been a joke, hadn't it?

Indignation burned inside her. Couldn't it just as well have been one of them in the tracksuit? The athletic Rob or Tania? Either of those two slim young men, Ben or Jake?

She walked towards David and Veronica, still seated at the bar. Customers unconnected with the crime course continued to chatter as before. But those who knew what was at stake watched her enter in an expectant silence. They were waiting to hear why CID had wanted to interview her again. She decided she would not give them that satisfaction. Let the detectives show them that sketch in their own good time.

Veronica and David had swivelled round on their stools. What had been going through their minds while they waited? Their faces were full of concern.

She stopped in front of Veronica. 'He'll see you next.' Then, in a softer voice, 'Nothing serious. They've found a witness with some new information. They need to check it out with us.'

She lifted her eyes to the rest of the group. Everyone there was still looking at her. Had they heard what she said to Veronica? Almost certainly Ben and Jake, just beyond Veronica, had. Perhaps Jo and Harry at a nearby table, too.

She was not going to say anything more. Not even to Veronica. Let DI Foulks and DS Blunt reveal this new evidence to whom they chose, in their own way. She had done her bit, though it hadn't been much help. Still, she reflected, even negative evidence could be significant. The lad in the tracksuit hadn't been in the lower lane by which Hilary and Veronica approached the well, or not within that narrow time frame. That *was* information. If he was the killer, he must have got away by one of the upper branches of the lane. Or hidden himself in the children's play-ground? She remembered the two of them peering through the gate. Had it really been empty?

How long had Melissa been dead when they found her?

She slipped into her place on the other side of David from Veronica. The stool had been left empty. She waited for David's hand to close over hers on the counter. A natural gesture of reas-surance. It did not come.

Veronica was moving away, a little unwillingly, it seemed. As she headed for the door, Hilary felt David move from beside her. He too stepped down from the bar.

'I'll see you across the quadrangle,' he said.

There was a stir of murmuring across the room. Heads watched the two of them retreat into the night.

Hilary suddenly felt very alone.

It was Jo nearby who said what she did not need to hear.

'Your friend's still a very pretty woman, isn't she?'

Hilary blazed inside. She wanted to cry out, '*And David's the kindest man I know. Every year since he retired as a doctor, he's spent time volunteering in a hospital in Gaza, or at a clinic in the Yemen, wherever they need his skilled help. He came here to*

Morland Abbey because he was as much concerned for Veronica's safety as a vital witness as he was for mine. What's so remarkable about him offering to escort her across the deserted courtyard after dark?'

But she dared not tell anyone else about the overheard conversation that had put Veronica in so much more danger than her.

Eyes were beginning to turn back to Hilary now, speculative or sympathetic. She was painfully aware that Veronica *was* a great deal prettier than she was, with her slender upright figure, her still-fair hair, softly waved around a heart-shaped face. Hilary, honesty told her, was not so very different in build and looks from Theresa. *Though at least*, she thought, *I do take a bit more trouble over my hair.*

She had to hold on to the memory of David's arms around her in the bedroom when she walked in and found him. And, to be fair, he had offered to escort her across the courtyard to her interview. She wished now she had accepted.

Ben leaned across, as eager as ever. Would he never get over treating this as entertainment? 'Go on then. Tell us. What's this new info that's got Foulks and Blunt back here working overtime? They've already interviewed all of us twice. Once for Dinah Halsgrove, and then to find out if we were anywhere near those Leechwells when Melissa was done in.'

Again, Hilary flinched from the lack of humanity in his avid curiosity.

Is that how a killer might talk, feigning not to know?

'I'm afraid that's not for me to say.' She was aware how curt she must sound. 'I'm sure the inspector will call back anyone else he thinks may be able to help him.'

It was her turn to cast a curious eye around the assembled writers. How many of them had gone into Totnes during their free time after tea? And would they have told the truth when the detectives questioned them about their movements?

The colonel had chosen the castle for his crime setting this morning. Had he said anything about going back to see more of the town this afternoon? Harry Walters, too, had said something about going to the castle, but she could not remember when. Probably while Jo was busy writing this morning. Could he have taken her back into town, later this afternoon, to show her, as Hilary had Veronica? And where had Ben and Jake been?

One name came back to her. A rounded rosy face. Ceri lived in Totnes. She had been at Morland Abbey for that tense session with Gavin this afternoon, ostensibly concentrating on their fictional characters, but interrupted at intervals as one by one they were called out to give evidence about Dinah's near fatality. Had she left for Totnes after tea? If anyone knew those narrow lanes leading to the well, which most of the group had missed, it had to be Ceri. Ceri, for whom the Leechwells apparently had a particular significance.

Yet she had baulked at the idea of using them as the setting for a murder, even a fictional one.

Hilary looked around her.

Two figures caught her eye on the far side of the room. Tania and Rob, seated at a table with others whom Hilary could not name. Tonight, Tania was wearing a chunky sweater with a deep polo neck. But this morning . . .

It came back to her with startling clarity. The athletic-looking Tania had come to breakfast wearing a black tracksuit with white flashes on the sleeves and legs.

Don't be ridiculous, she told herself. The tracksuit in the sketch had been navy, not black. The white stripes on the arms and legs had been continuous, not these partial bands.

But how accurate was any eyewitness?

She was seized by the thought that she should hurry back to the inspector and tell him. She was already slipping down from her stool.

Jo rose from the adjacent table.

'It's getting pretty crowded in here. Why don't we decamp to find some easy chairs? The book room over in the East Cloister is really quite a comfy lounge.'

The moment passed. She would tell DI Foulks, but later.

It was a short walk across to the East Cloister from the bar. A few people were already seated in the book room, but there were spare chairs and sofas.

The display of Gavin's books still dominated one wall, set out on tables and a perspex stand. Hilary paused beside it. By far the greater number of copies were of his one bestseller, *The Long Cripple.* The cover artist had made that blunt head seem sinister, even at the start of this weekend. Now it had a far more ominous meaning.

She picked a copy from the rack and examined the cover. She understood that puzzling iconography now. That blind, questing, reptilian head. The slowworm, or blindworm.

That was the long middle basin, where Hilary and Veronica had found Melissa, face down.

Gavin Standforth had obviously known about the wells.

She put it back rather hurriedly, as though her fingers did not want to prolong contact with it. There were too many bad memories.

'Have you read it?' she asked Jo, who was following behind her. 'I'm told it's rather good.'

'That!' The younger woman almost spat the word. Then she seemed to recover her smile. 'It makes you wonder, doesn't it, how he can do it just once, and never before or since?'

'Luck, I suppose. He just hit on a good idea.'

'Oh, yes, he certainly did.'

They settled themselves in the easy chairs, with Harry joining them. Relaxing into the cushions, Hilary realized just how weary she was. When David came back with Veronica she would suggest calling it a day.

The minutes ticked by.

David and Veronica, she realized would expect to find her still in the bar. She hadn't left a message. Would someone tell them where she had gone?

The door of the lounge opened. David and Veronica were laughing together as they came through. Hilary felt a momentary satisfaction that they had found her. Then the sight of them stabbed her with a pain she recognized a second later as jealousy. The realization astonished her. Had Jo's barbed comment really got beneath her skin?

But what could these two possibly have to laugh about? It was the end of a horrific day. She and Veronica had found a murdered body. Hilary felt exhausted, emotionally shattered. She did not think she would be able to shut out, even in sleep, the image of Melissa's dead face.

And yet those two were laughing. Not yet searching the room for her, but finishing something that had passed between them as they crossed the cloisters.

It was only an instant. They were suitably sober now as their eyes found her and they made their way across the room to join her. Whatever had happened out there in the quadrangle, it was something she was not going to be party to.

The room had filled up somewhat. Some course members had gone, rather dispiritedly, back to their rooms. Others sat talking quietly. Only those who had agreed to meet in the morning to brainstorm theories about Melissa's death still had a purpose. The rest, like Hilary, were just waiting out the DI's instructions until tomorrow afternoon. Making a pretence that they could still be of help.

Heads turned, of course, at Veronica and David's return, as they had to Hilary's in the bar. But something of the avid curiosity had gone. Was it because no one could conceive of sweet, elegant Veronica being arrested for murder? A different scenario had crossed the minds of at least some of them when Hilary was summoned.

Veronica sank into the easy chair beside her.

'A gin and tonic, please,' she said in answer to a question of David's which Hilary had not heard.

'What about you?' He turned to her.

'Tomato juice, please.'

'Not another whisky?'

'No, thank you.'

She did not know why she was being curt with him. He had done nothing to deserve it. Wasn't it a gift enough that he was here with her? That they would sleep together tonight?

While David went off to the bar, Veronica gave Hilary a rather tired smile. But the laughter had gone from her violet-blue eyes. 'That was a scary experience. Not at all what I expected. Did they ask if they could search your room?'

'No. Why? Veronica! They couldn't imagine it was *you* in the tracksuit?'

'I suppose they have to consider all possibilities. Still, it gave me a fright. Just for a moment, I wondered whether someone could have planted it in my room.'

'Surely not!'

Her unwilling mind was now including the slim Veronica in the list of course members who might have disguised themselves as a teenager in a hooded tracksuit. For all its improbability, might that have been how Inspector Foulks' mind worked?

'When it came to remembering someone in a tracksuit, I'm afraid I wasn't much help to them. I don't suppose you were, either?'

'No.'

'Though memory can play strange tricks on you. If you think about it long enough, you begin to imagine you *did* see what they asked you about. But it's only because they've implanted that image in your mind.'

'What image?' She was suddenly aware that Jake and Ben had crossed the room and settled themselves on the sofa opposite.

Jake was leaning forward in that characteristically eager way. While Veronica was away, the young men's conversation had drifted to singers and bands which meant nothing to Hilary. She had tuned them out, while her own thoughts raced uncontrollably over the events of that afternoon and who else might have been in Totnes when Melissa was killed. About whether the witness could have been mistaken about that tracksuit.

Now she was alert again, and on the defensive. She turned the questioning back on them.

'Where were you two this afternoon after tea?'

Ben and Jake looked at each other, speculation evident in their expressions. Hilary studied them. Jake still had something of the flamboyant adolescent about him, though he must be in his twenties at least. Ben, more square-shouldered, swarthier, dark hair shadowing his chin. At a pinch, either of them could have passed as that teenager in the hoodie whom the artist had sketched. The thinner Jake, certainly, if he hunched his shoulders to lower his height. Ben only possibly.

But how reliable had the description been?

If the inspector could suspect Veronica enough to search her room . . .

'We took a walk down to the Dart. There's a footpath alongside the river.' It was Ben who answered.

'A river path? How do you get to it?' Jo too had joined them. 'Might be an idea for my morning run.'

'Head down the drive. You'll see the footpath sign.'

'Did you go upstream or downstream?' Hilary persisted.

'Down. Look what is this? The DI's been all over this. He knows where all of us were.'

'Assuming everybody's telling him the truth,' Jake laughed.

Downstream, towards Totnes. Veronica and Hilary had walked into town themselves, though by the road.

'Then I think the DI might want another word with you. I wouldn't go to bed just yet.'

'Come on, Hilary! You can't just leave it at that,' Jake exploded. 'You have to come clean. Why is he questioning some of us again?'

Hairs prickled on Hilary's neck. Was that all the police were doing? Questioning them? Or was it possible that there were officers searching other bedrooms, looking for a navy tracksuit with white stripes on the sleeves and legs? A thought struck her. What might be hidden in the boots of cars parked across the road from the entrance arch? But surely, if that seeming youth was the killer, he'd have got rid of any clothing which might bear the faintest trace of Melissa's DNA?

She did not realize she had lapsed into silence until David said, 'I think we ought to get you to bed.'

He was standing over her, a glass of tomato juice in his hand. He cast a wide smile around the room.

'Sorry, folks! I didn't mean that the way it sounded. But Hilary looks all in.'

He sank on to the sofa beside her. Behind him, Veronica had risen to examine the book display while she sipped her gin and tonic. She turned to them, holding Gavin's most famous work in her hand, just as Hilary had.

'The Long Crippler again. It's eerie, isn't it? You said that was the name of the spring where we found Melissa. But if it was someone from the Morland Abbey course who killed her, and the Leechwells were meant to be significant, which they obviously are, why didn't they leave her in the Snake pool? She was the leader of the Snake group. The Slowworms are Gavin's lot.'

'Did someone want to throw suspicion on Gavin?' Ben suggested.

'Or was it *actually* Gavin? Obsessed with his own cleverness and his wretched book.' The question came from Jo. 'Flaunting it, and defying us to pin it on him.' Her eyes were sparkling at the idea.

'That sort of speculation will have to wait until the morning,' David said. 'Bed for us, folks.'

Obediently, Hilary rose with him. She really did want to be in bed.

It was natural that Veronica should join them on David's other side.

NINETEEN

They said goodnight to Veronica outside her bedroom. Veronica opened her door hesitantly and looked inside.

'It seems untouched. If they *have* searched it, they've put everything back in its place. All the same . . . it feels like a violation. They say that's how you feel when you've been burgled. A stranger going through your things.'

'But we know they couldn't have found anything.'

'Are you going to be all right?' There was concern in David's voice.

'Yes, thank you. It's an odd feeling, though. You know you're innocent, but the police can make you feel as though you're not.'

Hilary turned away. She felt an odd embarrassment about sharing her own room with David now. True, it had a generously large double bed. She had been unexpectedly glad to see him. She should welcome the comfort of his warmth beside her. Was it just the knowledge that Veronica was sleeping alone which made her feel awkward? Or that snide comment of Jo's about Veronica being so much prettier, and the shared private laughter of her friend and her husband as they entered the lounge?

Rather grumpily, she began to get undressed.

David had brought only a light overnight bag. He took out his pyjamas, his toilet things.

'Bathroom's across the corridor, she told him. 'They don't do en-suites up here.'

He had hardly reached the door on his way out when there was a quick knocking.

'Can I come in?' Veronica's voice.

David pulled the door open. 'We're more or less respectable.' He gave her a ready smile. 'What's up?'

Hilary paused in the act of unbuttoning her shirt. There was no reason why Veronica shouldn't see her in her underwear. They had shared a room many times. But it irked her that David had not even looked over his shoulder for her consent.

While Hilary felt unspeakably weary, there was an excitement about Veronica's face, despite the late hour and all that had happened in a dramatic day. Something Hilary had caught in Ben and Jake, eager to find their solution to the murder.

'There's a light outside. Just a pencil torch, by the look of it. But someone's going along the path towards the chapel.'

Veronica's room was on the other side of the corridor from Hilary's. While her own overlooked the cloisters, Veronica had a view of the path that ran alongside the Great Barn to the gardens beyond. A little way to the left, Hilary remembered, was the Lady Chapel, which was all that remained of the magnificent abbey church.

'You think it's significant?' David asked. 'It's certainly an odd time of night for someone to be going for a walk.'

'Security,' Hilary said dismissively. 'Fiona said there was someone on duty twenty-four/seven. They probably check the buildings at night. Or couldn't it be the police? I don't imagine for a minute that they've all gone home.' She heard the scepticism in her voice that this could be a further twist in the mystery. All she wanted was to get to bed.

'One person or more?' David asked. He was already on his feet, moving across the corridor towards Veronica's room.

'Impossible to tell.' Her voice was retreating. 'I couldn't actually see anyone. Just this moving light.'

Hilary sighed and buttoned up her blouse again. She followed them outside to Veronica's door. It was a much smaller room than Hilary's. They all crowded to the window.

Hilary was the last of the three, and the shortest. By the time she was able to glimpse through the curtains between Veronica and David's shoulders, the Great Barn opposite was in darkness. To her right, a bright overhead lamp showed where the path alongside it met the cobbled yard in front of the Chapter House. It was some moments before her eyes adjusted and she picked out the much smaller pinprick of light some way to her left.

'It certainly looks as if they're going to the chapel, unless they're going past it to the gardens.' She meant to keep her voice low, but it sounded louder than she intended in the darkened room. It occurred to her that Veronica must have put the light out before she opened the curtains.

The other two turned swiftly. David held his finger to his lips. Hilary felt idiotically rebuked. The window was closed on a rainy autumn night. It was surely impossible for anyone to have heard her.

'Are they going to meet someone in the chapel?' Veronica whispered.

'Only one way to find out,' David whispered back. 'Stay here.'

He made for the door, squeezing past Hilary.

A moment later, Hilary was out in the corridor after him. 'You don't know the layout,' she hissed. 'Or the quickest way out. And I'm more likely to recognize who it is than you are.'

David was still fully clothed. Hilary had shed her cardigan when she started to undress. She grabbed a rain jacket from the inside of the door of her room as she passed.

'This way.'

Veronica still stood at her bedroom door. 'I'd better stay and watch what happens,' she suggested, 'in case someone comes or leaves before you get there.'

'Good thinking.'

Adrenalin was pumping through Hilary. She felt more awake, now that she was doing something. There was a little triumph that she had managed to be the one to accompany David, not Veronica.

They crept down the first flight of stairs as fast as caution would allow. It brought them to the glass door where Hilary had bumped into Melissa that first evening. Hilary led the way to the fire exit on that landing on the side away from the courtyard. It was hard to see outside in the dim light from the corridor, but she knew that steps ran down to the path beside the barn. It would lead them directly to the chapel.

It was not totally dark outside. Clouds were torn across the night sky, letting through occasional flashes of moonlight or a tranche of stars. There was a spattering of rain.

The path beside the rough stone wall of the barn was now a dark gulf. There was more light to their right from the distant lamp on the cobbled square. They turned away from it. There was no sign of the torch ahead now. It was impossible to pick out the chapel at the end with any certainty against the background of dark trees. Was the night prowler, whoever it was, inside? Hilary had only an indistinct memory of the interior. Was it an arranged meeting place? Might whoever he or she had hoped to meet already be there? She strained for voices.

David strode ahead. Suddenly the hard surface under Hilary's feet gave way to grass. They were out in the confusion of the monks' graveyard. They had lost the path. She stumbled after David.

Hilary felt, as much as saw, the dark bulk of stone looming over them.

David whispered. 'There's a door here, but it's locked. Padlocked, I think.'

'The main door's round the other side.'

She had been here on previous visits to the abbey, but she could not remember it distinctly. An isolated memory did come back to her from earlier this weekend. Ceri from Totnes had chosen for her fictional crime scene, not somewhere in the town she knew so well, but this very chapel.

Could it be she who had arranged to meet someone here? And if so whom?

A shudder ran down Hilary that was not all to do with the rainy autumn night.

In a sudden moment of panic, she realized that she had lost David. She hurried round the corner of the Lady Chapel and found herself in the lighter space of the ruined church. A sudden shaft of moonlight showed her David crouched before a second, larger door down a short flight of steps. It was closed. Hilary hurried to catch up with him while the brief light lasted. Was he listening to something, or someone, or hearing only silence?

If that other person was not already inside . . . In alarm, she looked over her shoulder. Could someone else be following them, bound for this same rendezvous?

As she turned, her foot slipped off the top step. Something cracked under her heel. Glass, by the sound of it. In the silent darkness it had the effect of a gunshot. She was aware of David suddenly straightening up.

The door to the chapel flew open. There was a faint light inside, but it only served to throw the figure who stood on the threshold as a black silhouette.

'Who's there?' The demand rapped out.

Past David's shoulder, Hilary gasped, 'Gavin!'

Thoughts rushed through her tired brain, confusing her. Why should she be startled to find it was Gavin here? He had been the focus of her suspicions ever since Veronica had heard that conversation with Theresa. She had tried to push the thought away after Melissa's murder, seeing him instead as the bereaved husband, but it came crowding back. Yet why would Gavin and Theresa need to meet here in the chapel, when they probably had rooms on the same corridor in the East Cloister? That faint light inside was partially blocked by the half-open door. The moonlight had vanished behind hurrying clouds. The lamp on the Chapter House courtyard was now far away. Who else might be hidden inside there?

But Gavin turned on his torch again and swung the slender beam from Hilary to David.

'Who are *you*?'

'Hilary's husband.' David took a step back to stand protectively alongside Hilary on the darkened path.

'And what might you be doing at Morland Abbey, taking a walk in the dark through the ruins?'

We might ask the same question of you, Hilary thought.

Instead, belatedly, the terrible events of the day caught up with her. This was the first time she had seen Gavin since he had received the news of Melissa's death – or had he had reason to know that news before Hilary and Veronica found her corpse?

'Gavin! I'm so sorry. It must have been a terrible shock. I expect the police told you it was Veronica and I who found her.'

'What?' Gavin turned back to her. He sounded disorientated, but it had taken the focus of his attention away from David.

Her husband, however, could speak for himself. 'Naturally, Hilary rang to tell me what was happening. I knew it would have been traumatic for her, finding your wife like that, and not helped by knowing that whoever did it was still at large. Since she said the police wanted everybody to stay until tomorrow, I thought the least I could do was to drive over here and back her up.'

No mention of Veronica. It was a small satisfaction, an unworthy part of her heart told her.

'How chivalrous.'

Hilary took a step forward. She was craning to see past Gavin into the dimly lit chapel, but it was not going to give up its secret. Gavin stood firmly on the threshold, blocking the way.

'I think it might be a good thing if you went back to your beds.' Gavin's voice held a note of authority. 'This is not the sort of situation for people to be wandering around in the dark.'

If he realized the irony of that statement, he gave nothing away.

'We saw a light outside. David thought he should investigate.'

She caught the tilt of Gavin's head as he lifted his shadowed face up to the row of windows along the East Cloister behind them.

'I seem to remember you had a room overlooking the cloisters. Top floor. Am I right?'

Hilary remained silent, unsure how much more to give away.

She did not need to. She heard the knowledge dawn in his altered voice.

'Ah! Your friend, Veronica Taylor. Delightful lady. The two of you on the top corridor of the East Cloister, while most people are over in the West Cloister. We put ourselves and the speaker, of course, on the floor below you. Poor Dinah. And you two were only just overhead. Veronica's room is on this side, if I remember, looking out on the Great Barn. I expect she's watching us, even now, isn't she? Did the three of you come to the same idiotic conclusion? That the murderer would be stalking the grounds at night, on some nefarious errand, giving himself away by flashing a torch?'

Hilary felt her cheeks grow hot in that same torchlight. That *had* been what they were thinking. It sounded ridiculous now, summed up in that cool, amused tone of Gavin's.

Remarkably self-contained, under the circumstances.

It was left to David to ask the obvious question. 'As a matter of interest, what *were* you doing here at this hour of night?'

'This is a consecrated chapel. Would it surprise you to know that I came here to pray? My wife was murdered today. I asked Fiona for the key.'

Hilary felt the ground cut from under her feet. She was sure there was somebody else in the Lady Chapel, but it would have taken a very insensitive man or woman to blunder on after a statement like that.

It might even be true. Whoever had been waiting for Gavin might have been someone he trusted as a close friend. Perhaps the two of them really *had* agreed to meet here, in this place of worship that was all that remained of the great abbey church. Everyone else had gone to their rooms and there was no danger of encountering a member of the course, gushing with sympathy he did not feel he could handle.

It was just possible. But did she believe it?

There was nothing for it. With a gruff, 'I'm sorry,' she turned on her heel.

As she picked her way back along the path, with David following, she turned. A gleam of moonlight showed her Gavin still staring up at Veronica's window.

David and Hilary climbed the steps to the first floor of the East Cloister. Hilary nearly jumped out of her skin as a deep voice challenged them.

'Hold on there. Who might you be?'

The lights were on in the corridor. Hilary had time to make out the dark bulk of a uniformed figure beyond David.

'Sorry, Officer. It's Dr and Mrs Masters. We're on our way to bed.'

David's appeasing voice addressed the burly officer blocking their way.

'And what might you have been doing out there at this hour?'

Hilary inserted herself between them. 'There's something you need to know. Gavin Standforth is meeting someone in the Lady Chapel. We couldn't see whom.'

'Is he, indeed?'

'If you're quick, you might catch them together.'

'You seem in a hurry to get rid of me, ma'am.'

'Because you can insist on going past him into the chapel, and we couldn't.'

He studied them for a moment. Then he said, 'Well, then, if you'll excuse me.' He pushed past them through the open fire door. A much more powerful torch sprang into life, illuminating the uneven walls of the Great Barn.

'Damn,' said David, none too softly. 'That'll scare them off before he's anywhere near the chapel.'

Hilary went back to the fire escape. She watched the bright beam receding swiftly along the path. David was right. Gavin and whoever he had gone to meet could have vanished into the maze of paths through Morland's grounds before the policeman got there. A wasted opportunity.

'Let's go upstairs,' she said. 'It's been a very long day.'

Veronica's room on the top floor was still in darkness. She turned from the window as they entered, a slender shadow before the indistinct light beyond the glass.

'How did it go?' she said softly. 'Did you manage to see who it was, and whom he was meeting?'

'My fault,' Hilary admitted. 'I stepped on something that broke under my heel. It was Gavin inside, but we never got to see who was with him, let alone hear what was going on between them.'

'What's that?'

A sudden brightness outside had caught Veronica's attention. She swung back to the window.

'Only the police,' Hilary sighed. 'He caught us coming back indoors. We told him about the pair in the chapel. I hoped he might have the authority to get past Gavin and find out who the other person was. But instead of that, he switched on a torch as bright as a searchlight. They'll be miles away by the time he gets there.'

Veronica peered out into the night. 'You're right. There's no sign of anyone there now. So it was Gavin, was it? The one with the pencil torch? I thought it might be. There was something about that rather theatrical way he walks.'

'He seemed remarkably in control of the situation. If it was put on, then he's a very good actor,' David said. 'His wife was murdered today. That would probably be enough to break most of us in pieces.'

Hilary felt a surge of emotion as she sensed him turn his head towards her in the darkness.

More practically, she said, 'Unless, of course, he was the one who killed her.'

'I keep thinking over that meeting with Theresa,' Veronica mused. 'I wish I'd heard more of it. There was certainly complicity between those two about *something*. And it had to do with a death. Do you suppose it was her in the chapel? I forgot to tell you, but someone came out while you two were walking back to this building.'

Hilary and David were suddenly attentive.

'Who?'

'I couldn't see more than a glimpse. There was just a flicker of moonlight between the clouds. I caught a sort of pale gleam between the shadows. I got the impression that it was a woman, but I can't say why. Something about the way she moved, perhaps.'

'Theresa?'

'That was the first thought that came into my mind, of course. Her sort of figure ought to be easy to recognize. But I'm not sure. It could have been. But it seemed as if she was wearing an anorak with the hood pulled up. It could have made her look bulkier than she really was.'

The hood pulled up. Hilary's mind shot to the description of the youth in the hoodie in Leechwell Lane. But that had been a tracksuit, not an anorak. And the black would not have shown up against the shadowing trees. Still, the Lady Chapel was some distance away, and the path to it in near darkness. Veronica might easily have been mistaken about that detail.

'There was something else.' Veronica's voice slowed. 'The one I now take to be Gavin said something to her. Then the two of them looked up. I got the feeling that they were staring straight at this window. As though they knew I was here watching them.'

'They did,' Hilary said bluntly. 'Gavin has a remarkably accurate memory of which rooms we've been allocated. He knows we're here on the top floor. That my room overlooks the cloisters and yours faces this way. He even made loaded comments about how close we were to Dinah Halsgrove's room. As though *we* were the ones under suspicion. And yes, I'm afraid he'd worked out that you must be the one who saw his torch from your window.'

She was aware of Veronica's shiver.

David stepped in. 'Look, let's not get melodramatic. But how would it be if Veronica sleeps in Hilary's room tonight and I take this one. You've got a bed big enough for both of you.'

'Are you sure?' Hilary heard the relief in her friend's voice. 'I don't want to be a nuisance.'

'No problem. I'm travelling light. I've only got my pyjamas and wash bag to move.'

Hilary felt something precious being taken away from her. For all her jealousy of his shared laughter with Veronica, she really would have liked to snuggle against the comforting warmth of David tonight, of all nights.

The two women readied themselves for bed in Hilary's room. Veronica sat on the edge furthest from the window, brushing her fair hair.

'It's silly, but it does feel better having David here. Though I don't suppose anything would have happened to me.'

TWENTY

For all her exhaustion, Hilary could not fall asleep. She lay in the unfamiliar room listening to the even sound of Veronica's breathing on the other side of the bed. She twisted in frustration. Only a short time ago, she had felt a ridiculous resentment at sharing this room with David, who seemed more concerned about Veronica than about her. Now she longed for his warm reassuring presence in the same bed, only to find it taken away from her. For a moment, she even wondered whether she should pad her way along the corridor and creep into the single bed David had taken over from Veronica. Then she remembered. The object of the switch was so that Veronica should not have to sleep alone. She threw the bedclothes off her, then snatched them back again.

It was a wide bed. Veronica slept on undisturbed. She was the one who was supposed to be in danger, but it was Hilary who could not sleep.

She thought about the rooms on the corridor beneath her. In one of those, Dinah Halsgrove had been taken seriously ill. Was the elderly author still in hospital, or had they allowed her to go home? Certainly she would not be coming back to the room in which she had been so nearly fatally poisoned. What about Melissa and Gavin? Presumably they had shared a room as husband and wife. Melissa's side of the bed would be cold and empty tonight. Melissa herself no doubt lay in an even colder bed in a morgue somewhere. Was Gavin back in their room from that strange encounter in the Lady Chapel? Was he the grieving husband, or Melissa's killer? How was he living with that emptiness?

Theresa? Hilary shook off the thought that it might have been she whom Gavin was meeting in the chapel. Despite the conversation that Veronica had overheard, it made no sense for them to meet there. He had only needed to take a short step along the corridor to find her.

Who, then? Someone staying in the West Cloister? Her mind's eye took her across the lawn, fitfully lit by the moonlight between the clouds. That was where many of the course members were sleeping. Gavin would not have wanted to face them, in the wake of such a terrible bereavement. And someone from the West Cloister might well have been spotted skirting the cloister to visit him here. The chapel would make sense for a secret nocturnal meeting place.

But why? Why would Gavin be in collusion with one of the would-be novelists?

Always supposing the stranger in the chapel was indeed someone on the crime-writing course.

She sighed. It was scarcely likely that any one of this random collection of people would have a motive for disposing of Melissa, or of abetting Gavin in doing so.

But what did she know about them? What history of intrigue and unfaithfulness might lie behind that relationship? And yet, murder? It seemed to be carrying a failed marriage to ludicrous extremes.

She tossed restlessly. Who else, then? Someone on the Morland Abbey staff? The ever-helpful Fiona?

Stupid to think that she could solve this, when the police knew far more than she did, and had the authority to find out still more.

She twisted again, unable to get her body comfortable or her mind relaxed.

That figure in the hooded anorak. The one Veronica had felt was a woman.

She tried to picture the police artist's sketch that DS Blunt had pushed before her earlier that evening. The figure in the hooded tracksuit, who they thought was a teenage boy.

She startled awake to find Veronica's hand on her shoulder. 'Wake up, Hilary. It's breakfast in ten minutes' time.'

There was no answer from David's room. As they turned away, Hilary heard rapid footsteps on the stairs just out of sight below them. David's balding head appeared, the coronet of fairish hair circling it beaded with rain. As he came round the bend in the stairs, his lean face was aglow with health and a cheerfulness that belied the seriousness of the situation that had brought him here.

Something in the familiarity, the normality of seeing him here, contracted Hilary's heart. David returning from his run, as he did every morning. She was shy of telling him how much she cherished his presence. In the rush of gratitude at seeing him, she was ashamed of the jealousy she had felt yesterday.

He gave her a casual hug and kissed her, as though this was an everyday place for them to meet.

'You don't know what you're missing. The best part of the day's gone before you're out of bed. How can you stay indoors while you have all this to enjoy?'

The large wave of his hand took in the window behind him and the glimpse of the mist-shrouded cloisters. Beyond, Hilary knew, were the gardens and tiltyard, backed by a rising bank with flights of steps, shrubs, paths and statuary. How far had his run taken him?

'Later,' she said firmly. 'It sounds as though we've got plenty of time on our hands before lunchtime. And I doubt you could see anything much before this mist lifts.'

'You'd be surprised.'

He opened the door to what had been Veronica's room. The curtains of the window opposite had been drawn apart. David strode across to it.

'Our little foray last night seems to have borne dividends. They've taped off the area around the chapel. I went to have a look, but the arm of the law is guarding it.'

Veronica and Hilary joined him.

'Hmm,' Hilary said. 'So they can't pin enough on Gavin to arrest him, but they do suspect him. They're obviously hoping to find forensic evidence there to tell them whom he was meeting.'

'The woman in the anorak – if it *was* a woman,' Veronica agreed.

'Most murders are committed by someone the victim knows,' mused Hilary. 'Gavin does seem the most obvious target. Last night – I may be turning into a nervous old woman, but he gave me the creeps. The way he looked up at this window.'

David's hand rested on her shoulder. 'He certainly seemed to be trying to scare us off. But nothing happened. No one tried my door to strangle me in my sleep – Sorry, Veronica!'

Hilary's mind flew to her own door latch lifting, that first night.

'I have to admit I'd have felt scared sleeping here alone, after you told me that,' Veronica confessed.

'Today's a new day,' David reassured her. 'Let's find breakfast. I've worked up a prodigious appetite. Then all you have to do is sit it out until this afternoon. Then, home. You can put all this behind you.'

'I doubt it,' Hilary said. 'Some things never leave you.'

The sight of Melissa's body snaked over the lip of the Leechwells. Her face pale and lifeless when they turned her over. The feel of her cold lips.

They were not the only ones late to breakfast. The morning before, the would-be crime writers had assembled eagerly, curious to know what the first of their tasks would be. Sunday morning seemed to have left most of them with a feeling of purposelessness.

The shadow of death hanging over Morland Abbey was deepened by the presence of the police. DI Foulks, DS Blunt and three other officers, one uniformed, two in civilian clothes, were seated at a table of their own.

'Good morning, ladies, Dr Masters.' Colonel Truscott tried to cast an air of normal civility over the grim situation. 'It looks as though we shall be left to our own devices this morning. I hardly imagine from what you said that you will be joining our band of amateur sleuths for – what did they call it? – *brainstorming.*' He made the word sound like a newly invented and unsavoury occupation.

'I thought I might go to church.' The words surprised Hilary, even as she said them. And yet she was suddenly sure that this was what she wanted – no, needed – to do.

She turned to David. He nodded. 'I'm with you.'

'I'd rather like to come too,' Veronica said. 'Where were you thinking of going? The village church, or Totnes?'

'I hadn't really thought.'

She had assumed, as they all had, that Sunday morning would be the last full session of the course. If all had gone according to plan, they would have established their setting and one significant character and would now be working on their plots.

But a different plot had overtaken them and caught them in its snares.

'Do you think we need to clear it with the police?' Veronica asked, casting an apprehensive glance across at the table where DI Foulks sat sipping his coffee. 'He wanted to keep us all on hand as potential witnesses.'

'I shall tell him,' Hilary said, getting to her feet.

She felt the eyes of the dining hall on her as she made her way to the police table.

'Inspector.'

He turned courteously. 'Mrs Masters?'

'Is it all right with you if my husband and I and Veronica push off to church this morning? You don't need us for anything more?'

'You're coming back for lunch?'

'Of course. You asked us to stay until the course officially closes this afternoon. Though it's hardly much of a course with our leader in mourning.'

'People will have made plans, booked trains. I'm only asking you to keep to those plans. I have no authority to make you stay.'

Hilary looked across at a uniformed policeman tucking into bacon, sausage and eggs. She did not think it was the larger officer with the powerful torch they had run into last night.

'I suppose one of your officers told you that Gavin was out last night, meeting someone in the old chapel. All that's left of the abbey church. David tells me you've taped it off this morning.'

He studied her for a moment without speaking. The long intelligent face was creased with thought.

'Of course. Thank you for drawing that to our attention. It seems that you and Mrs Taylor have a knack for being in a position that makes you vital witnesses.'

Was that praise or an accusation? Or just a wry comment on coincidence?

It gave her a cold feeling in her spine to know that she did not herself believe in coincidences. Looked at from the detective inspector's viewpoint, it must seem strange that she and Veronica should be so conspicuously in the centre of the frame. What did he really think about them? His courteous demeanour gave nothing away.

Surely he must by now have questioned Gavin Standforth about whom he was meeting in the chapel? What had Gavin told him? And would it have been the truth?

What innocent explanation *could* there have been for such a clandestine meeting?

Gavin's own words came back to her. '*Would it surprise you to know that I came here to pray? My wife was murdered today.*'

It was not unlike the reason she had just given DI Foulks for leaving Morland Abbey for Totnes.

Was it even possible that it was true? That Gavin was innocent of his wife's death? That they had wronged him grievously?

She would have a lot to pray about this morning.

There was a stir of interest. Hilary looked up. It was something of a shock to see Theresa enter the dining room. Immediately she checked herself. She did not know why she should feel that.

Yes, she did. Even before Melissa's murder, had there not been something sinister about Theresa? The Toad, squatting, largely silent, over her group of writers.

She had to remind herself that, to the people of Totnes, the Toad spring was a source of healing. The warty reptile was said to cure skin diseases. Things were not always what they seemed.

The disquieting feeling continued. She tried to shake it away as she watched Theresa walk past their table and take an empty place beside Harry Walters. The plump-faced man seemed too embarrassed to know what to say. *We're all like that in the face of bereavement*, Hilary thought. *We can't find the right words. And Theresa is bereaved too, isn't she? She has lost at least a colleague, and probably a close friend, in the most appalling manner.* Hilary wished now that Veronica had not heard that conversation from the tiltyard. It had seemed that Gavin and Theresa nursed some anger against Melissa. She found it chilling to think that Theresa might be the murderer. To know that so much venom was sitting at the next table. Sharing food. Better to believe that it was someone she had never set eyes on who had done the deed. That stranger in the tracksuit.

David called her attention away. 'Ah, I beat her to it. Last time we met she was running past the Henry Moore statue at the top of the grounds.'

Hilary turned to see Jo Walters striding lithely across the room towards Harry. There was an enviable glow about her. Hilary sighed. She could never imagine herself donning a tracksuit or leggings and jogging round the paths of Morland Abbey before breakfast. Jo would have showered and washed her hair to emerge radiant and confident. She wore a high-necked green jumper, above which her cheeks were rosier than normal.

It was perhaps not quite in the best of taste to arrive looking so healthy and happy on a morning like this.

Hilary had just turned her eyes to spreading black cherry jam on her toast when a greater stillness fell over the room. Her eyes followed the direction of everyone else's.

Gavin.

The hush was more intense than that which had marked Theresa's entrance. It dawned on her that this was the first time most of them had seen him since news of Melissa's death reached Morland Abbey.

She remembered, with a mixture of fear and embarrassment, that encounter in the dark outside the chapel. There had been something malevolent about him then, hadn't there? The way he had looked up at Veronica's window, knowing exactly where she was and what she was doing there.

Or had Hilary let herself be carried away by the conventions of crime writing? To see a murderer where there was only a shocked and bereaved husband?

What were the rest of the company thinking as they watched him make his solitary way across the room?

She had thought he might take the empty seat beside Theresa, at the same table as Harry and Jo. But he found a small table where no one else sat. She tried to tear her eyes away, not to stare as he walked across to the buffet bar to help himself to fruit juice like everyone else. If he really was innocent, she must allow him the courtesy of privacy as he came to terms with his dreadful circumstances.

If he was not . . . That was for the police to decide. She could see heads turning curiously on that table too. What did they know? What did they suspect?

'Hilary,' Veronica said patiently. 'Did you hear? I'm suggesting we go to the parish church in Totnes. Is that OK?'

She turned back, distracted. 'Yes. Fine.'

Hilary looked around her ancient bedroom with a feeling of bereavement. It had been such a joy to open the door and discover it on Friday afternoon. That vast arching beam spanning the room beyond the foot of the bed. The view from the window across the lawn to the West Cloister, the arched gatehouse to the south. Even the tiles around the small fireplace had evidently not come from a DIY store on an industrial estate. She stroked the cream and brown chequerboard, and studied the occasional patterned tile. She found a canopied well, which reminded her of the nursery rhyme of Jack and Jill, a bird of prey, head bent over its victim, what looked like a leaping goat, a man like an onion seller, with his wares dangling from his outstretched arms. Were these random images, or did they mean something more than she could grasp? Her fingers found the pitted timbers of the room with the same nostalgia. Five hundred years or more under her hand. Whatever happened, this would be her last day at Morland Abbey. Although they were not leaving until the afternoon, she needed to pack her bag, vacate this room, and hand in the key.

She felt a flash of resentment she knew to be unfair. If things had been different, she could have woken this morning to feel David beside her in this large bed. Instead, it had been Veronica who shared the night with her, carefully distant across the wide mattress. There had been no privacy to cuddle up against him in the dark. No chance to let go of her self-possession and confess to him how scared she had been at finding Melissa's body in the well. No opportunity for him to cradle her and reassure her that it would be all right.

Instead, the first she had seen of him had been his balding head ascending the stairs, on his way back to Veronica's room from his run.

It was apparently Jo he had shared that early morning with him, out in the steeply sloping grounds with their sweeping flights of steps and hidden pools. Not his wife.

Veronica had come in behind her. 'I'd better go back to my own room and finish packing. Not that it will take me long.'

Was there embarrassment in her voice? Did she realize what she had taken away from Hilary?

Left alone, Hilary felt a pang of guilt. It was the possible danger to Veronica, more than to her, which had brought David here. But so much had happened since then. Veronica couldn't still be at risk from Gavin and Theresa, could she? Not now that she had made her statement to the police? It was too late to silence her.

Hilary let out a sigh and bent her mind to clearing the room of the few clothes and minor possessions she had needed for the weekend. She picked up her notepad with the novel she had started to write, sitting on the step that led down into the Leechwells. Hastily, she dropped it into her suitcase. She would not be returning to *that* again.

The door opened for a second time. It was David.

As she turned, a grin lit up his face. 'This is where I really need a wife. In the short time I've been here, I've scattered my few belongings across two bedrooms and at least one bathroom. What are the odds on my remembering to pick them all up?

David's and Veronica's clothes, mingling in that smaller bedroom.

'Here,' she said, getting to her feet. 'You hung these in the wardrobe.' She lifted down a raincoat and a heavy knitted jacket.

'Thanks. You're a miracle.' He dropped a kiss on her forehead, then his arm went round her shoulders and he pulled her close. That, at least, was something he would not do with Veronica, she told herself. She let her body snuggle into the warmth of his embrace. His jumper smelt of woodsmoke. She comforted herself that she might not look as fair and feminine as Veronica, but she had this when she needed him. It was ridiculous that she could ever have been jealous.

'Right,' she said, releasing herself and smoothing her rumpled hair. 'We need to clear our rooms, get all this into the boot of the car, and then it's off to Totnes.'

'I'm sorry your weekend has turned out so terribly. Do you think you might write about it one day? Turn reality into fiction as a catharsis? You could always transpose the story into the past.'

'No,' said Hilary curtly. 'Definitely not.'

TWENTY-ONE

There was a queue at the reception office in the West Cloister. The course participants were handing in their keys and settling bar bills. Hilary found herself behind Lin Bell. The older woman turned. Her smile seemed forced, a gallant attempt to put a civilized gloss on the profoundly shocking events of the weekend.

'It seems rather premature to be relinquishing our keys. As though the weekend were over. But there's still this morning to get through, and our final meeting with the Inspector. Do you have plans?'

'To get away from here as soon as possible,' Hilary answered. 'But we can't just yet. So I'm planning to go to church.'

'It must be nice to have that consolation. I lost that long ago.'

'It's never too late to change your mind.'

Lin ignored that. 'This meeting with DI Foulks this afternoon. Don't you feel it smacks rather too much of the old-style whodunnit, Agatha Christie vintage? All the interested parties gathered in one room for the dénouement. The clever inspector surveys the course of the plot and lists all the possible culprits, before pointing the finger triumphantly at the one person no one has suspected. Do you suppose that's what our current DI has in mind?'

'I'm sure that's not how the police work nowadays.'

'So am I. I fear it's just going to peter out inconclusively. He can't detain us any longer, but he wants us to let him know if any fresh evidence comes to mind.'

'That, I'm afraid, is real life. Not a neatly rounded scenario. Still, there's probably been lurid coverage of the murder in the press. Body in the Leechwells. I haven't been following it. Maybe one day we'll switch on the television and hear they've arrested someone.'

'Mrs Bell?' Fiona at the reception desk recalled Lin's attention to the matter in hand.

When it was Hilary's turn, she was struck by how changed the receptionist looked from the smartly dressed and elegantly made-up woman who had welcomed them to Morland Abbey what felt like ages ago. Friday afternoon. Less than two days.

Now Fiona looked strained, as though she too had been up in the night, searching for suspects in the darkened paths and shrubberies of Morland's grounds.

Perhaps she had, Hilary reflected, as a new twist presented itself. Why do we assume that the culprit has to be someone who came here for this course? What if the fact that it happened *here* was more important than any of them realized? Gavin and Melissa must surely have been to Morland Abbey before, either attending a literary event or organizing one of their own. What else might have happened at the abbey, some time in the past, involving Fiona? Could yesterday's calamity be the playing out of an old enmity, and nothing to do with this week's would-be crime writers?

'See you at lunch then.' Lin Bell was at her elbow, bidding her a temporary farewell.

'Yes. Yes, of course.' Distracted, Hilary struggled to remember the pin number for her credit card.

It was her turn to move away from Fiona's desk. She had paid no attention to who might be waiting behind her. It was a pleasant surprise to meet the knowing smile of Jo Walters through those heavy-rimmed glasses. Harry stood, as always, a supportive shadow at her side.

'Nearly the end,' Jo said, with an attempt at lightness. 'We have to crack this by this afternoon, don't you think? I couldn't bear to go away not knowing.'

Hilary ran an assessing eye over the blonde young writer. From the very first afternoon, Jo had impressed her with the seriousness of her ambition to make a go of this. Hilary had an inner conviction that she would. Most of her fellow writers, Hilary knew, would founder in unfinished manuscripts or the discouragement of rejection letters. But there was something about Jo's bright intelligence, her determination, which convinced Hilary that this woman would not.

Jo Walters. Her imagination painted the name on the cover of a crime novel, possibly even a bestseller like Gavin's. Might she and Veronica come back to Morland Abbey one day and find that name prominently on display in the book room, Jo sitting at the table writing autographs?

The week's events caught up with her. Would she and Veronica *want* to come back?

'I'm sure DI Foulks is doing his best. I've no doubt he must have all sorts of evidence he isn't sharing with us. For all we know, he may have his finger on a suspect by now.'

A shiver seemed to run through Jo. Her eyes brightened. 'Yes, I know we're at a disadvantage. We can't know a fraction of what he knows. But wouldn't it be wonderful if someone here got the answer before he does?'

'I can't think of anything about this weekend I'd describe as "wonderful".' Hilary sharply cut the conversation short.

Harry moved to take her place, fumbling in his wallet for his credit card.

Fiona leaned forward. 'That one, Mr Walters?' pointing to one of his many bits of plastic.

'Oh, yes! Thanks. I seem to be all fingers and thumbs today.'

Hilary left the Walters to it. David and Veronica were waiting by the door.

'All done?'

'For the moment.'

Hilary paused before stepping out into the quadrangle. The early mist was receding, leaving a glory of autumn leaves against a background of grey stone. She breathed deeply. All around her rose the medieval buildings which had withstood so much turbulent history.

'It's strange to think that it's all still here, unchanged by everything that's happened within these walls.'

'Perhaps that's why we keep coming back,' Veronica said. 'The lovely permanence of it.'

'And why it's not entirely ridiculous that Gavin might actually have gone to the Lady Chapel to pray when he thought the rest of us were on our way to bed. I wish I knew what to believe.'

Some of the early birds were already making their way across from the West Cloister to Lady Jane's Chamber. Ben and Jake were walking briskly, chatting with animation. Ben held a notepad in his hand.

'Look at them,' Hilary exclaimed. 'This has made their day. Not the fictional crime they came for, but a real-life murder. They're going to be dining out on this for years.'

'Only it isn't actually real life to them, is it?' Veronica asked. 'They can't seem to separate what's happened on the ground from what they were making up in their heads yesterday.'

Others were also converging on Lady Jane's Chamber. Many of them Hilary did not know by name, from the Snake and Slowworm groups.

'Are you sure you don't want to join them?' David asked. Was that a gleam of mischief in his eyes?

'Ugh!' Hilary gave a shudder that was not entirely feigned.

They had almost all disappeared through the door when a last figure came hurrying across the dew-beaded lawn from the direction of the car park to join them.

'I didn't expect to see *her* with them.' Hilary watched the small upright figure of Lin Bell making for the same door into the East Cloister as the two young men. Although she was heading indoors, she carried a walking stick and had a knapsack on her back. Probably she planned to take a walk after the meeting.

Her animated face swung round to them as she passed.

'Have you heard? They've taken Rob to the police station for questioning.'

A shock ran through Hilary. The long-legged, bespectacled companion of Tania. The young man with *Wirral Whippet* emblazoned on his sweatshirt.

Then memory flooded back to her. Could someone have told the inspector about Rob's macabre description of his imagined murder scene? The body lying in the pool below the water wheel. Had DI Foulks made the same connection between that fictional image and the pools of the Leechwells?

Frantically, she tried to reorganize her thoughts. She had had her suspicions about Tania, whose tracksuit had resembled the police sketch in some respects. But Rob had been no more than one name on a long list of possible suspects who might have been mistaken for a lanky teenager. A list so wide, it had even included Veronica.

She thought quickly back to what she remembered about Rob. Athletic certainly. He had been wearing rather inappropriate shorts when she first saw him. Could he have been the figure emerging into the cloister in the mist of early morning? And what if he had been?

'Why?' Veronica was demanding. 'What motive could he possibly have?'

Lin shrugged, her eyes still sparkling. 'What motive does anyone have? We don't know enough about each other. Are you coming?'

With that, she was off up the stairs to Lady Jane's Chamber.

The three of them were left standing nonplussed in the cloisters.

Hilary was the first to break the silence. 'Do you remember yesterday morning, when we were sharing our ideas for where to set a murder? Can you recall Rob's?'

Veronica frowned. 'No–o . . . No, hang on. Wasn't it something rather nasty about a waterwheel?'

'Dartington Tweed Mill. He had his victim caught up in the machinery, and ending up as a mangled corpse in the pool.'

The significance struck the three of them into silence.

Across the drive, more of the course members were putting luggage into the boots of their cars. Hilary raised her hand to Dan Truscott.

This morning he wore a flat tweed cap. Hilary felt that, however he dressed, he could not disguise what he was. A retired colonel, with the discipline of a lifetime ingrained in his habits and beliefs.

'Good morning, ladies, Dr Masters. Bad business, this. Your husband will be glad to get you safely away from it all. You too, Mrs Taylor. No place for a woman.'

'We're all caught up with it, whether we like it or not,' Hilary retorted. 'Though I don't mind admitting I shall be glad to drive away from here this afternoon. I just hope they've found the culprit by then. Did you hear they're questioning Rob?'

'Are they, indeed? Well, you can leave it to the police, dear lady. Finding a murderer is a man's job.'

'They have women in the police now, you know.'

When they were safely out of earshot, David chuckled.

'Is he real? He's so much the stereotype of the retired military gentleman. Do you suppose there are darker depths he's not allowing us to see?'

'What you see is what you get. He may actually be the original the caricatures are based on.'

'I don't know.' Veronica's light voice held a note of speculation. 'I've sometimes wondered what he's doing here. You look at people like Ben and Jake, or Jo. They're obviously hooked on the crime genre. They've read authors I haven't even heard of. They genuinely want to succeed. But I doubt if our good colonel has read anything later than the Father Brown stories. And when he read out his own bit of writing, well . . . Hilary, you were the only one who was brave enough to say what we all felt. It was, well . . .'

'Leaden. Oh, dear. I hope I didn't demolish the poor man completely.'

'But why did he come here?'

'Another mystery we're unlikely to solve.'

*　　*　　*

Hilary drove them down the sweeping drive of Morland Abbey and into Totnes. It was good to be away from the insistent police presence at the abbey. The mist had been torn away. The sky was a cheerful blue, with white clouds scudding across it and no sign of the overnight rain. As she got out of the car, the screams of seagulls made her feel how close they were to the sea.

'This way,' she said, heading resolutely for the opposite side of the High Street, away from Leechwell Lane. She would try not to let herself think of that this Sunday morning.

The bells were ringing out for morning service. Some shops were open, but there was still something of a Sabbath atmosphere. It felt cleansing.

David, she knew, might have preferred a simpler non-conformist chapel, or a Quaker meeting. But there was something about the history of Morland Abbey and Totnes which called for its centuries-old parish church to complete the experience. To put the murder in the context of the centuries of violence the town had seen. It had survived and flourished, a resolute part of her mind told her.

'We didn't get to see the church yesterday,' she told David. 'What with one thing and another.'

It was a colossal understatement.

The narrow hill of the High Street widened to reveal the landscaped churchyard in front of the priory church of St Mary's. The red sandstone tower, surmounted by pinnacles, soared into the sky that was turning blue.

'Built with wool money, I shouldn't wonder.' The historian's part of her brain took over. 'When Devon cloth was at the forefront of the export trade.'

Veronica turned back to look down over the town. 'It's strange to think of the Dart estuary crowded with sailing ships setting out to sea, where now it's just the occasional cruise boat and motorized yachts.'

'Nothing stays still.'

The interior under the wagon roof was dimly lit after the sunshine outside. Hilary felt the hush fall over them and was glad of it. They found a pew towards the back of the morning congregation. All three sat awhile in prayer. When Hilary raised her eyes again, her active mind was back, assessing her surroundings.

For a while, her brain was busy with stone and wood, stained glass and plaster, fitting the carvings to their century. She let her eye pass over her fellow worshippers without curiosity. It had not occurred to her to study the human content of the church. Then a familiar face recalled her to the twenty-first century. She should not have been surprised to find that some, at least, of those on the study course at Morland Abbey should be here at morning service, but she was.

Harry, looking rather disconsolate on his own. So he had not chosen to join Jo at the brainstorming session, then. Hardly surprising. And curly-haired Ceri, the one local resident from the group. It was this fact that had made her stand out from the rest. Unlike all the others, who were requested by DI Foulks to remain at Morland Abbey, Ceri had the freedom to go back to her home in Totnes for the night. She must know the town so much better than the rest of them, better than Hilary and Veronica, for instance. Ceri had clearly felt strongly about the Leechwells. Strongly enough to resent Gavin's rather jokey appropriation of its presiding deities.

The Long Crippler. The blind Slowworm.

Melissa, the leader of the Snakes, was dead, but she had been lying in the Long Crippler pool.

People were rising from their seats, spilling into the aisle. Hilary realized with a start that she had not given the service the full attention she had meant to. When the congregation exchanged the peace before the Eucharist, David had kissed her on the cheek. She had shaken hands automatically with the people in the pew in front of her, but had not turned round to those behind. Her still agitated mind had been darting off in all directions.

'Sorry!' she said to God. 'But I really did come here because I needed you. I'm all of a muddle this morning, but you're used to that, aren't you? It's a blessing that you know what I need before I ask you. Only I should have been putting more work into praying for those who need you even more than I do.'

'Good morning,' she heard Veronica say to someone in the pew behind them. 'I didn't realize you were here too.'

Hilary turned to find that Theresa had been sitting directly behind her for the past hour.

She gave a small shudder, then felt a rush of confusion. She wished she could make up her mind what she felt about their group leader. A co-conspirator with Gavin, behind Melissa's back? A secret lover, even? Or a colleague who, beneath the composure which gave nothing away, had been knocked sideways by the shocking loss of her friend?

Instead, Hilary took refuge in what she did know.

'You know what they say about that hole in the wall of the chancel? That it's a leper squint, so that the lepers of St Mary Magdalen's hospital could sit in the side chapel to watch the sacrament. Nonsense, of course. Like Leechwell Lane being a leper path. They'd hardly use one so narrow that you'd be rubbing shoulders with them on the way to the healing well.'

'The healing well. Where you found the body.'

Theresa's expression was unreadable. But Hilary was shocked by the crassness of what she had just said.

'I'm sorry! I didn't mean . . .'

'It wasn't exactly healing for Melissa, was it?'

Theresa turned and walked away.

'There's something about that woman that unsettles me,' Hilary confided to David as they stood in the aisle. 'I'm probably being grossly unfair, but when I'm within a ten-yard radius of her I feel as though ants are walking up my spine.'

'She does seem a bit strange,' David agreed. 'I mean, I know it must have been a terrible shock, the course leader's wife dying like this, and in the worst possible way. But someone should have taken charge. If Gavin's out of commission, then the obvious person is Theresa. Yet she seems content to let the rest of you muddle on as best you can.'

'I suppose she thinks we wouldn't even be here if DI Foulks hadn't insisted that we stay till the end. He's obviously still hoping something new is going to turn up, that one of us will remember something, and any one of us might be needed as a witness.'

'Still, there's only a few more hours to go. I have hopes of the Chapter House's Sunday lunch. And then it's home. You'll be glad to see the back of this place. Morland Abbey, I mean.'

'Yes . . . and no. I hope it doesn't spoil it for me completely. I've so enjoyed coming here in the past. I'm glad at least the murder didn't happen there.'

Veronica was making her way up the aisle towards the chancel. Hilary assumed she had gone to inspect the magnificent rood screen which separated it from the nave. Mercifully, it had escaped the ravages of the Reformation. Fifteenth-century, she recalled, intricately and surprisingly carved, not out of wood, but sandstone.

Her attention was snatched back to the present. Veronica had not been heading for the screen. Instead, she had stopped to talk to someone. Her head was bent solicitously towards a middle-aged man in a brown jacket. Harry Walters.

'Excuse me,' Hilary said to David. 'I'd better go and have a word with Harry. He looks a bit down this morning.'

'Unlike his wife. She was a picture of health, jogging round the grounds before breakfast.'

'She's brighter than Harry. She's got caught up with this group who think they can solve the mystery before CID do. I've called them callous, but I suppose it's a way of taking their minds off the emotional reality of what's taken place. Turn it into an intellectual game. Keep your mind so busy that there's no time for the heart to get involved. I guess that's what the police have to do, let alone the pathologists who conduct the autopsy. If they cared too much they'd go under.'

'Yes,' said David. 'That's kind of how it works.'

'Oh, I'm sorry!' Hilary was conscience-stricken. 'I wasn't talking about you. I mean, I know you're a doctor. You've seen terrible things. Gaza. Yemen. But you're the most caring person I know.'

'No offence taken.' He smiled at her fondly. 'There's a lot in what you say. We call it professionalism.'

Hilary approached Harry and Veronica. Close to, she found to her astonishment that Harry's face was wet with tears.

'Morning, Harry,' she said, with a forced cheerfulness to cover her embarrassment. She did not know whether she should mention the tears. Veronica was better at the sympathy thing than she was. 'I see we're not the only ones seeking solace in the arms of Mother Church. It's good to know that places like this are always here when we need them.'

Harry made a gallant attempt to swallow back his emotion. 'Jo's braver than I am. She said life has to go on. She kept saying we had to find out who killed Melissa. As if . . . But . . . but I keep remembering. It was only this time yesterday we were sitting in Melissa's group in Morland Abbey. I never pretended to be much of a hand at this writing business. I only came along because of Jo. But Melissa was so kind . . . She treated me as though I was as good as any of you others. She said if I couldn't manage to put a plot together this morning, she'd help me. She was a lovely lady.' Fresh tears spilled over. 'I'm so sorry!'

Hilary put out an awkward hand and squeezed his arm. 'No need to be ashamed, just because you've got a warmer heart than the rest of us. I think we're all waiting for DI Foulks to drop the starting flag, so that we can be off home.'

'Apparently the police have a suspect,' Veronica added. 'Rob.'

Harry shook his head blankly.

'Tania's partner. The Wirral Whippet. Oh, I forgot. You're not in our group. You may not have met him.'

Harry brushed his tears away. 'The police will never find the true killer. Someone who's much too clever for them.'

TWENTY-TWO

They were on their way to the church door and the contrast of bright sunshine outside.

'Do you want to stay behind for a coffee?' David asked. 'Say hello to the congregation?'

'I'm not sure I'm feeling that sociable yet,' Hilary replied. 'Perhaps not.'

Someone was chatting to the rector at the door: Ceri. When she moved on, David, Hilary and Veronica took their turns for a handshake and a word of welcome.

'Sad business, I'm afraid,' he said when he heard they had come from the abbey. 'It must have been a terrible shock for all of you.'

'It was kind of you to remember Melissa in your prayers,' said Veronica.

'It's the least that any of us can do. If it would help to talk . . .?'

'Thank you. We're managing fine.' It was not true, but Hilary longed to be quiet now.

When they stepped out on to the churchyard path, Ceri was waiting. Her dark eyes smiled briefly at them.

'I'm glad somebody knows what to do with a Sunday morning. I was never happy about giving up morning service to write a crime novel. I said something to Gavin about it, but he just laughed and told me I could go to Evensong if I was that keen. As it turned out, it wasn't necessary. We have this morning.'

'You seemed upset about Gavin's attitude to more than one thing,' Hilary observed. 'His use of the characters from the Leechwells, for instance.'

A strange expression came over Ceri's face. A mixture of indignation and something else. Fear? 'I thought he was mocking them. Toad, Snake, Crippler.'

'You speak as though they're real people,' Veronica said.

Ceri rounded on her. 'They *are* real. Not people. But real just the same. We don't leave flowers and hang ribbons just for the sake of an old folk tale. But something angered them. Crippler in particular. You can hardly have failed to notice that Melissa was leader of Gavin's Snake group, and she wasn't found in the Snake pool.'

'We're hardly likely to forget,' Hilary told her through tight lips. 'We found her.'

'Yes, of course! I'm sorry. I should have remembered. Poor you . . . All the same, I can't help being glad we're in the Toad group. Touch wood, nothing's happened to us. I'd be scared if I was in either of the others.'

'Like poor old Harry, you mean? He looked in a bad way. He's really cut up about it.'

'So he should be. There's a meaning behind this.'

They parted from her at the church gate. As the three of them walked back to Hilary's car, she felt a heightened sense of the short, fragile time allowed to them. They had just less than an hour before Sunday lunch. Then DI Foulks wanted a final meeting in Lady Jane's Chamber, before the shattered course disintegrated.

Nothing more could happen between now and then, could it?

As he opened the passenger door for Veronica, David said, 'I've been thinking. What you said about the detective sergeant showing you a drawing of a boy in a tracksuit. She wasn't wearing a tracksuit when I met her out running this morning, but she could have got rid of it. I think Jo Walters could pass for a teenager under a hood. She's slim enough. If she hunched her shoulders a bit, stuck her hands in her pockets . . .' He closed the door and got into the back seat, behind the two women. 'Sorry! It's ridiculous to make an accusation like that when I don't know the woman from Eve, and on such a flimsy supposition. But it's an idea.'

'You know,' Veronica said, 'that could just explain why Harry was so upset this morning. He said it was because of Melissa, which is reasonable enough. But what if Jo has said or done something to make him wonder the same thing?'

David's voice came from the back seat. 'Harry would know whether Jo had a navy tracksuit with white stripes. She was wearing grey leggings and a pink tee shirt when I saw her this morning.'

'But I doubt he'd tell the inspector if she had,' Veronica countered.

'You two think *she* could have killed Melissa?' Hilary swung the car out into the traffic. 'But why ever would she?'

'What do we know? Somebody had a reason for it,' Veronica replied.

'The woman in the anorak.' David leaned forward suddenly. 'The one you saw last night leaving the chapel. Could *that* have been her too?'

'Meeting Gavin?' Hilary asked. 'After she'd killed his wife?'

David sat back. 'I suppose not.'

They had driven some way out of town before Hilary started so violently, she nearly drove into the kerb.

'We're forgetting! What if it wasn't a woman at the chapel? Could that have been Rob? Yesterday, Tania was wearing a black tracksuit. It wasn't navy, and the white stripes didn't go right down the sleeves and legs, but it was close enough. What if Rob borrowed it?'

There was a breath-held silence.

Then Veronica said, 'But surely, if he was wearing that tracksuit when he did it, he'd have got rid of it, wouldn't he?'

But the alternative possibility nagged at Hilary on the short drive back from Totnes and up the tree-hung drive of the abbey. For a time that half-heard conversation between Theresa and Gavin in the tiltyard had made her suspect an affair involving the two of them, necessitating the removal of Melissa. She had dismissed this as extreme in these days of easy divorce. Yet what if Gavin's mistress was not the plain-faced Theresa, but Jo Walters? Lively, youthful, a surprisingly attractive mate for poor old Harry.

Jo and Gavin. She pondered the combination. It made more sense. Jo, hooded and anonymous in Leechwell Lane. Jo, meeting Gavin in the chapel at night, while Theresa would only have had to walk along the East Cloister corridor.

Did it make more sense than Rob?

Still, she ran up against the same problem, like a physical barrier. Why would either of them resort to murder?

Somewhere in the distance came the wail of an emergency vehicle's siren.

'I hate it when they do that,' Hilary muttered. 'I can never tell where it's coming from, and what I'm supposed to do.'

She pulled over to the side of the road as an ambulance went racing past, followed soon after by two police cars.

'Accident, by the look of it,' David remarked.

Hilary took the turning for the Morland Abbey estate.

An insidious thought was creeping into her mind as the car mounted the slope to the abbey's car park.

Jo had seemed more eager than any of them to engage with the murder mystery weekend and produce a bestselling crime novel. Jo had reacted with enthusiasm to the idea of a brainstorming session about Melissa's death. What if some aberration of her personality had led the intellectual challenge of committing a successful murder to trump the normal rules of morality and common sense? For her own satisfaction and to prove to bestselling author Gavin that she could do it too? Only in real life?

It was a chilling thought, but there were psychopaths who did think like that.

That babyish face, beneath the blonde curls.

'Something's happened,' Veronica said suddenly. 'Look at all those people at the gatehouse.'

In front of the arch that led to the cloisters and the Great Barn, members of the crime course were gathered. Knots of people were discussing something with a suppressed excitement. Even from inside the car, Hilary could feel the tension. She swung into the nearest space in the car park. In moments, the three of them were out and hurrying across the drive to join the others.

Heads lifted at their hasty approach. Some eyes brightened at the thought that this time they would be the ones to tell the newcomers the startling truth.

'What's up?' Hilary barked as she sped with dangerous haste along the cobbled entrance.

It was Jake who got in first, his grey eyes avid with the news.

'It's Jo,' he said. 'Jo Walters. She's been attacked. On the path down by the river.'

'Is she . . .?' Veronica's words trailed off.

'Dead? Apparently not. But unconscious, Fiona says, with a nasty crack on the head. It's anyone's guess if she'll pull through.'

'Do they need medical help?' David was urgent, practical.

Ben chipped in. 'The person who found her – apparently Lin Bell – called nine-nine-nine, then rang the abbey. We heard the ambulance siren just now. We were all for going to help her, but DI Foulks ordered us to wait here, damn him. CID have gone racing off.'

Did you really want to help her, Hilary thought, *or to satisfy your morbid curiosity about how the victim looked?* She thought of the diminutive Lin Bell, with her neat silver hair. A small slight figure, probably in her seventies. So the walking stick and knapsack *had* meant that she planned a riverside walk after the brainstorming session. And so, apparently, had Jo.

A shocking thought occurred to her. It was not just Jo who could pass as a teenage boy in a hooded tracksuit. And Jo was now the victim herself.

Hilary could feel the blood draining from her own cheeks. Only minutes ago she had been casting Jo Walters in the role of murderer. Now someone else had attacked her, evidently with murderous intent. Wherever Jo fitted into this mystery, it could surely not now be as Melissa's killer.

The suspicion was swinging inevitably back to Rob.

Or . . . It had been Lin who had made that phone call.

TWENTY-THREE

Hilary looked around suddenly. 'Where's Harry?' Nowhere in the press of anxious faces could she see the broad, usually genial countenance she had last seen streaming with tears in St Mary's church.

Ben and Jake's looks questioned those around them.

'Sorry. Haven't seen him.'

'He was probably down by the river with Jo when it happened,' Jake suggested.

'He wasn't,' Hilary said firmly. 'He was in church with us.'

'Ah! The God Squad.' Ben grinned.

'If you like to call it that. Some of us have an idea what to do with Sunday morning other than point the finger at people for murder on precious little evidence.'

'Ouch!'

'As it happens,' Jake supplied, 'the session didn't last all that long. We were a bit short on numbers. Rob and Tania were out of it, of course. You heard he'd . . .?'

'Yes,' Hilary said curtly.

'And Jo wasn't there . . .' His voice tailed away. 'We never imagined why.'

'I guess the rest of us ran out of ideas,' Ben added, 'apart from wondering where on earth Rob fitted in.'

'Unless you count that old theory that Gavin set this all up for the publicity.'

'And happened to have an expendable wife.'

Was that a twinkle in Ben's eye? Even at a time like this? Hilary stared him down. 'You two are impossible. A third woman may be at death's door and you think it's a *joke*?'

'Sorry, ma'am.' There might have been contrition as well as mockery in his expression. It was hard to tell.

'Anyway, that was Rob and Tania's idea, wasn't it?' Hilary pointed out.

'You mean they put it up to divert attention from Rob?'

'How can any of us know? Anyway, there's a very real possibility that poor old Harry is on his way back here from church, not yet knowing his wife's been attacked.'

There was another emergency siren approaching. It stopped further down the hill, just out of sight. Hilary made a decision.

'I've got to go and see.'

'Hilary, the inspector asked us to stay here,' Veronica intervened.

'He didn't tell *me*.'

She went clattering back over the cobbles, wishing she had not chosen to wear heeled shoes to church, in a vain gesture towards respectability.

As she turned on to the drive, she was aware of David just behind her shoulder.

'I'm a doctor. But there's nothing you can do,' he said. 'They won't let you anywhere near her.'

'I know. But I have to do something.'

Out of the corner of her eye she saw that Veronica was following them at a little distance.

They rounded the bend and saw the reason for the wailing sirens that had fallen silent now.

The drive bent sharply past the lowest of the abbey's surrounding complex of modern buildings. A police car was drawn up at the side of the road.

'Look!' Veronica pointed. 'Down there.'

A meadow sloped down to where the River Dart was hidden among the trees. A wide footpath had been mown through the tall grass and clover. Just where the wood began, a flash of green and yellow was visible. The ambulance. Two more white and blue police cars were parked alongside it. Someone had opened the wide field gate for them, alongside the smaller one for walkers.

Hilary strode through. The ground was soft beneath the wet

grass. As she plunged on down, she cursed her inappropriate heels more than ever.

'This is as far as they could drive,' David said as they neared the vehicles.

Ahead, the track mown through the grass ended in a narrow footpath disappearing into the trees.

Hilary hurried on past the vehicles into the little wood. There was a shout from the path in front of her. A policeman had turned.

'You can't come down here, missus. They'll have closed it off.'

She strode past him, though she could hear David apologizing. She was in the little wood now. There were autumn leaves underfoot. Still she could not see the water or the riverside path.

A very few minutes of swift walking brought her through a wicket gate and out on to the bank. The River Dart was wider here than she had expected. A moorhen scurried among overhanging branches. There was a narrow footpath along the edge in either direction.

Hilary stopped, as the other two caught up with her.

'Which way?' she asked.

'I can hear voices,' Veronica said, turning left, upstream.

'And there are a lot more footprints going that way.' David was examining the muddy path. 'CID won't be too pleased with us. There might have been clues, but the damage is already done.'

They turned that way at the water's edge, trying to keep away from the footprints. The earth underfoot was puddled with rain. Hilary's court shoes were not coping well.

There were trees and bushes on either side of the path, obscuring their view. They rounded a bend and the foliage opened out to reveal a wider stretch of river. There seemed to be a crowd of people bent over something. Uniforms. Green for the paramedics, black for the police. A small, solitary figure stood beside them: Lin Bell.

'Are you sure you want to see this?' David said at Hilary's elbow. 'You won't be able to do any good.'

She did not answer. She hardly knew herself what was driving her. Guilt? She had almost convinced herself that it was Jo, not Gavin, who had killed Melissa. Jo, the athletic one, running through the grounds in the early morning. Jo, who might well have brought a tracksuit with her. Jo, with that sharp intelligence and determination behind those dark-rimmed glasses. Yet now Jo was the victim.

A policewoman was beginning to stake out the area with plastic tape saying: *Police. Do not cross.* But Hilary's eyes were going beyond it. What was happening in that huddle of figures bent over something on the riverside path?

As they watched, a steam train pulling cream-and-brown coaches chugged its way incongruously along the opposite bank. Holidaymakers were leaning from the windows, pointing in excitement across the water.

David went forward to the tape. 'I'm a doctor. Can I help?'

The police officer straightened up. 'The ambulance crew's with her now, sir. They've given her emergency first aid. I think they want to get her to hospital as soon as they can.'

'She's still alive then?' Hilary burst out.

The policewoman's eyes went to her shrewdly. 'Why? What do you know about this? Name?'

'Hilary Masters. I heard Jo Walters had been attacked. I'm on the course with her, at Morland Abbey.'

'Guvnor!' the woman called.

An older sergeant came striding out of the wet bushes. Had he been searching for something there?

'More of them, Sarge.' The policewoman indicated Hilary, David and Veronica. 'From the same lot as that woman who found her.'

'Lin Bell, yes.' Hilary looked ahead at the little elderly woman with the knapsack. Was it just coincidence that she had been walking along the path at the same time as the more athletic Jo? *Found her* did not suggest that the two of them had gone for a walk together.

'Is Jo's husband here?' she asked.

'We're the ones who ask the questions,' the sergeant interrupted.

But Hilary's eyes already told her that there was only one other person in civilian dress in that attendant group beside the victim. The lean figure of DI Foulks.

There was sudden movement now. The paramedics were lifting a stretcher. Two police officers lent a hand. The little procession began to retrace their steps beside the tranquil water, heading for the path which led up to the meadow. The policewoman lifted the tape aside to allow them through. David, Hilary and Veronica pressed back among the foliage. Hilary felt a bramble snag her tights.

The first thing she looked for as the stretcher party passed them brought an overwhelming relief. The bandaged head was not covered with the blanket. Jo was still alive.

Hilary did not have long to savour that moment of relief. Another figure came into view, emerging swiftly from the screening trees further upstream. He was studying the ground around him, even peering over into the water. It was the shorter, sturdier form of Detective Sergeant Blunt. He joined his inspector and seemed to be reporting something.

The inspector looked up to where the stretcher party was still making its way towards the field path and the ambulance. He visibly stiffened as he saw, between the green uniforms of paramedics and the black of police, the civilian clothes of Hilary, Veronica and David. Hilary's insides knotted as he quickened his pace and strode along the muddy, leaf-strewn path towards them. But David, at least, had a very good reason to be here, didn't he?

Foulks towered over her. 'You again! How many times do I need to tell you that this a police matter? We do not need your well-intentioned help.' His eyes swivelled to David. 'I don't believe I've interviewed you yet, have I? You're not on the course.'

David put out a hand, which the inspector ignored. 'David Masters. *Doctor* Masters. Husband of the lady who appears to be causing you so much aggro. I know the feeling.' His lips twitched in a half-smile.

Hilary's back stiffened, in an attempt to regain her dignity. 'What did you expect me to do? Emergency vehicles go screeching past us, and then come to a halt. We've already had one murder and an attempted one. Did you not expect us to be the least little bit curious? Apprehensive even? And not without reason by the look of it. How bad is Jo? There was blood on that head dressing.'

DS Blunt intervened. 'We could have done without three more people adding their footprints to the unholy mess we have here already. We've given clear instructions for everyone from Gavin

Standforth's course to assemble in Lady Jane's Chamber this afternoon. Yes, I know you're all hoping to get away soon, but this is going to mean another round of questioning.'

'Yes, of course,' Veronica said, in her gentle, reasonable tones. 'We understand. I'm sorry if we're being a nuisance. We did try to keep away from the footprints.'

'We're not the only ones who were out this morning and missed your orders,' Hilary countered. She decided she would conveniently ignore the fact that the rest of the group had told her about them. 'And besides, Ceri was in church with us. She was scheduled to have Sunday lunch with the rest of us here, but under the circumstances, will she come back to the abbey? She's not living in.'

'She knows very well that we want her to stay until this afternoon,' Blunt pointed out.

'And then there's poor Harry,' Veronica said. 'He was already in tears this morning. What will he be like when he learns about this? Poor man!'

Hilary could not miss the sudden alertness of Inspector Foulks. 'Harry Walters was upset, you say? When was this?'

'At the parish church this morning,' Veronica told him. 'St Mary's in Totnes. We went to speak to him afterwards and . . . well, the tears were rolling down his cheeks.'

'What time was the service?'

'Sung Eucharist at eleven fifteen.'

'So, while his wife was lying injured on the footpath,' David mused. 'Inspector, do you have any estimate yet of the time she was attacked? No, silly.' He threw up his hands. 'You wouldn't tell me, even if you knew. You must forgive a medical man's natural curiosity.'

'You can't suspect *Harry*!' Veronica exclaimed. 'He doted on Jo. The tears were because of what happened to Melissa. He and Jo were in the Snake group. Melissa was their leader. He knew her better than we did. He said she'd been kind to him. He'd come to pray for her, and her family. For Gavin. And then I suppose it all got too much for him. He seems a kind-hearted soul.'

'I'll still want to talk to him. To all of you.' The inspector had recovered his impassive calm. The canine features were sharp and watchful again. He was giving nothing more away.

Hilary's mind struggled with the tangle of events. What could the attack on Jo possibly have to do with what had happened, first to Dinah Halsgrove and then to Melissa?

An involuntary shudder ran through Hilary. All of a sudden, she wanted nothing more than to be back in the medieval Chapter House of Morland Abbey, enjoying the chef's no doubt excellent Sunday lunch. Comfort food.

This was the third and final day of Gavin's course. This afternoon, he should have been bringing together setting, character and plot, and sending them home eager to write it up as a novel. Instead they'd had one violent death, two near fatalities. It was a long time since it had seemed amusing that they had come here to learn about writing crime novels. Would any of them finish their stories now? The murderer among them might have killed more than flesh and blood.

She thought of Tania and Rob's early theory that Dinah Halsgrove's collapse might be nothing more than a publicity-grabbing hoax.

It had gone far beyond that possibility.

'OK, folks,' David said. He was looking along the path to where police officers were still busy on the river bank. The spot where Jo had fallen was now screened by a white tent. 'It's clear we're not wanted here. They'll be going over the area with a fine-tooth comb, looking for evidence. We're only muddying the water. Let's get back to the abbey and see if we can work up an appetite for lunch.' He turned back to the inspector. 'You won't have me on your list of writers. I only arrived yesterday evening. Though I did have a run-in with one of your men last night. But you'll know about that already. If you think there's anything to be gained by questioning me, I'll be glad to make myself available.'

'Thank you, sir,' Inspector Foulks said stiffly. 'I may need to take you up on that. You seem to have forgotten the reason for that "run-in", as you call it. My officer found you and your lady wife returning from the Lady Chapel to the East Cloister late last night.'

Hilary turned to her husband. His mouth had fallen open. Could the inspector really think there was anything suspicious about the story of the two of them following that torch to the chapel?

* * *

The three of them walked slowly up the grassy slope towards the abbey. Sheep munched their way incuriously across the hillside. No one had much to say. Hilary led the way through the archway that gave that iconic view of the cloister garth and the Great Barn opposite the Chapter House. She stopped dead. There, in front of that stunning backdrop, a large wedding party was posing for photographs.

The incongruity of this scene of hope and happiness, in the midst of all the dark and dreadful things that had been happening, silenced her normally ready tongue.

Veronica caught her up. 'Doesn't the bride look ravishing? Mind you, she must be getting goose bumps in that strapless dress, but still . . .'

'Do you think we can tiptoe round them?' David asked. 'I need the bar before lunch.'

They threaded their way around the cobbled courtyard, until they could reach the outdoor tables of the Chapter House's beer garden. Hilary subsided on to a seat and waited for David to return with a pint of local beer for himself and glasses of sherry for her and Veronica. Some of the others from the course were there, but the mood was subdued. Ben raised a half-hearted glass to them. The mocking laughter had gone from Jake's face. No one could pretend any longer this was a joke.

'Well,' Hilary said, as the golden liquid warmed her. 'What do we think of *this*?'

'Why would anyone want to attack Jo?' Veronica asked. 'And what could she possibly have to do with Dinah Halsgrove going into a coma? Still less murdering Melissa.'

David twisted his tankard in his hands. 'I've been thinking about that. It bothers me. Yes, it's quite possible to go into a coma if you overdose on diabetes medication. But from all accounts, your novelist was a very intelligent woman who knew about multiple ways to poison people. It seems highly unlikely that she would do it by accident, and it's hardly the method you would choose for a suicide. But if someone else administered the drugs to her, it would be a chancy thing to judge the effective dose. You said she joked that she was rattling with tablets.' He glanced at Hilary for confirmation, and she nodded. 'From what I remember of the standard medication, those tablets wouldn't readily dissolve in water. I'd expect a woman as bright as her to notice something wrong.'

Hilary frowned. 'Once they'd given the kitchen a clean bill of health, we thought it must have been Theresa. Apparently, she was the one who took the tray from the waiter in Dinah Halsgrove's room. She was the only one who had the opportunity.'

'Dinah had a cup of tea in the garden with us,' Veronica reflected. 'But she refused the cake.'

'Hard to see how anyone could slip her a serious dose of non-soluble tablets between collecting a cup from the tea urn and giving it to her, let alone persuade her to drink it.'

'It was Gavin who brought her the tea,' Veronica recalled.

'And there was no other opportunity, between the tea and the supper tray?' David asked.

The other two sat silent.

'There was a jug of water on the table in the Great Barn when she gave her talk,' Veronica ventured. 'But powdered tablets would show up in that, wouldn't they?'

'If she took the trouble to look,' Hilary ventured. 'If it was me, I might have been so caught up in what I was going to say that I might not notice.'

She sat in silence, pondering this scenario. Suddenly she brought her fist down on the table with a thump. She felt a quiver of excitement run through her. 'There *was* something else. I was standing in the book room afterwards, wondering whether it was worth queuing up for her signature, when Melissa pushed past me. She seemed to be acting as Dinah's minder from the time she picked her up at the station. While Dinah was signing books after her talk, Melissa gave her what looked very much like a glass of whisky.'

David's head went up. 'A strong enough taste to disguise the flavour. A situation where she was under pressure from people to answer questions and sign their books. She just might not have noticed . . . But . . . well, I'd have expected some of the residue to remain at the bottom of the glass. It's a highly imprecise way of ensuring that she took the necessary overdose.'

'And how would Melissa have known what the necessary overdose was?'

'Necessary for what? To kill her? Or something less than that?'

No one would ever be able to ask Melissa now.

'We're assuming it *was* Melissa,' Hilary said into the pause which followed. 'Only Melissa's dead.'

'And it makes sense to assume that both attacks – and now the one on Jo this morning – are all part of the same plot. That certainly rules Melissa out.'

They sat in the thin sunshine, hearing the sounds of merriment from the wedding party outside the Great Barn.

'Unless . . .' Veronica said after a long interval. 'Do you remember *The Name of the Rose*?'

'Yes, but what's that got to do with anything?'

'What I've always loved about that book is that there are a string of bizarre murders conducted in this labyrinthine monastery up in the mountains, and we're desperately trying to think who could be behind them all. The answer is . . . no one. Every murder is committed by a different person for a different reason.'

Hilary and David stared at her.

'You mean,' David began, 'it doesn't have to be the same person who poisoned Dinah Halsgrove, killed Melissa Standforth and bludgeoned Jo Walters this morning? We could be looking for three different people?'

'Or two,' Hilary corrected him. 'It's possible there's a connection between two of them, but not the other one.'

They sat back, looking out over the grassy slopes of the grounds, thinking through the implications.

Hilary broke into their thoughts. 'I always did have my suspicions that Melissa was behind what happened to Dinah Halsgrove. For a while, it seemed unlikely, because she was on the boat with us and it was Theresa who stayed behind to look after our distinguished guest and give her supper, but I've not got over that time I met her in the corridor just before Dinah Halsgrove's talk. I could swear she was on her way to do something and was angry to run into me. She thought we were all safely in the Great Barn.' In spite of the sunshine Hilary felt a small shudder. 'I did have a theory that she might have been on her way to steal some tablets from Dinah Halsgrove's room. Only then, of course, I thought it couldn't be her, because she was dead. I didn't stop to think that her killer might not have been the same person as the poisoner. Well, it seemed logical. Two murderers, or would-be murderers, loose in the same place on the same weekend. But as you say, it could happen.'

'I was scared to death by the conversation I overheard,' Veronica leaned forward, 'between Gavin and Theresa. I thought it meant that they had something against Dinah and that's why they tried to arrange her death. But what if . . .'

'It was Melissa they were angry with?' David finished for her. 'They may have felt sure she was at the back of that. And from what you've said, it sounds as though her mental balance was not all that it might have been.'

'Angry enough to murder her?' Hilary's voice was still sceptical.

'We don't know enough about Jo, though,' Veronica reflected. 'There *might* be something that links her to Dinah Halsgrove or to Melissa.'

'There was one thing,' Hilary recollected after a pause. 'At Dinah Halsgrove's talk, I forgot my badge and had to go back for it before they would let me in. I didn't know you were saving a seat for me at the front, so I ended up in the gallery. And guess who I was sitting next to? Jo. I did rather idly ask her why she was up there, and not at the front with the rest of you. Thought perhaps she'd gone to the loo or something. But I thought at the time she wasn't telling me the truth. What if *she* was the one stealing Dinah's medicine, while everyone else was in the Great Barn?'

'I don't buy it,' David put in. 'We've more or less decided that it would have to be Melissa doctoring the whisky. But what about the teenager in the hoodie you were telling me about? The one you say a witness saw near the Leechwells around the time of Melissa's death? I met Jo Walters out running before breakfast this morning. She has that sort of lean figure that could be mistaken for a teenage boy, given the right clothing. *That* could be her.'

'Jo murdered Melissa?' Veronica exclaimed. 'What possible reason could she have?'

'There was something else I don't think I've told you,' Hilary reflected. 'There *was* something strange between Melissa and Jo. Yesterday morning, when we met in our groups for the first time, I caught Melissa looking agitated. She was saying something to

Gavin and looking at her Snake group. I couldn't see just what it was who had upset her. But it might have been Jo, mightn't it? Could the two of them have met before?'

David shrugged. 'I know no more than you do. I'm just following up your idea. There may or may not be a connecting thread between all three attacks. Not necessarily the same person, but a chain reaction. One person does something that brings down anger on them, and then so on.'

Hilary looked at her watch. 'Lunch! There are good smells coming from the kitchen. And come this afternoon, we should all be free to go home, whether the inspector's solved his case or not.'

'Solved his three cases,' David pointed out. 'Have you noticed, they don't seem to have called in another investigating officer to take over the attempt to kill Jo? The police appear to be assuming they're all part of the same story.'

TWENTY-FOUR

They moved indoors to the high-raftered bar-cum-dining room. All the long tables where Hilary and Veronica usually ate were taken. The three of them found a smaller one that seated four. A young man was already there on his own. Black hair was swept back from his forehead to fall just below his shoulders. Although alone in a communal setting, he had an air of self-containment.

'Do you mind if we join you?' David asked.

'Go ahead.'

As Hilary seated herself she looked around at the setting with a feeling of regret. Part of her longed to be away from here, with all its recent tragedy, and safely home. And yet she was filled with longing for the weekend it should have been in this evocative place. She looked around her, feeling she must imprint all this on her memory. The two colossal alcoves which had held the cooking fires for the Great Barn after the Reformation. The lofty windows in their deep embrasures high above her head.

She had to crane her neck to look up to the immensely high rafters which followed the pitch of the roof outside. And here she was, awaiting lunch in a space which would once have been bustling with cooks, potboys, scullery maids and serving men in Tudor times. Would she ever feel able to return here after this? It felt like a loss of a precious innocence.

She came back to the present as a surge of whispering ran round the tables, and then a profound hush. She looked behind her. Gavin was walking across the room, followed by Theresa.

He looked white and strained.

Jake rose from one of the long tables to offer him a seat. Gavin shook his head, with a pale attempt at a smile.

He paused, looking around at them all, as if not entirely sure what they were doing here. When he spoke, his voice was hoarse.

'I'm sorry about all this. It's not how I intended it to be.'

There were awkward murmurs of sympathy. Nobody knew just what to say.

Gavin turned away. He and Theresa took seats at another of the smaller tables.

'He doesn't somehow look like a killer,' Veronica said quietly. 'Just profoundly shocked.'

When the conversation in the dining hall had resumed, David turned to the young man beside him. 'Are you on the writing course too? Do you know these ladies?' He made the introductions.

'George,' said their companion, putting out a hand. 'Yes, I'm into crime too.'

Hilary studied him. She had only a vague recollection of seeing him at their sessions, but then, there were nearly thirty of them, and the programme had not run as planned.

'Which group were you in?' she asked.

'Snake,' he said. The smile dropped from his face. 'Bad business. Melissa. And now Jo.'

'She and Harry were in your group, weren't they?' Veronica said.

'Yes.' There was something about the shortness of his answer which aroused Hilary's curiosity.

'Did she . . .?' She must feel her way carefully. 'Did Jo get on with Melissa?' She was not sure herself just what she meant. Why had there been that abruptness in the young man's voice?

His dark eyebrows came together. 'Now why would you ask that?'

'I'm not sure.' She was reprieved by the arrival of the young, slim-hipped waiter with their soup. When he had gone she found that George was still looking at her expectantly. 'Just something in your tone of voice,' she confessed.

George looked down for a moment, absently crumbling a piece of bread in his fingers. Then he sighed.

'I don't know myself whether it's relevant or not. The first session, when we met in groups after we'd come back from choosing our settings, we went round the circle introducing ourselves. When it came to Jo, Melissa said, "We've met before. You were on Gavin's writing course in Salisbury, weren't you?" But Jo came back at her like a crack of gunfire. "No!" And Melissa looked sort of flustered. "Sorry. I could have sworn it was you," she said. "I know it was four years ago. And your hair colour was different then. But . . ." Then she just carried on to the next person and it passed over. Only she kept looking back at Jo. But I've asked myself ever since. *Did* Jo know Gavin and Melissa? And if so, why would she want to deny it?'

They finished their soup in silence. Hilary could feel her companions' minds racing, as hers was. It had seemed hard to imagine why anyone in this random group of would-be writers, meeting their leaders for the first time, should want to murder one of them. But there had certainly been that moment of alarm she had observed between Gavin and Melissa. If Jo already knew them, and had been dismayed that Gavin's wife recognized her, then . . . But her sharp mind refused to take her any further.

'Did you tell the inspector this?' David asked, when the soup bowls had been removed.

'Of course. I'm not an idiot.'

'And?'

'He'll have stored it away in that canny brain of his, but he's obviously not letting us in on what he thinks.'

'But now Jo herself has been attacked. A blow to the head that could have killed her,' Hilary reflected. 'If she *did* kill Melissa – and I can't imagine any reason why she should, even if they had met before – then could what happened this morning be Gavin taking revenge?'

'For what?' David asked.

'And if he suspected her of lying, why not just report what he knew to DI Foulks?' Veronica asked.

Hilary eyed the plate of roast beef that had been set in front of her with more enthusiasm than she had anticipated. She was feeling a little more like her normal self. It was a relief to get her brain working again, instead of that sense of helpless bewilderment.

David was saying, 'Unless there is something about all this that Gavin doesn't want to tell the police?'

'You mean, whatever it was that made Jo angry enough to kill Melissa?' George asked. 'Just supposing for the moment that she did.'

'You did say that the supposed teenager in the hoodie could have been Jo,' Veronica reminded David. 'That at least makes some sort of sense.'

'But what could that have to do with whatever happened at Salisbury – if anything did?' Hilary finished. 'And since none of the rest of us were there, how can we possibly know?'

'We could ask Harry.'

'He's not here.'

'Probably at the hospital.'

'But they may not have been married then. Otherwise, why didn't Gavin and Melissa recognize her name?'

The speculation petered out. Hilary bent her mind to savouring her Sunday roast.

'You know,' said Veronica later, as the raspberry pavlova arrived, 'Jo was – is – very clever. What if she'd worked out who killed Melissa, and that person found out?'

Hilary could not resist turning round. Gavin and Theresa were sitting on their own at the next table.

A shudder went down her spine. Two people eating in silence. It was scary not knowing if the folk you were sharing lunch with were guilty of murder.

George pushed his hair back and wiped his lips with his napkin. His chair legs scraped on the wooden floor.

Hilary started. Her mind had been so busy running over their speculations that she had forgotten there were four of them at the table, not three. Her mind raked over what they had talked about. Had she given away anything she should not have? And did she have a right to keep knowledge to herself?

Her heart sank as she realized that they had indeed recalled that seemingly incriminating conversation between Gavin and Theresa yesterday morning. She was fairly sure they had not said anything explicit about its content, but it would be enough to identify Veronica as a key witness.

Or was she? What those two at the next table had said in the tiltyard had been in the hands of the police for nearly twenty-four hours. If Veronica's testimony threatened them, the damage was already done. And even if it were not, it should have been Gavin and Theresa she was anxious about overhearing talk about it, not George.

A sudden memory made her sag with relief. Surely, the three of them had been on the outside table, drinking beer and sherry, when they talked about that sinister conversation, not here in the dining room with George.

George, from the Snake group. Since the waiter had brought them dessert, their fellow conspirator had lapsed into silence, a quiet, listening presence. What else had they said? It was like the discovery that you are in the presence of an adder. Not a sudden movement on its part, but a sharp realization that you have been at close quarters with a poisonous snake, unknowing.

She looked with alarm at the youngish man with the back-swept hair. He stood arrested in the act of leaving them. His dark eyes teased her now.

'I seem to remember you were the one who read the riot act to Ben and Jake because they proposed a brainstorming session, wanting to toss over theories about what's going on. And here you are, the three of you, falling over yourselves to swap possible scenarios for murder and poisoning. A little hypocritical, don't you think?'

Hilary felt her cheeks warm. 'It's only natural. We've been rather more closely involved than the rest of you. It's not the same as sitting down cold-bloodedly to construct possible plots, as if this were just another crime novel.'

'Isn't it? You'd have to plan a real crime that way, wouldn't you?'

Veronica leaped in to rescue Hilary. She gave George a disarming smile, part motherly, and just a little flirtatious. 'Were you there this morning in Lady Jane's Chamber? How did it go? I heard you were short of numbers.'

'Less than a dozen of us. And not Jo. It's a scary feeling. She might already have been . . .'

'I know. Poor Harry was at church with us. Really upset.'

'How do you mean, *upset*? Wouldn't that have been before Lin found Jo with her skull stove in?'

'In tears, poor man. And no, it couldn't have been about Jo. He was crying because of Melissa.'

'So, did you discount the idea that it was Rob? You knew by then that he was at the police station. Have you come up with any astounding theories that the finest minds of CID haven't thought of?' Hilary asked crisply, wanting to restore something of her dignity.

'Not really.' A rueful grin. 'All sorts of ideas. Gavin's jealous of Dinah Halsgrove's success, since he can't seem to write more than one good book. Sends her into a near-death coma. Theresa's got a thing about Gavin, so she bumps off Melissa. No, nothing that's halfway plausible. We gave up after less than an hour. Lin said she was going for a walk by the river to clear her head. She said she thinks better on her feet. She'd remembered Jo asking Ben about the riverside path. Apparently he and Jake were down there yesterday afternoon.'

'So your brainstorming group already knew that Jo might be going there?'

'I . . . suppose . . . so.' George stopped, as though the idea had only just occurred to him.

'Including Rob.'

'I hadn't thought of that.'

'Well, it's not the sort of place where anyone who wanted to do her in was likely to come upon her by accident,' Hilary pointed out.

'I guess not. At least . . . well, Lin obviously did. She's that straight-backed little lady over there. Must be in her seventies.'

'We know her. She's in our Toad group. So, she asks about the path where she knows Jo might be running and takes a walk there.'

'You surely can't be suggesting . . .'

The three of them followed his eyes to the long table where Lin sat at the end, finishing her dessert. A small, self-contained figure, who said little to the people around her.

'Doesn't seem likely, does it?' said George. 'A woman her age, getting the better of an athletic type like Jo.'

'Unless she had the advantage of surprise,' David put in. 'From what I could see, there are plenty of trees along that path. Easy enough to lie in wait behind one, and deal her a blow with a hefty branch as she runs past.'

'But why?'

The question silenced all of them.

'And didn't you say Jo must already have been attacked, since she didn't make it to your meeting?' Hilary put in.

'So you think Lin only pretended to find her by accident?' Veronica asked.

'Did she think it would make her look more innocent?'

Hilary thought back to the artist's impression of the unidentified figure in a tracksuit. It had come to her with a sudden revelation this morning that Lin, as well as Jo, had the slender build and modest height that could have passed for a teenage boy in a hooded top.

But common sense took over. Why would a woman of Lin Bell's age be bringing a tracksuit to a crime-writing weekend? Unless she had reason to know that Jo would be there, and had planned it all beforehand. She shook her head. It was too like a closely plotted crime novel, as George had said.

'We ought to keep our voices down,' Veronica said, suitably low. 'Gavin and Theresa are watching us.'

The two leaders, sitting at the table only a little distance away, had indeed turned, as if to wonder what George could suddenly have to discuss that was of such importance that it detained him in the act of leaving the room.

As she watched, a waiter passed between their tables. It was the much younger one, in tight-fitting black shirt and trousers, with a long grey apron wrapped round his narrow hips.

She remembered again seeing him on other occasions, carrying trays from the kitchen. Had she dismissed too easily that passing idea that he would have had the opportunity to doctor Dinah Halsgrove's supper with ground-up tablets? She pictured him now, carrying that tray around the paths skirting the lawn from the Chapter House kitchen to the East Cloister.

She studied his back view with renewed interest. That same slender build again. Could he . . .?

But the question came back, like that about Lin. *Why* would he? And were the next two crimes connected to the first?

Was it possible this had something to do with Morland Abbey, not the writers' course? Could he have been in league with Fiona? Fiona, who had been on duty on the night of Halsgrove's collapse. Fiona, who had the key to the chapel?

Hilary shook her head, trying to clear her thoughts. 'Nothing about this makes sense. You think you're on to something, then another thing happens and all your theories are out of the window. Coffee?' She turned to David.

He looked at his watch. 'Half an hour before the detective inspector wants to meet you for the final time. Meet *us*, I suppose I should say. I'd better be there. He has a rather suspicious view of my activities around the chapel last night.'

'*What* activities?' George was suddenly alert, all thoughts of leaving gone.

'Long story.' David got to his feet unhelpfully. 'How about if we leave these upright chairs and make for the sofas in the Gatehouse for our coffee? I need to go to the loo first. I'll see you there.'

'What's this about the chapel?' George demanded as David left.

Hilary led him away from Gavin and Theresa towards the door to the courtyard. 'Hush. I'm not sure this is something we should make public knowledge. The police know about it, but I doubt if other people do.'

'Come on, now! You can't hold out on the rest of us. Something happened at the Lady Chapel last night?'

'Something and nothing. My lips are sealed.'

'Bollocks!' George stared at the two of them angrily, then he strode ahead of them out of the Chapter House.

TWENTY-FIVE

Hilary and Veronica came out on to the courtyard which looked more disconsolate than before. A few fallen petals were all that remained to show where the laughing wedding party had posed on the steps to the Great Barn. The first fat drops of rain flattened them against the cobbles.

There were lights on in the Great Barn, though it was only early afternoon.

'Hmmph!' said Hilary. 'We were lucky to get a good Sunday lunch, if they've got all those to feed as well.'

'I'm sure the kitchen are used to it. And what a romantic setting to get married!'

'In the midst of life we are in death, didn't you say? It's a good job they don't know what else has been going on here this weekend. It would rather have taken the shine off the happy couple's day.'

'They must have wondered, though.' Veronica nodded across the lawn to the entrance arch, where two uniformed police officers stood under its shelter. 'I don't fancy they're just standing there to keep out of the rain. We're under guard.'

'I hope you're not suggesting there's going to be another attempted murder. And talking of rain, we'd better get a move on, or we'll be soaked before we get to the Gatehouse.' As she spoke, Hilary set off for the archway at a brisk pace.

'I see David's remembered where to find the loos.'

On the far side of the entrance, David's tall form was visible going up the short side path between the lavender bushes on the left. To the right, steps led down to the Gatehouse Café.

'Did you know this used to be a roundhouse? They don't have to be round. It's where a horse walked round in a circle, turning a wheel.'

'Yes, Hilary.' Something in Veronica's voice made Hilary turn to examine her friend's face. Veronica's expression was studiously blank. She reminded Hilary of one of her too-innocent pupils.

'I like to *know* things,' Hilary burst out in self-defence. 'I know you think I'm an incurable school-marm. I can't help it.'

'Just like you have to know who put the overdose in Dinah Halsgrove's food or drink. Who murdered Melissa. And now who has had a go at killing Jo. And why. George was right about you. However much you pour scorn on the brainstorming group, you want to find the answer as much as they do.'

'Did you expect me to switch off my brain, just because the local constabulary shows up? Talking of which, who's that under the arch with the representatives of the law?'

'It's Harry!'

Hilary quickened her pace. Veronica kept up with her. Now she could see that there were, not two figures, but three in the shadow of the entrance arch. Two tall and uniformed. The other shorter, rounder. Clouds were darkening the early afternoon and the rain was falling harder. It was with relief that the two women reached shelter.

There were no tears on Harry Walters' cheeks now. He had reached refuge before the rain could wet his face. But he seemed to be responding monosyllabically to the policemen questioning him. Sorrow had pulled down the lines of his usually cheerful countenance.

It occurred to Hilary suddenly that Harry could have come back to Morland from Totnes in all innocence, the only one of them not to know that his wife was lying in hospital, very possibly with a brain injury.

Jo. That bright, sharp intelligence. The determined would-be crime writer, who had struck Hilary as the one among them most likely to succeed. How life-changing might that attack be?

'Have you told him? Can we be of help?'

The larger of the officers, whose chevrons pronounced him a sergeant, swung round. 'I'm afraid this gentleman seems a bit knocked out by the news. We didn't know he was the husband until he showed up, or we'd have handled things a bit more delicately. I think he could do with a good strong cuppa.'

'Leave it to us. This way, Harry.'

The light of recognition lit Harry's mournful features for a moment. 'I want to go to the hospital. But this officer phoned through for me. They won't let me see her yet. They say she's in surgery.' He sounded desolate.

All sorts of thoughts raced through Hilary's mind. When Jo came round – if she *did* come round – would she remember who had struck her down? Had she even seen her assailant? She thought of David's theory, that someone could have stood behind a tree, down there by the river, armed with a heavy branch. Even someone as slight as the diminutive Lin Bell.

They led Harry through a side door under the arch and down the steps to the Gatehouse Café. A massive beam spanned the room, from one white-painted stone wall to the other. The building projected into the garden. Rain darkened the wood of the outside tables.

'You're right,' Veronica observed, looking around. 'It's not round at all. It's a hexagon.'

But Hilary stopped short on the point of lowering herself on to a sofa. She was suddenly aware that Tania and Rob were coming forward, their faces creased with sympathy.

Hastily Hilary tried to rearrange her face to hide her surprise that Rob was not under arrest. She was aware of Tania's hostile stare. She evidently hadn't been successful.

It occurred to her that the police might have released Rob, but that didn't necessarily mean they'd cleared him.

'Harry! We're so sorry!' Tania gushed. 'What a terrible thing to happen. And on top of everything else.'

'How is she?' asked Rob.

Harry shook his head. He looked bewildered. 'She's in surgery. That's all they'll tell me. They even told me to stay away from the hospital. Said there was nothing I could do until she comes round.'

The tears had started to roll down his plump cheeks again.

Veronica guided him to the settee facing Tania and Rob. 'Sit down. Tea or coffee?'

He shook his head once more, as though the choice was too overwhelming for him.

'Tea, then. With plenty of sugar.' She went to the counter and ordered tea for Harry and coffee for themselves.

Hilary subsided into the seat next to Harry. 'I used to love the old sagging sofas here, knee-deep in newspapers. Hmm. I suppose these are tolerably comfortable,' she admitted, then felt a spasm of conscience for the inappropriateness of the thought.

A silence fell over the group. Hilary found it difficult to know what to say to Harry. She studied Rob's bespectacled face instead, but could read nothing there.

Once the first rush of sympathy had subsided, Tania and Rob seemed to have run out of words too. They were the ones, Hilary remembered, who had begun by treating the events of the weekend as a source of hilarity. They had joked that Dinah Halsgrove's sudden illness was all part of a deliberate hoax, dreamed up by Gavin for publicity purposes. The unfolding tragedies had gone far beyond that, and left them stranded in isolation where the tide of violence had cut them off.

Where could Rob fit into this? And was Tania involved? Or was she taken as much by surprise as the rest of them?

Other people, not all of them associated with the course, looked across at the group around Harry with open curiosity. Hilary thought she recognized three from Gavin's Slowworm group. They were evidently listening to Harry's replies, yet they made no move to offer condolences. Veronica came to join them, carefully carrying a loaded tray.

'I got a coffee for David. He takes it black, doesn't he? He should be here in a moment.'

She poured three spoonfuls of sugar into Harry's cup. 'I don't know how you usually like it, but you need it good and sweet now.'

Harry gulped at it, spluttered, and set the cup down shakily. 'Hot,' he mumbled, by way of excuse.

'So it should be.'

Veronica pulled up one of the wooden chairs for herself. The rain continued to fall outside the windows, closing them in.

There were footsteps on the stairs down from the gateway. Hilary brightened, anticipating David's return.

She was wrong. A pair of long grey-clad legs appeared, then the rest of the rangy Detective Inspector Foulks. He stood for a moment, surveying the scene. Behind him, Hilary saw DS Blunt and a uniformed policewoman. This was the way it had begun. These same three officers in Lady Jane's Chamber on Saturday morning. Her fears and surmises had been growing. All the same, she was surprised by the reaction of shock as she thought, 'They're going to arrest Harry!'

Hadn't something inside her known the inevitability of this all along?

Yet she felt suddenly, inexplicably, protective of this tearful man, who had come to the course seemingly in such a genial, relaxed frame of mind, indulging his wife's ambition to write a successful crime novel.

But DI Foulks merely came across to the sofa where Harry sat and said in a gentler voice than usual, 'Mr Walters? I'm sorry to have to intrude at a time like this, but we need to ask some questions about your movements and your wife's.'

Harry looked up, a dazed expression in his wet eyes. 'I don't know what I can tell you.'

'Let's do this in private, shall we?'

Harry got clumsily to his feet. 'I told her not to come. I said it would only make her angry all over again. Best to leave it. But she wouldn't listen.'

'This way, sir, if you wouldn't mind.'

Harry mounted the stairs with the two detectives, the policewoman bringing up the rear.

Their departure left an awkward hush.

'What did he mean by that?' Rob broke the silence with the question in all their minds.

Hilary paused, wondering whether to speak out. She decided it was too late in the day to keep secrets.

'We had lunch with George. Long-haired lad from the Snake group. He told us Melissa said she thought she'd met Jo before. Jo vehemently denied it. But it fits in with something I saw for myself. It was when we were dividing into groups, and the leaders were getting ready to join us, I saw Melissa looking over at the Snake group. She seemed really upset. She said something to Gavin and he looked where she was pointing. I couldn't see who it was they were looking at, but I think it came as a bit of shock to Gavin too. From what George says, I can only imagine that was Jo.'

Tania objected, 'That doesn't make sense. If they already knew Jo, they'd have picked up her name on the list of applicants, wouldn't they?'

A thoughtful pause.

'Not if Theresa handled the forms,' Rob suggested.

'And not if Jo wasn't married to Harry then,' Veronica said. They turned to her. Her cheeks grew pink.

Where mine would have been an uncomfortable red, Hilary told herself.

She rallied. 'Jo did sound a bit venomous when I drew her attention to Gavin's bestseller. Maybe there was more behind that than I thought. I assumed it was just jealousy. She really does want to make it big in crime fiction. She was not just passing a pleasant weekend in lovely surroundings, like us.'

'Speak for yourself. I wouldn't mind getting my hands on Ian Rankin's sort of income myself,' Rob put in.

They sat in thought. Hilary watched the rain bouncing off the wooden tables outside.

It was Veronica who turned her head to look back at the stairs to the entrance arch.

'What's happened to David? His coffee's getting cold. He should have been with us by now.'

Hilary felt a sudden anger, with herself as much as Veronica. She was David's wife. It should have been she who had noticed his absence. But her mind had been busy turning over the possibilities of Jo's previous encounter with the Standforths and how that might be connected with the attack on the eager would-be crime novelist as she ran the riverside path. Could it be, after all, not Harry, but Gavin and Melissa who were responsible?

Not Melissa, she remembered with a start. Melissa was dead.

Veronica's question pulled her back to the here and now. She looked around the café, as though expecting her husband to materialize. David should have been here now. It was only a short step across from the toilet block to the café entrance.

She turned to look at the stairs again, though she knew there would be nothing to see.

His mug of coffee stood forlornly on the low table in front of her, cooling.

She looked the other way. French windows led out to a picnic area. Beyond that another flight of steps led up to the drive opposite the loos. He might come that way.

The Gatehouse Café was emptying. The rain was easing. Visitors would be setting off to tour the gardens. The course members would be gathering for their final meeting.

'See you in Lady Jane's Chamber,' Tania said, as she and Rob stood up to go.

'We'll be right behind you. We'll just hang on for David.'

In a little while, there was only one couple left besides themselves. The man had a rather lean and distinguished bearing. Hilary felt sure she would have recognized him if he were on the course. Just another of the day visitors, then, here to enjoy a Sunday afternoon at the splendid Morland Abbey. Everybody else on Gavin's weekend must be in Lady Jane's Chamber in the cloister by now.

'It's two o'clock,' Veronica said.

Hilary rose. 'I'm going to see where he's got to.'

Veronica followed her up the stairs to the entrance arch. Now that the rain had stopped, the two policemen on duty were standing further apart. The broad-shouldered sergeant was patrolling the path around the inner lawn, the younger constable surveying the occasional traffic on the drive that swept downhill between the entrance and the car parks.

'I see they haven't closed the grounds to search for evidence,' Hilary observed.

'They taped off the path down by the river, where Jo was found.'

'If you'll excuse me. I'd better check that David hasn't had a heart attack in the loo.'

'Hilary! You can't just go charging into the gents.'

'Watch me.'

She strode up the narrow path to the public conveniences.

'David!'

There was that cold echo of plumbing and tiles.

A startled man in a leather jacket burst out of one of the cubicles.

'Sorry!' he exclaimed. 'I thought . . .'

'Just looking for my husband.' She forced herself to smile.

'Ah. I see . . . Want me to try the other cubicles?'

'If you would.'

But none of them was engaged. The leather-jacketed man

pushed open the doors, just in case. He shrugged. 'Sorry,' he said again, and ran the tap to wash his hands.

Hilary stood baffled. Feelings of panic were not yet rising in her gut, but she could feel them beginning to stir. Instead, her busy mind whipped through the other possibilities. David had forgotten he was supposed to be meeting them in the Gatehouse. He had gone straight to Lady Jane's Chamber. But no. It had been David's idea to decamp to the sofas in the café. She thought of the cold cup of coffee still standing on the table.

Perhaps he had met someone who had urgent information . . .

She turned abruptly back to the entrance and marched up to the sergeant. 'Have you seen my husband? He went into the toilets about . . .' She glanced at her watch. 'Twenty minutes ago. Greying hair. Going bald on top. Slight limp. Might have been talking to someone.'

'What was he wearing?'

She stared at him. Her mind froze. David was such a familiar figure, it did not occur to her to identify him by his clothes, as she might a stranger. What *had* he been wearing this morning?

Her memory jolted into gear. Of course. They'd been to church in Totnes. David was never a man for over-much formality, but he would at least have put on a jacket.

'A sports jacket, I think. Greenish sort of check. Hairy tweed. You know the sort of thing.'

The sergeant nodded. 'Seem to remember him. Went to the toilets, didn't he?'

'That's just what I said. But he hasn't come back. He was supposed to join us in the Gatehouse Café, but he never showed up.'

'Want me to check the gents for you?'

'I already have.'

'Yes,' said the sergeant, looking her up and down. 'I imagine you would.'

They stood in unhelpful silence. Raindrops dripped from the guttering. There was a faint waft of music from the wedding party in the Great Barn.

Suddenly the sergeant stiffened. 'You're from the writers' course, aren't you? I thought you were supposed to be meeting DI Foulks in Lady Jane's Chamber now. Better get a move on.'

Hilary looked over her shoulder. Veronica, she realized, was having the same sort of conversation with the younger constable on the outer side of the archway. She came towards Hilary now, shaking her head. A frown of worry creased her usually smooth forehead.

'No luck, I'm afraid. Our friend's been keeping an eye on the comings and goings along the drive. Though he did admit to taking a break under the arch here when the rain was heaviest. No sign of David, I'm afraid.'

Hilary came near to stamping her foot. 'This is ridiculous. He can't just have vanished.'

'There's one place he could be. Where we should be now. Though you'd have thought at least one of them would have seen him crossing the courtyard.'

Even as they skirted the wet lawn, Hilary had a sinking certainty that David would not be in Lady Jane's Chamber waiting for them.

TWENTY-SIX

T he sounds of music and laughter from the wedding party in the Great Barn swept across the courtyard towards them. There could not be a greater contrast, Hilary thought, between that joy and hope for the future and the story of murder and hatred that was playing out so close to it.

Common sense was telling her agitated mind that David could not be in danger. He had played no part in the violence of the weekend. He had overheard nothing, he had found no corpse. If anything, it was she and Veronica who should be victims – or suspects. The police had only their word for it that they had found Melissa already dead. But she was still dreadfully afraid. There was so much else about this weekend which did not make sense.

She prayed that David had not become part of that.

She and Veronica hurried up the stair to Lady Jane's Chamber. Hilary held her breath as she opened the door. It took only a

second to scan the crowd of faces that turned to them with
anxious curiosity. The one face that mattered, David's, was not
among them.

Inspector Foulks and DS Blunt stood where Gavin had
previously addressed them. These were real-life sleuths, not the
authors of fictitious crime. The DI's face, which had softened
when he spoke to Harry, was now taut with anger. Hilary strode
towards him, intent only on one thing.

His voice cut like a scalpel. 'I distinctly recall summoning
this meeting for two p.m. It is now quarter past. Is it a matter
of no importance to you that one murder has been committed
and two others attempted, and that you might be vital witnesses?'

'What you should be worrying about is not that we're late,
but that someone who should be is not here at all. I demand that
you send out a search party for my husband.'

A gasp of surprise came from the others in the room. Heads
turned to check the rows of chairs, the half-familiar faces. DS
Blunt conferred with his inspector in a low voice.

'Hilary,' said Veronica quietly behind her, 'David's not the
only one who is missing.'

Hilary turned her eyes from the inspector, but the only face
that counted with her was David's. If there were others who
should be here, she could not identify them.

The inspector's voice supplied the information her baffled mind
could not. 'Mrs Masters. Your husband was not even on the
crime-writing course. He didn't arrive until after Mrs Standforth
was murdered. Yes, there was that incident in the chapel. But
what concerns me more is that Mr Standforth is missing, and
Miss Blackall.' Hilary's mind puzzled for a moment, then
concluded the second name must be Theresa's.

'And Colonel Truscott,' Jake's voice added from the front
row.

Fear rushed back at Hilary. She had hovered between
suspecting Gavin and Theresa early on to eliminating them
from her suspicions, but what if she was wrong? What if David
had stumbled upon new evidence that pointed back to them?
Someone must have wanted to silence Jo down there on the
riverside path. Could that someone have sought to silence David
too? Was it too ludicrous to imagine that he might have heard

something in the men's toilets which he should not? But what would Theresa be doing there?

'Have you seen them?' DI Foulks was asking. 'Any of them?'

'No,' Veronica answered for both of them, her voice calmer than Hilary's had been. 'We're late because we were waiting in the Gatehouse Café for David, but he never came. Under the circumstances, we're desperately worried about him. We asked your policemen on duty in the entrance, but neither had seen him leave. Please, will you start a search?'

DI Foulks stared at her for a moment, then gave orders to the detective at his side. DS Blunt spoke into his radio.

The rest of the room was a buzz of speculation. Lin Bell, sitting close to where Hilary and Veronica stood, leaned over and caught Hilary's arm. 'We were getting concerned about you. This whole thing has been ghastly. I couldn't bear to think that something else might happen. Where did you last see your husband?'

'Going to the loos opposite the café.' The unromantic nature of her answer hurt. Was this the explanation she would have to give people for the rest of her life about the last time she saw David? The quality of their lifetime's relationship demanded something better than this.

And how sincere was Lin Bell's sympathy?

There were growing voices in the courtyard below the window, mostly male. DI Foulks strode past her to the stairs, leaving DS Blunt like a sheepdog ordered to guard the flock. Hilary hurried to the window. Uniformed police officers and a few in plain clothes, who must be detectives, were gathering in the courtyard, almost under the windows of the Great Barn. While the wedding celebrations went on, DI Foulks was organizing the search that might find what Hilary most dreaded.

Veronica was beside her again. 'I don't see where Colonel Truscott fits into all this. He seemed such a straightforward, old-school type.'

'Appearances can be deceptive. You said yourself, he seemed too true to type to be real.'

The orderly meeting was breaking up. Chairs were pushed back. Voices were rising. Hilary's eyes were drawn to the knot of people converging on the hapless DS Blunt.

A couple from the Slowworm group addressed the sergeant in loud protest.

'We've got a train to York to catch. You can't keep us here. We were told this was the final meeting.'

Blunt was obviously trying to calm them, to persuade them to wait a little longer.

'You'd think they didn't know there was a murderer loose among us. Or perhaps that's why they're in such a hurry to leave,' Hilary commented.

'I don't know. You have to sympathize. It's Sunday afternoon. For people who live in the north of England, there may not be that many more trains today.'

The mutinous crowd was falling back, some still bristling with indignation, others resigned to the delay. One last couple approached the sergeant. Tania and Rob, whom they had last seen in the Gatehouse. Tania's mouse-brown hair was damp with rain.

Hilary's attention focussed suddenly. There was a change in DS Blunt's body language. No longer was he holding up his hands to placate irate travellers. He was bending forward, his notebook out. As she watched, he reached for his radio.

Hilary forged her way across the room. Rob and Tania were just turning away. An expression almost of guilt passed over Tania's face.

'Hilary! I'm sorry. I didn't realize it was important. Or not till you came in.'

'*What* was?'

'David. We'd just left the Gatehouse Café to come to this meeting when we saw him.'

'*Where?*'

'Where you said. Coming out of the gents' loos. Only then Theresa came round the corner from the drive. She was looking really distraught.'

'Yeah,' Rob cut in. 'She grabbed him by the elbow. We were sheltering from the rain under the arch with a couple of police bods. It was too far away to hear what she was saying.'

'And then the two of them dashed off together.'

'*Which way?*' demanded Hilary.

'Sorry. I didn't see,' Tania apologized. 'Away from the cloisters.

That's all I can say. I don't know whether they turned up the hill or down, or crossed over to the car park.'

'We had no reason to follow them,' Rob said. 'With the rain coming down, we just made a dash for Lady Jane's Chamber, the other way.'

Could she trust anything Rob said?

'But we asked the policemen at the entrance,' Veronica protested. 'Both of them said they hadn't seen him after he went into the loos.'

'They wouldn't. They were further in under the arch, keeping out of the downpour. From what we saw, David and Theresa didn't turn into the quad. The loos are set back a bit. They'd have been out of the line of vision of the fuzz.'

'The sergeant's radioed his inspector,' Tania tried to comfort Hilary. 'They'll have a search party on to it. They'll find him.'

Hilary's imagination took in the route away from the abbey. The cobbled approach that led out to the drive. The car parks beyond. And somewhere past that, another of those paths that led down to the river. Where Jo had nearly died.

'I can't stand this!' she exclaimed. 'I have to see where Theresa's taken David!'

She heard the detective sergeant's shout behind her as she made for the stairs. She knew he was calling her back, but she didn't care. The buzz of the crowded room heightened in consternation. There were footsteps pounding across the floor. But she was flying down the stairs at precipitate speed.

A bizarre sight met her. More uniformed police were converging on the quadrangle, some of them at the run. They were coming, she supposed, from the further corners of the gardens and grounds. The DI was giving them urgent directions. Most made off through the entrance arch at speed.

But Hilary was not the only spectator. A few Sunday-afternoon tourists had stopped on the far side of the cloisters to gape. Some were taking photos on their phones. And down the steps of the Great Barn the wedding guests in celebratory suits and dresses were spilling out to discover what could be more exciting than the bride and groom's festive day. There was a flash of white and black as the couple themselves appeared at the head of the steps.

DI Foulks himself set off, not running but walking briskly. He was following the stream of police to the arch that led outside the cloisters.

A hand grasped Hilary's arm. 'There's nothing for you to do, ma'am. Leave it to us.'

She rounded on DS Blunt. 'Get lost!'

She glared at him, and he let go of her. With a grim look at Veronica, Hilary followed the stream of police. Outside the cloisters, the two of them paused on the drive opposite the car park. They could see uniformed figures diverging in all directions. It had a random, scattergun look. Hilary knew each officer would have precise instructions from DI Foulks about where to search, but also that the detective inspector had no more idea which was the right way to go than she had.

She and Veronica were left alone, with no clear directions.

It was Veronica who said, with an attempt at calm reasoning, 'If they'd gone straight ahead, or to the right, the policeman would have seen them, even from under the arch. They have to have turned left if they stayed out of sight.'

Hilary followed her gaze. The drive sloped upwards between outlying buildings and on round a bend. This was the way that would take them through the Morland Abbey estate and out to the village on the corner of the main road. There would be any number of possible ways a couple on foot could diverge from that route.

She started up the drive, hurrying, but with a sense of hopelessness. Why, oh why, had David not popped into the Gatehouse to tell her where he was going? What could be so urgent that he couldn't spare time for that?

She was overcome by a surge of remorse that she should feel angry with him even now. Ever since he had arrived she had experienced stabs of jealousy that he seemed more concerned about Veronica than about her. And now he himself was in danger, taking off into the blue with someone who might be a murderer, and all she could do was feel mad at him because he hadn't told her where he was going.

She redoubled her speed, panting up the incline.

'Hilary!' Veronica's voice came from surprisingly far behind.

Hilary turned. Veronica had stopped by a smaller car park, just past the end of the East Cloister. She was beckoning.

Reluctantly, Hilary trudged back downhill to join her.

There was a glow of excitement in Veronica's eyes.

'They've all gone charging off, away from the abbey. But what if they're going in the wrong direction? I can only imagine that Theresa was wanting to take David to Gavin, though I shudder to think why. Suppose he's injured. Gavin, I mean. Suppose Theresa attacked him and he needs a doctor? Anyway, whatever the reason, don't you remember where you found Gavin before?'

Hilary's mind was a blank. She had seen Gavin in so many places this weekend.

Veronica gestured behind her, to the path that led between the back of the East Cloister and the tithe barn.

'*Here*. Don't you remember? Last night I saw a torch on this path. You and David went haring along it and discovered Gavin . . .'

'In the Lady Chapel!' Hilary exclaimed. 'You think . . .?'

Without waiting for an answer, she sped off along the path.

The soaring roof of the Great Barn rose above her on her right, the Tudor chimneys of the East Cloister to her left. She glanced up at the top floor as she sped past. It was from one of those upper windows that Veronica had watched her and David, the same window Gavin had turned to look up at with such venom. She was coming in sight of the rose garden now, behind the Great Barn. The neatly raked paths and carefully tended flowerbeds, with their glowing roses, seemed at odds with the horror of the weekend.

A sudden thought made her stumble, as though she had caught her foot on a stone. Someone else had been missing from Lady Jane's Chamber. Colonel Truscott. But what could *he* have to do with David's disappearance?

Then suddenly she was out in a wilder setting. The old monks' graveyard beside the ruined abbey church. She remembered that unexpected transition from path to grass in the near darkness the previous night. Now, she saw how the path curved away to the left. In front of her, east of the slab that marked the site of the high altar, was the only part of the church that still bore a roof. The Lady Chapel was built of yellowish-grey stone. On this nearer side was a small padlocked door. But there was another door, out of sight around the further side. As she came in sight of it, the outline of an arch at the west end showed where the sanctuary had once joined it.

She nerved herself for what might be waiting for her down that short flight of steps.

TWENTY-SEVEN

Hilary was in sight of the second door now. This was the chapel that had been appropriated for the Woodleigh family's use. There were voices from within. A man's and a woman's, though she could not yet distinguish whose.

Then, overwhelming her with gladness, she heard David's.

'You can't keep this a secret.' And then in alarm, 'Colonel! This isn't helping.'

He was still alive. She would not allow herself to admit until now how much she had feared something worse.

David's voice broke off with a gasp. The door was almost closed. Hilary pushed it open and almost fell down the step.

She had to pull up short. It was a small chapel, but it seemed full of heaving people. They jostled in the narrow confines with their medieval carvings. It took her moments to sort out how many of them and who they were. David, in his tweed jacket, seemed to be struggling, with his back to her. For a moment she could not see his opponent. Even so, it was immensely reassuring to feel that prickle of cloth against her outstretched hand.

She could hear Gavin's voice, though she could not see him. He seemed to be crouched beyond David, on a red-cushioned kneeler in front of the altar.

'I didn't do it. But nobody's going to believe me.' From between the other men's legs, his voice came almost as a whine.

Theresa, glimpsed now on Hilary's right, was bending over him, her arm round his shoulder, as though she was trying to comfort him.

It was the voice on her left which startled her.

'Liar!' Colonel Truscott trumpeted. 'I don't know what this

secret is you keep blathering about. But you've made it clear it gave you a reason to murder poor Mrs Walters.'

She could see him now, wrestling to break free of David.

'Is she dead?' There was even more alarm in Gavin's question.

'For all I know, she may be by now, poor lady,' Truscott panted. 'No thanks to you if she's not. And a cad who could do that to an attractive young woman, who came here to benefit from your advice, is surely capable of killing his wife as well.'

'I didn't . . .'

'What happened? Did your good lady find out you were plotting to do away with Jo? Did you have to silence her before she told the police?'

He threw himself forward. He was a big man. David was trying to hold him back. The red-faced colonel lunged at Gavin, hands outthrust, as though he would break his neck. The two of them, Truscott and David, struggled in the confined space. On the wall beside them, the plaster figures of the be-ruffed Sir George Woodleigh, his wife and children clasped their hands in prayer. From a roof boss above, foliage spilled from the grinning mouth of a Green Man.

'Colonel Truscott!' Theresa reared up. Her short figure seemed for once to tower over her colleague protectively. 'Gavin was more devastated by Melissa's death than anyone. It's ridiculous to accuse him of murdering her.'

'Then who did?' grunted the colonel, still wrestling to get out of David's grasp. He was a powerful man. Hilary felt herself grow pale. Neither of them was a young man. David kept fit on his morning runs, but she fancied Dan Truscott might be stronger.

'I've no more idea than anyone else. Nor who tried to kill Jo.' Gavin groaned, and buried his blond head in his hands.

'You see?' Dan Truscott's accusation was cut off short with a cry of pain. David was attempting to force his arm behind him. Hilary retreated up the step, out of the way of flailing limbs and heaving bodies.

A peripheral part of her mind was aware that there was an emptiness behind her where Veronica had been.

'Leave it to the police,' David gasped, as though he too was in pain.

Watching them struggle, Hilary winced. She remembered the shrapnel wound in his side, a relic of an air strike when he had spent time in Gaza last year as a relief doctor.

It was maddening to feel there was nothing she could do. Would dialling 999 bring the police officers already on the estate? She fumbled for her phone, and realized she had dropped her bag. The chapel was so small that she could not even work her way around the fighting men to join Theresa in protecting Gavin.

Did she *want* to protect him?

Above her, memorials to more ancient warriors looked down on this scene of chaos.

'Stand aside, ma'am.' The masculine voice behind her rang with such authority that Hilary obeyed instantly.

An impossibly tall-seeming police officer launched himself into the fray. In seconds, he had done what David had tried to but could not. Truscott's arms were pinned with professional ease behind his back.

'That's quite enough of that, sir. Or do you want me to arrest you for obstructing the police?'

Dan Truscott's reddened face now turned towards the door, so that Hilary could see how mortified he was to find himself on the wrong side of the law. This was a man who had been accustomed to giving orders, not to receiving them, or not in such peremptory terms.

'I was attempting to do your duty for you, officer,' he gasped. 'There's a very good reason this gentleman isn't at the meeting with your Inspector Foulks, why I found him shivering with fright because I'd got on to him. I don't know what this secret is he was blabbering about to Dr Masters, but I can make a pretty good guess.'

'The police deal with more than guesswork,' came a cool observation from behind Hilary.

The daylight of the abbey ruins had been darkened again. This time it was the tall figure of Veronica in her violet rain jacket and the even taller one of DI Foulks.

Foulks stepped down past Hilary. Now that the fighting had stopped, the group of five people seemed smaller than it had been. There was just room for Foulks to stand on the chapel floor between David and Theresa. The latter stood her ground, still comforting the shivering Gavin Standforth. She looked more like a bulldog than a toad now.

David had let go of the colonel, to Hilary's relief. Truscott now stood resentfully in the police constable's grasp. She felt the weakness of gratitude as her husband turned to her. There were beads of sweat on the side of his nose. She wanted to reach up and wipe them away. She had feared for him many times in the past. Now the two of them moved together and he held her silently.

'Take the colonel outside,' the DI nodded to the constable. 'Reinforcements are on their way.'

'Do you want me to charge him?'

'I'll deal with him later.'

Even as the constable led the indignant colonel up the step past Hilary, two more officers appeared around the corner of the chapel.

Without the colonel's flailing presence, the Lady Chapel seemed larger, lighter. The cross on the altar had become visible. It was possible to imagine this place once again as a place of prayer. There was even space to notice the bramble shoot snaking up through a hole in the corner.

'Get up,' DI Foulks ordered Gavin. 'If you can.'

The author got shakily to his feet. He had to lean against the chest for support. Theresa hovered anxiously at his elbow.

'The colonel made a very serious accusation against you. Does he have any evidence to support it?'

Gavin tried to speak, but no words came. Hilary wondered whether Dan Truscott might really have had his hands around the novelist's throat before David pulled him off.

Theresa answered for him. 'I suppose you have to know this, but I beg you to keep it secret. It has nothing to do with anybody's murder, I promise you.'

'I'll be the judge of that.'

Theresa was staring past him at Hilary and David and Veronica. Her intention was plain. David made to turn, but Hilary glared defiantly back. It was not going too far to say that David had risked his life to protect Gavin. She was staying.

Theresa shot a look of apology at the author. Reluctantly she spoke.

'It was four years ago. I wasn't working with Gavin then, so I had no idea anything was wrong when she turned up here. It appears Gavin and Melissa ran another crime-writing course like this. Jo Walters was there. Only she wasn't Walters then. She married Harry a year or two later. Jo . . .'

Gavin moaned and hid his face in his hands again.

'It seems Jo came up with a plot for a novel. A particularly good one. Gavin had been writing murder mysteries for years, and getting them published with small-time firms, but he could see that this was streets better than anything he'd ever thought of. Something that would really make the publishers sit up and take notice . . . I'm sorry, Gavin. They have to know. It will be much worse for you if Jo comes round and tells them herself . . .'

'I didn't try to kill her!'

'I know that. But the inspector still needs to hear the truth. It's best if it comes from you.'

Gavin groaned again. He had difficulty getting the words out. When he did, they were almost a whisper.

'It's true. It was a brilliant plot. And what little I saw of her writing showed a cracking style. The moment the course was over, I went back and got the whole thing down on my computer. I dropped everything else to write that book in record time. I was scared she would finish hers ahead of me. I'd given her as many objections as I could, to make her think she couldn't write it up just as it was. But she could have. It was stunning. You'd never have thought she was a first-time author. So I wrote it myself, as nearly in her style as I could. It was the best thing I'd ever done. *The Long Crippler.*'

'The one that made you fame and fortune!' Hilary exclaimed. 'Your bestseller.'

The title which had dominated his display in the book room.

He hung his head. 'It wasn't entirely her work,' he defended himself. He was struggling to prevent his voice from becoming a whine. 'I do know a bit about characterization. How to keep up the tension, prolong the mystery. But she did too, right from the start. She had all the right instincts of a writer.' His voice fell further. 'She could have done it herself, without any help from me.'

'But didn't she get back to you?' David asked. 'Threaten to unmask you? She must have found out.'

'She did try. But I'd done all the obvious things, like change the names of the characters and their personal details. Set it somewhere else. I told her there was no copyright in ideas.'

'And that there was no such thing as honour,' Hilary remarked.

'She was bitter. But she seemed to accept it. At first.'

He left a silence.

'And then,' the inspector said, 'she turned up again on this course.'

'I didn't recognize her straight away. She'd dyed her hair as well as changed her name. But Melissa . . .' He choked on the name. 'Melissa did.'

'And you thought that now you'd reached the heights of fame on the strength of that one book, she really could do you serious harm. If she let the world know what happened, where you got the idea for that bestseller, that would have wrecked your reputation.'

'It was getting hard to keep up sales, anyway,' Gavin whispered. 'The next one sold on the strength of *The Long Crippler*, but the reviews weren't so good. Since then . . .'

'You saw your already tottering career ending in failure and disgrace.'

'*I didn't kill her.*'

'She's not dead yet. At least I very much hope she makes it through surgery. It isn't Jo Walters who was murdered. It was your wife. Why? Did she threaten to unmask you too?'

'That's ridiculous!' Theresa shouted. 'It had nothing to do with this! Melissa was doing everything she could to advance Gavin's career. She even . . .'

The words died away within the chapel walls.

'Even what?' prompted the inspector.

Theresa looked to Gavin for help.

'They know so much, you might as well tell them the rest. She's dead now.'

Theresa sighed. 'Melissa had this harebrained scheme. She desperately wanted to get Gavin back on the A-list. She thought we could use this weekend to stage a real-life murder mystery. Or something close to one. Headline publicity. Crime writer struck down on murder mystery weekend.'

'Deliberately poisoning Dinah Halsgrove with her own medication.' Hilary got there before her.

Theresa turned surprised eyes. 'You knew that?' Her eyes widened. 'So Melissa was right! She was sure you'd guessed why she was heading for Dinah's room while the rest of you were supposed to be in the hall.'

'So she came to my room in the night to – put a stop to me.' Hilary felt David's hand close round her arm.

'Like I said. She was highly strung. I'm sorry,' Gavin muttered. 'Anyway, you were right. She took the chance to steal some of Halsgrove's medication.'

'It seemed the only explanation,' David said. 'Under the circumstances.'

'Yes. Not a fatal dose, of course.'

'Pretty difficult to be sure of that, especially at Dinah Halsgrove's age.' The doctor's condemnation was evident.

'Do you think we didn't realize that, Gavin and I? We were horrified that she might actually die. We did everything we could to talk Melissa out of it. That's why Gavin insisted I should be the one to stay with her at suppertime, while Melissa and the rest of you went on the cruise.'

'Only the drugs weren't in her supper, were they? I'd guess they were in the whisky which Hilary tells me Melissa brought your distinguished author when she'd finished her talk and was busy signing books. There was a good chance she'd be too tired and preoccupied to notice there was anything wrong with her drink.'

Theresa's eyes widened further. 'So that's how she did it! We never knew.'

'Very likely.'

The detective inspector turned his intelligent gaze on David. There was a flash of admiration.

'Well spotted, doctor.'

'I wasn't there. But Hilary was.'

Was that the merest flush on the inspector's cheeks?

'I may have underestimated Miss Marple.'

'But Melissa is dead,' Hilary stated the obvious. 'I hardly think it likely that it was Dinah Halsgrove's revenge. She was still recovering in hospital. So if it wasn't you two, trying to cover up, who could it have been?'

'I've no idea,' Gavin said in a small voice. 'And after all that, all Dinah's illness got was a small column on the inside pages. And she could have *died*.'

TWENTY-EIGHT

'I suggest you leave it to us to find the culprit,' said Inspector Foulks, not for the first time.

They were interrupted by the sudden appearance of DS Blunt. He looked flustered.

'It's that crowd in Lady Jane's Chamber, sir. They're getting mutinous. You can see their point. Some of them have got trains to catch. They've booked taxis. Begging your pardon, but we gave them to understand we'd be finished with them by three.'

A shadow of annoyance passed over the inspector's face. 'I was investigating a murder then. I didn't know there was going to be another attempted murder today. And that's even supposing she pulls round. They're writers. You'd think a group of intelligent people could understand that.' Then the creases in his face sagged. 'I suppose you're right. We can't keep them here indefinitely. They've cleared their rooms and checked out. We have to let them go. Just make sure you've got all their contact details and that everyone's accounted for their movements this morning. Tell them I'll be along in a minute.'

'Yes, sir.' The sergeant set off, almost at a run.

Theresa broke the silence in the chapel. 'You're not going to charge us, are you? And please, *please*, don't say a word about what we've told you.' Her usually impassive face creased into an expression of pleading.

'I can't promise that. It may be relevant evidence. But no. I've no hard grounds to arrest you for Mrs Standforth's murder, and I think we have to see what Mrs Walters says about her assailant when she comes round. If she does.'

Hilary was pulled up short by the realization again that Jo's life was hanging in the balance. She remembered vividly their first meeting over tea in the garden. That sense of a sharp intelligence beneath the white-blonde hair. The spark of ambition as she told Hilary of the novels she intended to write. Hilary's own perception that, of all the course members she had talked to, Jo was the one most likely to succeed.

And she would have . . . if Gavin had not stolen the story that should have launched her career.

She could still write another one. She had it in her. But still . . . Hilary grieved for the younger woman's loss.

And then there was that memory of Harry, bewildered and in tears.

Her mind was a confusion of possibilities. None of them she wanted to confront.

The inspector was already striding out into the graveyard. Sunshine was bejewelling the raindrops on the grass. With a sag of her emotions, as the drama in the chapel receded from her, Hilary followed him. Veronica was still standing on the threshold.

'That was a pretty heartbreaking story, wasn't it? Poor Jo. And you even have to feel for Gavin. He got the success he always longed for, but ever since, he's been desperately afraid she could take it away from him.'

'There's one thing that puzzles me,' Hilary said, feeling the sun warm on her face after the chill inside the chapel. 'With all this social media stuff, Twitter, Facebook, you name it, why didn't she just spread the word around before now? She could have told the whole world he's a cheat and thief. Why come back here on another course?'

David fell into step behind them. 'I think perhaps that may have been too vague for her to get real satisfaction. There are so many false rumours bandied about on social media. Who would have believed her? She may still have been planning to do that, but I think what she wanted was to see him face to face. From all accounts, she's a clever woman. I don't know what she was plotting in the way of revenge, but she may have wanted to see the expression in his eyes when she told him.'

'Do you think she was planning something for this afternoon?' Veronica asked. 'The final session of our crime-writing course. Like the classic dénouement, when the detective surveys the case and points his or her finger at the guilty party. Was she going to unmask him in front of us all?'

'If so, then she couldn't have planned for Melissa's murder to put a stop to the course,' Hilary pointed out. 'That final session isn't going to happen now.'

'No,' Veronica sighed. 'I suppose not.'

Hilary felt a pang of nostalgia, retracing the path along the back of the East Cloister with its tall medieval chimneys. She let her eyes range along the line of bedroom windows. She had already expressed her doubts to Veronica about whether she would ever be able to come back here. Would she? Might there be some time in the future when she could forget the look and feel of Melissa's cold flesh, could stop remembering the living woman, with her long patterned skirts and flowing hair. The woman who had bumped into her in the corridor that led to Dinah Halsgrove's room, on her way to steal her medication, the same corridor they were passing now? She did not think so.

She did not realize she had slowed her pace to look, perhaps for the last time, at the buildings she had loved for years. She was startled by Veronica's call, and saw that she and David were standing on the path some way ahead.

'Come on, Hilary,' Veronica said as she caught up with them. 'We're supposed to be at the inspector's meeting. He disappeared round the corner minutes ago.'

'What's the point?' Hilary said. 'We know what he's going to say. He'll give us one last warning to tell him everything we know, however insignificant, and then he'll let us go. We might as well head straight for the car park from here.'

'Hilary!' Veronica's voice trembled with laughter. 'Why do you always think you're a special case and the normal rules don't apply to you?'

'I don't!'

'Hilary, I love you dearly, but that remark shows a certain lack of self-knowledge.'

'I don't, do I?' she appealed to David. 'Think I'm above the law?'

'Well . . .' His own lips quivered. 'Let's just say your interpretation of the rules can be a little flexible.'

'Oh.'

They had almost reached the drive. All they needed to do now was to walk downhill a little way and double back under the archway into the courtyard. Unless they did the obvious thing, from Hilary's point of view, and simply crossed the drive to their cars.

The afternoon peace was shattered by the grinding of gears, as one of the parked cars was thrown into violent life by its driver. There were stuttering bursts of an engine firing, then silence. The noise started again. It was violent enough to stop the three in their tracks. Hilary thought that in that brief silence she might have heard a faint shout of authority from further down the hill.

'Someone's in too much of a hurry to get away,' David observed. 'More haste, less speed.'

As he spoke, a dark green Range Rover hurtled its way round the corner of the car park, careering off the kerb as it did so. It came charging towards them, ignoring the one-way signs, out on to the drive right in front of them.

David threw out a protective arm, forcing them back against the wall. The Range Rover took the turn at a reckless speed that threatened to overturn it.

Hilary glimpsed the driver's face as the vehicle lurched past her. Dark red, mottled, under a tweed cap jammed over grey hair. For a moment, she thought it was Dan Truscott. Then she remembered she had last seen him in the custody of a police constable.

'That's Harry!' Veronica exclaimed at her side.

Grit spattered against Hilary's legs from the spinning wheels. Her mind was racing.

'Do you think they've told him Jo's come round? Is he going to see her?'

'If he drives like that, he'll be dead before he gets to the hospital,' said David.

'What's up now?'

There were more shouts from lower down the car park. Police officers running. A WPC shot out on to the drive, frantically flagging down the hurtling Range Rover. It swept past her, making her leap back.

'Or Jo's dead,' Veronica said quietly. 'And poor Harry's out of his mind.'

A police car flew out of one of the lower exits and raced in pursuit. It switched on its siren. The blue light flashed. The three of them gasped as it swerved past the careering Harry, who was steering an erratic course down the hill. For heart-catching seconds, it seemed as though the two vehicles, one dark green, the other white with chequered bands, must collide. But the police car drove expertly past.

It came to an abrupt halt, just before the road bent out of sight. An officer leaped out of the passenger seat. He seemed to throw something out across the road. For a bizarre moment, Hilary thought he was casting a fishing net. The Range Rover charged on. The officer sprang out of its way.

For a moment, it seemed that it would disappear round the bend. Then there was a screeching of metal against tarmac. The Range Rover slewed violently off course. As David broke into a run towards it, the vehicle skidded in a half circle and toppled over on to its side. It lay on the verge of the road, wheels spinning, the engine still racing.

Harry, Hilary knew with a lurch of her heart, must be trapped on the underside.

The two officers were sprinting downhill towards the crash. More were coming out of the car park. Hilary and Veronica shot each other panicked stares, and set off after David. Veronica's longer legs pulled her ahead of Hilary.

'I was very much afraid,' she panted as she passed, 'he was wanting to kill himself. He may just have done so.'

The first officer to get there climbed up to pull the passenger door open. As he reached an arm inside, the noise of the engine fell suddenly silent.

Hilary ran past the parked police car. Only now could she see the mesh of spikes that had punctured the Range Rover's tyres. They had meant to stop Harry, but what if they had killed him instead? She was very much afraid of what sight might meet the officer who was leaning, head down, across the front seats of Harry's car.

She prayed David would be able to do something. He was a doctor. She was thankful, as she had not been before, for all his experience of violent bloodshed in war-torn parts of the world. Surely he would be able to cope.

She had to convince herself that Harry was still alive.

Her steps were slowing. One of the policemen had called on her to stop, but she had taken no notice. She knew that she did not want to see. She did not need to be here. There would be nothing she could do that trained professionals could not do so much better than she could. She should have listened to Veronica. She could have been back in Lady Jane's Chamber with the rest of the course. She could still hear DS Blunt's voice, ordering her back.

But she was here, with a sick feeling in her throat.

David had reached the Range Rover. Instead of climbing into it, as she expected, he seemed to be remonstrating with the policeman who had got there first. She watched him back away from the car and look instead at the still-smoking engine and the petrol which, Hilary could now see, was trickling from the fuel tank down the hill. She knew David would rather have left the injured man where he was until the ambulance crew arrived with the proper equipment. But he seemed to change his mind. He hoisted himself up on the footboard. Most of his body disappeared into the car. The police officer flattened himself to one side to let him past.

Now she could see them both straining to lift Harry's body from the wreck. Hilary was now horribly conscious of the leaking fuel.

They were lowering him out. David was supporting his neck. The second policeman strode across to help them. Together they carried him a safer distance from the car, to lower him on to the grass almost at Hilary's feet.

Veronica caught hold of her arm. 'You don't have to look.'

But Hilary did.

There was less blood than she had feared. It streaked David's fingers as he laid Harry's head on the ground. David, she noted, was the one giving orders now. He was supporting Harry, care-fully arranging his back and limbs to do the least possible damage. The driver of the police car was back at his vehicle, urgently radioing messages.

Hilary looked behind her. She was not surprised to find the long-legged DI Foulks coming down the drive at a loping run, followed by DS Blunt. There was a group of course members spilling out of the archway further up the hill.

Her ears strained for the wail of an ambulance siren.

Harry moved his blood-streaked head with a groan.

'Thank God!' Hilary gasped. 'He's alive.'

The uniformed officers stood aside to make room for the detective inspector. He bent over the injured man.

'It's all right, Mr Walters. Didn't you get the message from the hospital? Your wife's come round from surgery. They think she's going to live.'

'You don't understand,' Harry moaned. 'She was meant to be dead.'

TWENTY-NINE

Hilary's heart sank. Ever since she had heard about Jo being struck on the head, and remembered Harry's seemingly premature tears, a little part of her mind had wondered. Could all those tears really have been for Melissa? And if they were for Jo, how else could he have known?

'Lie still,' David was saying. 'The ambulance will be here soon.'

Even as he spoke, Hilary could hear sirens in the far distance.

But DI Foulks was also bending over the injured man, more urgently.

'What do you mean, Mr Walters? Who wanted her dead?'

Hilary already knew the answer before Harry spoke.

'I did.' There was an eternity of grief in his voice.

'*You* did? You're telling me you hit your wife? I'm not arresting you yet, but I ought to warn you that anything you say may be used in evidence.'

'Leave him,' ordered David. 'He ought to stay quiet.'

But Harry turned his head with a low cry of pain. Hilary knew it was not all physical.

'I made a mess of it, didn't I? Will you arrest her now?'

'Arrest her? For what?'

'For killing Melissa Standforth.'

'Bingo!' said one of the uniformed policemen quietly.

Hilary looked down at Harry's tortured face. She stepped round him, into the line of the inspector's vision.

'I think I can explain.'

'I know what you're going to say.' The DI lifted his grey eyes to hers. 'You think it has to do with what Gavin Standforth said in the chapel. But don't you think it's a bit extreme, to kill a woman just because her husband stole your idea for a book?'

'You need to appreciate the sort of person Jo is. Extremely intelligent. Very good at plotting. Perhaps more intent on the machinations of a murder and how the perpetrator might get away with it than just lashing out in sheer revenge.'

'You're suggesting that she killed Melissa Standforth as an intellectual exercise?'

'Given the circumstances, I think it's very possible, yes. She could have denounced Gavin on Twitter, or something like that. But would people really be that interested? Sour grapes, they'd say. She wouldn't be the first writer by any means to claim they were the unacknowledged source for a bestselling author's book. People have gone to court over it. No, she wanted to get her revenge in such a way that she could see in Gavin's eyes his understanding that she had done it, and why. For her, this was better revenge than killing Gavin himself. That would all have been over in a few seconds. No, Harry's right. She killed Melissa instead, so that she could look forward to Gavin knowing for the rest of his life why she did it, and being unable to say anything. Not without wrecking his own reputation. You saw him in the chapel. You heard him. He was reduced to a quivering wreck by the thought that what he did to her might get out in open court. Not just the social media. That's trivia. And can you just imagine the headlines if he shopped her? *Wife murdered to reveal author's shame.* I wouldn't be surprised if Jo met him in the chapel after dark yesterday to tell him what she'd done and taunt him with it. No, Gavin was going to keep quiet and suffer the knowledge of the truth. Jo thought she could see how to plan the perfect crime.'

'She would have done,' Harry groaned, causing all of them to recall his presence, bloodstained, on the grass at their feet. 'You asked us all if we'd seen that tracksuit. Nobody but me had. She'd taken care to bring other clothes for her morning runs.'

'Black leggings, I remember,' said David. 'With a pink tee shirt. I met her jogging in the grounds this morning.'

'But I'd seen the tracksuit in her holdall. I was putting our bags away after we'd unpacked. I asked her if she'd like me to hang it in the wardrobe, but she said no.'

The sirens were screaming closer. More than one of them. Time was running out.

'So she knew you'd seen the evidence. That you knew what it meant. Did she threaten you?' the inspector asked.

'She trusted me. I *loved* her. I still do.' His voice was trembling. Tears started down his face again.

'Hush, Harry. Lie still,' David told him.

'I knew if I kept quiet it would never come to court. She was far too clever. But Melissa was dead. Someone had to answer for that. Jo thought she'd committed the perfect crime. I couldn't bear to think of her being arrested and knowing that she hadn't. It wasn't just being sentenced to life for murder. It was the . . .'

'Humiliation,' David supplied.

'She couldn't have borne it. I thought I could spare her that. It was meant to be quick and painless. Justice to Melissa done. Jo would never have known what happened. But I couldn't even get that right.'

His voice was failing. David took his pulse.

Next moment, they seemed to be surrounded by uniformed paramedics, with a fire crew following hard on their heels. David and the inspector stood back. The paramedics put a neck brace on Harry and transferred him carefully to a stretcher. Not far below them, firemen were shovelling sand on to the leaking petrol, dousing the smoking engine with foam. For a few moments, there seemed to be a whirlwind of professional activity.

As the ambulance doors closed, Hilary felt utterly exhausted.

The inspector got to his feet, brushing grass from the knees of his trousers.

'You crime writers! I'll never understand you. Can you really get so caught up in a fictional murder that you'll commit a real one to settle a score?'

'I think it was more than revenge,' Hilary said uncomfortably. 'Jo needed to prove to herself that she could. That she wasn't just capable of writing a blockbusting novel, but that her plot was watertight enough to turn it into a reality. And I wouldn't put it past her to have planned to write a novel afterwards about what she actually did.'

'Defying the world to make the connection,' Veronica agreed.

'As a result of which, Harry Walters took it upon himself to see justice done in his own ham-fisted way,' the detective inspector said grimly, 'rather than hand the evidence over to me.'

'For love,' Hilary reminded him.

The ambulance siren was fading in the distance. Hilary watched the fire crew packing up, preparing to go. Some of the police officers were starting to disperse.

'He was going to get into his car and kill himself, rather than be made to testify against her,' Veronica said. 'Poor, poor Harry.'

THIRTY

'That wasn't meant to happen.' The uniformed policeman's voice was high and nervous. 'They told us that spike strip just brings them to a gradual stop. They showed us videos.'

'He swerved deliberately,' the driver tried to reassure him. 'Must have.'

'He would have done,' Hilary heard herself say. 'He wanted to crash.'

She saw with an irrational irritation that the rest of the Morland Abbey people were swarming down the road towards them. Honesty told her she would have done the same. She imagined the deluge of questions they would be bursting to ask. But she did not want to talk to them. To anyone.

David's hands were still smeared with Harry's blood. He was wiping them with handfuls of grass.

Random thoughts skidded through her mind. Weren't you supposed to wear gloves for that sort of thing nowadays? David wouldn't think about himself, of course. Still, Harry was hardly likely to be carrying HIV. On the other hand, how did she know? How much did she know about anybody, after this weekend?

David had been at worse scenes than this, seen streets running with blood. She had always tried to avoid thinking about that.

They were surrounded by excited people.

'That was Harry, wasn't it? Crashing his Range Rover. Was he running away? Does that mean he's the one who killed Melissa Standforth?' Jake was almost shouting in his eagerness.

'Poor man,' Ceri was saying. 'Is Jo dead? Is that why he went off the road?'

'Oh, dear.' Lin Bell looked pale. 'It was bad enough finding one body. At least, I *thought* it was a body when I came across Jo on the footpath. But two in one day.'

'Harry's alive,' Veronica reassured them. 'They're taking him to hospital. And Jo's come round.'

'So she can tell the police who attacked her!' This time the eager question came from Tania. 'Has she?'

'Sorry.' Veronica sounded as tired as Hilary felt. 'I've no information on that. And I don't expect the inspector will tell us if she has.'

There was a hesitation, then the crowd reluctantly began to break up. Most were heading, not back to the abbey, but to the car park. It was, Hilary realized, finally over.

Fiona the receptionist had David, rather cautiously, by the arm, anxious to avoid contact with his bloodied hands. 'Let's get you cleaned up. You can't go home like that.'

The young police officer, still looking worried, was gathering up the spike strip he had thrown in the path of Harry's Range Rover. Hilary made an effort and walked back up the hill towards him.

'It's not your fault. You tried to stop him safely. He was just off his head with grief.'

The policeman shook his head, as if he could still not believe what had happened.

'I never thought I'd be on the spot when, you know, somebody coughs up to a murder. Or an attempted one. It's sorted now, isn't it? All the stuff that's happened here this weekend?'

Hilary sighed. 'I suppose so. I don't know at what point DI

Foulks will decide Jo is fit to be charged with murdering Melissa. Harry will have to testify. He's not clever enough to get out of it. He really will wish he'd killed himself when they sentence her.'

The officer stopped in the act of folding up the spikes. 'Do you think he'll try again?'

'Killing Jo?'

'No. Suicide.'

'Probably not. The stuffing's been knocked out of him. Now he's told the inspector everything, he'll think it's finished. He's no idea what they'll put him through if she pleads not guilty. The courts. The press. He's too honest to take anything back. But I doubt if even Jo is clever enough to lie her way out of this now.'

'That's it, then.' The police constable grinned, suddenly brighter. 'Job done.'

'You could look at it like that. Three case files closed for your statistics. But for those two, it's only just beginning.'

Veronica joined them. 'I wonder what Dinah Halsgrove will think, when she reads about all this in the paper.'

'It will probably be in her next book.'

The River Dart bubbled clear over its stony bed beside the road. On the opposite bank, a steam engine puffed its way towards Totnes, pulling its cream-and-brown coaches. Autumn was colouring the banks of trees on either side of the valley.

As they drove away from the abbey, Hilary lifted her eyes to Dartmoor ahead, where she knew the skylarks would be singing. It should have been idyllic.

It was David's decision to bid farewell to the Dart with a cream tea at the magnificently restored Buckfast Abbey.

'This one's still functioning as abbeys were meant to.'

They turned off the main road to where, across the bridge, the abbey fields sloped down to meet the river. They parked under the trees and strolled down the path through the entrance to where the pinnacles of the great church soared up to greet them.

Soon, they were sitting on the roof terrace of the café in the autumn sunshine, watching the Sunday visitors exploring the grounds and the magnificence of grey stone and golden window tracery. Hilary could picture the brilliance of the modern stained glass inside, crafted in the monks' workshops.

'There's something hopeful about Buckfast, don't you think?' she asked. 'Of course, it's terribly romantic to see the old ruined abbeys like Morland, not to mention Glastonbury, Fountains, Rievaulx, Whitby and the rest. They're a telling witness to just how drastic the Reformation was. Past glory, deliberately pulled down. But here you got a handful of twentieth-century monks who weren't content to let destruction have the final say. So they set to, with their own bare hands, and rebuilt, well, all this.' She gazed across at the church and the abbey buildings beyond it.

The other two sat in silence. She sensed that they knew she meant more than reconstructed stone walls.

'It's going to be pretty hard for those folk to rebuild their lives, isn't it?' Veronica ventured. 'Jo and Harry.'

'It's in the hands of the Crown Prosecution Service,' David suggested. 'If Jo makes a full recovery, my guess is that they won't press Harry too hard for his part. "While the balance of his mind was disturbed", that sort of thing.'

'They can hardly say that about Jo,' Hilary retorted. 'Her mind was working all too sharply.'

'I don't know,' Veronica said more softly. 'It must have been a terrible shock to her when Gavin stole her work. A betrayal of trust. The opposite of what she hoped when she came on their course. She wanted so much to hit the A-list.'

'But it was all so calculated. She must have scared Melissa into agreeing to a secret meeting at the Leechwells. How else could she have known Melissa would be there? And that business with the hooded tracksuit. That was all planned beforehand. She knew when she packed that this was how she was going to do it. It had to be the Leechwells. There must have been a particular pleasure for her in killing Melissa in the Long Crippler pool. To use the title of Gavin's stolen book against him in such a horrific way.' She shivered, remembering the feel of the water in the ancient well as she lifted the sodden body.

'Men often get away with things on the grounds that it was a "heat of the moment" thing. I'm not sure that works so well with women,' David mused. 'Lashing out with brute force. It's less of an option if you haven't got the physical strength. Instead it smoulders, for years, maybe, until it can't be held in any longer. That's how she must have felt about Gavin.'

'Yes, poor Gavin,' Veronica exclaimed. 'Oh, I know, what he did was absolutely rotten. But you imagine him, starting out with high hopes, just like Jo. Getting his first mystery accepted. And then seeing it all fizzling away. Low sales. Hardly anybody's heard of him. Just another hack writer, only surviving because crime fiction is today's favourite genre. And then seeing this brilliant opportunity, *knowing* that this was the big one. I'm sorry!' She spread another scone with clotted cream and strawberry jam. 'I know I shouldn't make excuses for him. But it's going to be awful for him now. It's all going to come out. Jo will get her revenge, though at a terrible price. It's not just the shame. Gavin will know for the rest of his life that what he did cost Melissa hers.'

Hilary got up. 'I think I'll go into the abbey church for a while. I need to be quiet.'

David walked across the sunlit grass beside her, with Veronica following. His voice was comforting.

'You will go back to Morland, you know. Totnes. All that. You're a historian. You know that violence is never the end of the story. Some things fall. Others survive. The scene changes. Sometimes for the better, in ways you can't imagine.'

She knew he was thinking of the places he'd worked in. Gaza. Yemen. Stricken countries.

They stepped into the cool shadows of the nave. Tall Romanesque arches led the eye to the high altar. Hilary looked around her, marvelling. 'To think that half a dozen monks with wheelbarrows and wooden scaffolding did this. Less than a hundred years ago. Think of all the scores of people who must have told them they couldn't do it, that they were mad to dream of it. And here it is.'

'And in a smaller way, that's what Dinah Halsgrove does, year after year,' said Veronica behind them. 'Puts one stone upon another, day after day, to build a beautifully crafted book. Right into her nineties.'

Hilary swung round, a smile chasing away the serious set of

her face. 'Is that what you're going to do now? Write that crime novel about your lovers in the tiltyard?'

Veronica's laugh answered hers. 'I don't think my mind's devious enough for that. And I never even managed to complete the first exercise, remember? I got sidetracked by hearing Gavin and Theresa. You were the one . . .' She stopped dead.

'No,' Hilary said firmly. 'Not the Leechwells. That's one crime novel that's definitely not going to get written.'